Bear County,
MICHIGAN

Bear County, MICHIGAN

STORIES

JOHN COUNTS

TriQuarterly Books / Northwestern University Press
Evanston, Illinois

TriQuarterly Books
Northwestern University Press
www.nupress.northwestern.edu

Printed in the United States of America

10 9 8 7 6 5 4 3 2 1

Library of Congress Cataloging-in-Publication Data

Names: Counts, John, author.
Title: Bear County, Michigan : stories / John Counts.
Description: Evanston : TriQuarterly Books/Northwestern University Press, 2025.
Identifiers: LCCN 2024034751 | ISBN 9780810148017 (paperback) | ISBN 9780810148024 (ebook)
Subjects: LCGFT: Short stories.
Classification: LCC PS3603.O88644 B43 2025 | DDC 813.6—dc23/eng/20240819
LC record available at https://lccn.loc.gov/2024034751

For Meredith

CONTENTS

Big Frank

They left the windows unlocked in his wing of the Bear County Rehabilitation Facility. The authorities figured that if you ended up there, you had followed all the other court-ordered mandates and sobering up was a personal choice, not just a condition of probation.

It made it easy for Big Frank Dombreau to escape.

He was a large man, three-hundred-plus pounds, but that didn't stop him from climbing out the first-floor window next to his bed one late summer night two weeks into his stint. If caught, he'd be hauled back to jail. But he couldn't take three more weeks of the place. Big Frank was thirsty.

The facility was at the top of a hill, a Soviet-looking cinder block building that used to be a school, overlooking the northern Michigan coastal town of Bear River. Frank had gone there for junior high before the county turned it into a place where alkies, dopers, and criminally inclined addicts could dry out. Sobering up in the building wasn't all that different from attending school there, Frank decided: boredom intermingled with the smell of industrial disinfectant.

After launching himself into the warm night, Frank could have gone home, but Lisa would be there and he'd rather stay sober than see her. He still had a scar on his face from the frying pan attack that landed him in this mess six months ago. They'd been hammered, sucking down cheap wine in the kitchen of the house they rented on Spruce Street, before their friend Tommy showed up with whiskey. There was a fight about money. Lisa attacked him with the pan she'd just used to cook tacos. It was still hot. Ground beef and grease smeared on his face along with blood.

"You fat lazy piece of shit," she kept saying.

The insult didn't make much sense. Lisa was bigger than him and he was the one with a job, loading and unloading trucks at the cardboard factory. Frank, a dozen drinks in, defended himself and smacked her good after the fifth or sixth blow from the frying pan.

Tommy and Lisa both jumped on Frank and began beating him. He knew they'd been screwing too.

But when the Bear River cops showed up, Frank was the only one arrested, charged with felonious domestic violence and left to rot in the Bear County jail for months while his case moved to trial. He behaved, and when sentencing rolled around, his court-appointed attorney talked the judge into letting him serve the remainder of his time at the rehab facility.

Now Big Frank, as he'd been called since his days as a right tackle on the Bear River Bears football team, had run out of patience. He knew where to go, however. He struck out on the highway north toward LaFleur Lake, where there were dozens of vacation homes, walking in the dark. The September chill was settling in. Some folks might still be up enjoying the rest of summer, but there would be plenty of houses already shuttered for the season. Big Frank didn't see any reason for those cozy cabins and all the liquor in them to go to waste. If he was smart, he could last the whole winter there, crawl into a nice den and hibernate like a bear.

The first place that caught his eye was a little deer-hunting cabin. It looked just like his Uncle Dino's, where Frank first sipped beer at seven and lost his virginity to his cousin's friend Amber ten years later.

Big Frank still blushed at the memory.

Deer season wasn't for another month and a half and the cabin was closed. It was a safe bet there'd be booze.

The lock was a joke. Frank only had to nudge the door a little for it to give. He decided to fix it before he left.

But for now, there was booze to find. He wasn't disappointed. A glass bottle stood out on the kitchen counter next to an ancient toaster. Frank looked at the label and didn't know what was in the bottle. He tried to read it aloud to the empty room.

"Sanbooka."

He shrugged and poured himself a drink in a smudgy glass he pulled out from a cupboard. Before taking the sip, he lifted the glass and said "Cheers" to the ghosts in the room, perhaps the ghosts of his past too. He didn't wait for them to cheers him back, greedily sucking down the drink that tasted pleasantly like licorice and pouring another, filling his stomach with that familiar golden, glittery feeling he'd missed while living like a goddamn priest for half a year in custody.

The cabin consisted of three simple rooms: a kitchen, a sitting room with a fireplace, and a large bedroom with four bunk beds. Big Frank would have eight beds to choose from. But it was September, and even though it was warm during the day, by night it could get cold, so Frank decided to sleep on a pullout couch next to a kerosene heater in the main room.

First, however, there was drink to attend to. He poured himself another sambuca and walked around looking at the framed pictures on the walls. The pictures dated back to the 1940s, when the place was probably built, black-and-white pictures of stiff-looking guys in plaid wool coats just home from war standing next to slain deer hanging from trees or tied onto the hoods of large sedans. By the 1960s, pictures with similar poses were in bright

Technicolor, with the colors improving throughout the ensuing decades, as well as newer, younger faces, undoubtedly the men's children.

There were also several military plaques on the wall, and Frank soon deduced that all the men who belonged to this hunt club had served in the war together. The only picture that gave Frank pause showed six or seven shirtless men in a wrestling pile. Their smiles were exuberant.

Big Frank returned to the kitchen for more sambuca, but the bottle was drained. He needed more booze. He opened and rummaged through every cupboard, finding nothing but dusty plates and mugs. There was an unplugged fridge from the '50s where Frank found three warm cans of beer. He cracked one and kept looking.

He turned the joint inside out, finally ending up in the bunk-room, where he found a closet blocked off from the room by a sheet tacked to the wall. There was a footlocker at the bottom, hidden by a row of coats.

Frank opened the footlocker, which was filled with magazines and pictures and an old box of condoms. The front page of *Adonis: The Art Magazine of the Male Physique* featured a picture of a smiling, muscular man in a tight bathing suit on a beach, flexing for the camera.

Frank crouched down and dug a little deeper. At the bottom were Polaroids. One showed two naked men in a tight embrace, standing in this same room decades earlier.

Frank admired the look of contentment on their faces. He thought of Lisa and shuddered. In the increasing depths of his booze buzz, Frank pondered if he ever really liked women. Maybe I'm gay, he thought.

Frank dragged the footlocker over to a lower bunk bed, stretched himself out, pulled down his pants and tried beating off while looking at the beefcake mags and various Polaroids of the men engaged in a seemingly endless variety of sexual actions.

But he couldn't get an erection. It was nice that the gents in the pictures were having such a good time, but to even get anything stirring in his groin, Frank had to shut the locker, tightly close his eyes, and think about rolling around in the sleeping bag with Amber that first time. She had smelled like Tootsie Rolls. She'd eaten them constantly on that trip. Frank had only lasted a minute or two then. Now it wasn't long before he was messy and panting on the bottom bunk.

He cleaned himself up, put the footlocker back like he found it, fixed the lock on the door, and sat down at a table to write a note:

> *Sorry I drank your booze but I really needed it and*
> *I promise to buy you guys more if I ever can. IOU.*
> *Big Frank*

He left the note underneath the empty bottle and left.

It was dusk now and Big Frank's body and brain were demanding more booze. He wanted to be sure the next place had better supplies. He walked down to LaFleur Lake, which stretched and swayed a few miles toward Lake Michigan. There was only a half-mile of sand and dune grass between the little lake and the big lake. Dozens of houses ringed the water. One of them had to be the refuge he was looking for.

He settled on a small, newly built cabin right on the water. There was no one home—the blinds were all shut tight—and it didn't look like anyone was at the neighboring older cabins. There was also a rowboat under a tarp behind the house. Big Frank thought fishing might be fun.

The biggest selling point was the tacky sign hung next to the front door: "It's 5 o'clock somewhere." My kind of people, Frank thought. There was bound to be booze in there. The lock on the newer house was hard to jimmy. Since there was no one around, Big Frank just kicked it in. He wasn't disappointed in the offerings. Simple, but comfortable. Frank spotted a bar with a multitude of bottles and his heart melted. Whiskey. Rum. Vodka. Gin. All full. He looked in the garage. Three jugs of wine and two full cases of beer. There was also a freezer filled with steaks, chicken breasts, bratwursts, and pork chops.

Big Frank didn't know where to start. Standing before the little bar by the bay window overlooking the lake, he closed his eyes and reached out to grab a bottle. When he opened his eyes, his paw had the whiskey. He toasted the ghosts of the house and his past and started guzzling straight from the bottle while watching boats far out on the lake. He kicked his shoes off, sat down, and watched the water.

As he got settled in, drank more, and looked around the place, Big Frank noticed things in more detail. There were three laundry baskets of baby toys in the main room. In one of the bedrooms was a crib. He began inspecting the photographs in frames around the house. A couple his dad's age, their adult children, and at least a half-dozen small kids shared the cottage. There were pictures of babies everywhere.

Big Frank thought he could handle it, given the grand provisions at hand. Instead, he sat at the table and almost finished the fifth of whiskey as darkness spread across the sky over the lake. He was soon sobbing, pain rising from a deep and uncontrollable place that Big Frank was more afraid of than anything else. The tears streamed down his face into his beard as he looked at the lake and thought about Joey.

His son never made it to three. Ten years earlier, he'd been hit by a car and killed while Lisa was drunk on the couch, the television playing in the background. Big Frank had been at work. He never trusted Lisa's version of events, but it did no good to question his wife. The boy had somehow unlatched the screen door, walked across the front yard, and wandered into the middle of the street wearing nothing but a diaper and an undershirt. A teen in a pickup couldn't even see the poor little guy. Police ruled it accidental, but Lisa still got charged with neglect and served five years of probation. She was so destroyed Big Frank felt obligated to stay with her even though he was haunted. The collision played over and over in his imagination as he watched the dark come in over the lake, a vision powered by the pictures of all the staring babies.

He had to flee.

Frank didn't trust the next place would have such great food and drink, so he found a wheelbarrow in the garage and loaded it up with as much meat, liquor, wine, and beer as he could. A mostly full moon was out and he was sloppy from the whiskey. He wasn't sure how far he'd make it, especially because all the bottles made a racket clinking together in the wheelbarrow. He briefly thought about taking his haul out into the woods a few miles down the little gravel road. Maybe he could lift a tent and some camping supplies from a garage. But that would be a long walk. And it was late. He was drunk, tired, and hungry.

A house a few doors down seemed dark, so Big Frank parked the wheelbarrow next to the side door and clumsily tried breaking in. But he couldn't get the door to budge. He grabbed a bottle of vodka from the wheelbarrow, opened it, and took a swig before walking around to the screened-in front porch.

He got on the porch but couldn't get the main door open even when he kicked with all his weight. He slumped down and sat next to the door. The vodka was stifling his hunger, so he drank more. The moon shone down on him as he drank and drank. It was the last thing he remembered seeing.

Big Frank felt a poke in his belly. He forced his eyes open and his heart sank. A goddamn cop was hovering over him on the porch. Frank noticed it was daylight.

"Hey, big guy. Get up."

Frank was in a fetal position, clutching the bottle of vodka. He saw there were a few swigs left in it.

"Don't even think about it," said the officer, a young guy with short hair and wraparound sunglasses. "You're trespassing, bud. You scared this family half to death."

Frank noticed a concerned man, woman, and their teen daughter standing way back from the porch as if Frank had cooties. He noticed the cop was wearing latex gloves.

"And we know you broke into the place a few doors down. Come on, bud. I'm gonna have to take you in."

Frank sat up and caught his breath. Everyone was staring at him.

"First, give me the bottle. Then get up," the cop said.

Big Frank sighed and looked at the bottle, then unscrewed it and guzzled the rest of the vodka. This did not make the deputy happy. He lunged at Big Frank, who clocked him on the head with the empty bottle, which left Frank's hand and rolled down the porch. The deputy fell over howling, clutching his bloody head as the family screamed. Big Frank ran past them and found his wheelbarrow full of booze and thawing meat. It was heavy but he was strong. He quickly walked the wheelbarrow down the gravel road. He felt even stronger now and started trotting. Soon, Big Frank felt bigger and stronger than he ever had in his life, running down the road with the wheelbarrow as fast as he could.

The Women of Brotherhood

Debbie Somsel stood behind the counter at the EZ Mart flipping through a celebrity magazine. The pages fluttered from the whirring of a small fan set to high that was clipped to the lotto display behind her. It was 92 degrees, as tropical as it got this far north in Michigan. It was nearly noon and there had only been two customers all day, fishermen hauling boats who pulled up to the pumps, where they paid with credit cards and left without stopping inside to peruse the mart's wares of pop, beer, chips, and locally made venison jerky. Out the smudgy window, a police cruiser with its lights flashing but sirens off zipped by on the highway at high speed. Debbie assumed the cop had clocked a drunk fisherman going too fast.

The stuffy old building lacked air-conditioning and it was sweltering inside. Besides the rush for salmon fishing in early fall, business was always slow. Debbie couldn't convince owner Howdy Denver, a wealthy white-haired businessman who lived in the larger town of Bear River, to get the place air-conditioning. Howdy owned a half-dozen gas stations in Bear County and the Brotherhood location was the least-performing operation, something he always mentioned to Debbie during his monthly visits.

To survive the heat, Debbie wore cutoffs, a tank top, and, despite the No Shoes, No Shirt, No Service sign hanging on the door, no shoes. She was sweating so much her shirt felt heavy on her shoulders. Her body bore only a slight resemblance to the twig girls in the celebrity magazine. It was as if she and these Hollywood ladies were different subspecies. Debbie knew the women didn't really look that way, that computer programs airbrushed away all their imperfections. This seemed desperate to Debbie, who never thought much about how she looked, just that she was comfortable. Her body was a few sizes bigger and a few inches shorter than the girls in the magazine, with wide gray eyes, light brown hair in a clip, and chipped nails she couldn't stop chewing.

Debbie lingered on a page showing celebrity moms carrying their babies through parking lots of chic L.A. grocery stores, where they had probably never even heard of venison jerky, and felt a shiver of longing and jealousy along her spine. She let the magazine drop from her hands and gnawed her thumbnail while studying the glossy page. A familiar, haunted feeling welled up in her.

Debbie wasn't moved by the celebrities. She concentrated on the beautiful, wonderful babies who would grow up in a charmed and luxurious world and probably never hear of Brotherhood, Michigan, population 349. The town's only claim to fame was that the old chemical plant had ruined the uteruses of two generations of women, prompting several nationally televised news stories in the early 1990s. Many of the men had since disappeared, and six girls leapt to their deaths from the Old High Bridge over the Bear River Valley. The Brotherhood Chemical Plant, which had once employed nearly every man and woman in town, was shuttered and dismantled by federal authorities in hazmat suits. The building was long since gone, the land surrounded by two six-foot fences with barbed wire because the very earth was poisoned.

That was on the other side of Brotherhood from where Debbie stood at the gas station counter with the magazine. The EZ Mart was on LaFleur Highway at the edge of the tiny downtown, which consisted of a bar, a shuttered post office, a school, and a building with three storefronts, two of which were vacant and the third housing a taxidermy shop where an old stuffed deer with glassy eyes peered out at Debbie through the window all day long. The whole town was surrounded by miles of federal forest.

In the center of town was the Church of the Brotherhood, a simple brick structure built by the founders, who had forged their way into the northern wilderness in 1852 behind a man who claimed himself king and divine interpreter of the words of Jesus Christ. His name was Jason Morgan, and he was eventually stoned and drowned in Bear River by his own followers for heresy during what current church leaders called the Great Revolt of the Brothers. Nearly all the town's inhabitants were descendants of the church, including Debbie, but only a handful of elderly people still regularly attended anything besides funerals.

Debbie's celebrity baby reverie was interrupted by an old Pontiac pulling up quickly into the parking lot. The car came to a crunching halt on some gravel next to the propane tank display, and her best friend, Krystal, hopped out, a Newport dangling from her mouth. From the frantic way she was moving, Debbie knew something was wrong. Krystal bounded inside, still smoking, even though she knew it was against the rules. She had long, unruly red hair and green eyes, and was wearing cutoff jeans and a T-shirt.

"It's Melissa," she said. "She's on the bridge. I think she's gonna do it."

For a moment, Debbie didn't feel the heat. She didn't feel her fingers, her toes, or anything else.

"Oh my God," she said, closing the magazine and switching off the fan. "Let's go."

Krystal started the car while Debbie locked up the gas station. Debbie swiped some old fast-food bags off the front seat to make room and they sped off toward the old train bridge, past the fenced-off land where the chemical plant had been. Somehow weeds and scrub trees had started growing on the poisoned earth.

Even in catastrophe and ruin there was some kind of life.

Debbie was twenty-five now and the jumping had started when she was a little girl. She knew the stories of all six girls who died by suicide—including one she'd been close with, Renee Stonecipher. While restocking shelves during slow times at the EZ Mart, her mind often drifted to the bridge and the water and the rocks a hundred feet below. It was all so terrifying she would sometimes put down the bag of chips or peanuts and sit in the aisle, weeping into her hands. Then she would compose herself and get back to it. Debbie considered herself an optimist; no matter what happened there was some good in life if you looked hard enough, at least that's what her internet friend Pha Vong said. Even if that good was just weeds and scrub trees growing on poisoned land.

Her mother never talked about the suicides. The women of her mom's generation, the last in town able to bear children, dwelled in a silo of denial and silence. But the town gossip was enough for Debbie to know each case intimately. Each girl had her own reasons to jump. Some were booze and drug cases. Some were about money—everyone in Brotherhood was broke, but some girls were broker than others. Some suffered from debilitating depression or other mental illnesses, and men figured into a few situations too. All the cases, Debbie decided, were bound together by a lack of future and hope. A few girls, like her friend Renee Stonecipher, who killed herself two years earlier, tried to leave town but failed. It was as if the girls were fated to both Brotherhood and each other. The bridge was the only way out, a portal of escape. Renee had been in Debbie's same class of thirteen kids at Brotherhood High. She'd tried moving to Grand Rapids but found the city too big and scary, returning to Brotherhood, where she started using meth in the woods until she lost her head. Debbie knew her case the best because she was dating Renee's brother, Rick.

But now sweet and shy Melissa was out there, a hundred feet above the river and the rocks.

"I wish we could get Tommy on the phone. He could talk to Melissa, get her off the bridge," Krystal said between puffs of a new cigarette.

"I don't think anyone knows where he is," Debbie said, chewing on her nails again.

Melissa was a different story. She was a quiet, black-haired girl who looked at her feet when someone spoke to her. She'd had a boyfriend, Tommy, the taxidermist's son, who unexpectedly packed up and left a few weeks before, no note or message. This happened regularly in Brotherhood. Everyone quietly understood why the men were leaving.

"I heard Tommy drove up to the U.P. and found work as a dish-washer at a golf course," Krystal said.

"You know there's nothing we can do about him leaving," Debbie said.

There was a strained silence. Debbie's boyfriend, Rick, had pledged his undying devotion, promised he would never leave. It was common knowledge among those in town that Rick was also unable to have children. He'd had mumps as a child, the only case to hit Brotherhood in years. His subsequent infertility was a topic of discussion among mothers worried about their own children and the current generation of women keeping tabs on any available men. As for Krystal, she had never liked boys or babies. She had an ongoing secret affair with a married woman in Bear River and called babies "parasites," said they sucked the life out of the parents. "No one expects jackshit from us. We're free. It's awesome," she had once told Debbie.

"You're lucky with Rick," she said now, flicking the cigarette out the window. "The whole town knows you'll never end up on that bridge. You got too much going for you. Including that job."

While Debbie found the EZ Mart soul-sucking, it was one of the few full-time gigs in Brotherhood and therefore sought after by people like Krystal, who currently worked fifty hours per week at the Burger King in Bear River, a half hour away.

They were out of town now on Old Bridge Road, which went through the Matwa National Forest, ending abruptly where the earth descended into the river valley. Only a train bridge crossed the river. It was constructed in the roaring 1890s, when the timber trade boomed in the area and competing lumber companies owned by the Radke and Powers families got together to fund a 1,200-foot-long truss bridge. The bridge was put out of service in the 1950s, and became a popular destination for thrill-seeking local youths who dared each other to walk its breadth.

That was before the jumping began.

As they reached the bridge, Debbie could see police patrol cars and fire trucks parked where the gravel road ended at a waist-high metal railing, sirens off but red and blue lights still swirling. A dozen other cars were also parked in the area, and a crowd of locals had gathered in a clearing that overlooked the bridge.

After quickly parking the Pontiac, Debbie and Krystal rushed toward the crowd. They knew everyone but greeted no one. Melissa stood on a tie in the middle of the bridge, her black hair blowing in the wind, sobbing. The valley was a deep drop below. Debbie noticed Melissa was wearing a striped tank top she had recently borrowed, revealing creamy-white arms covered in small brown moles. Debbie wanted to run to her friend but couldn't. The authorities had the trail to the bridge blocked off.

"That asshole isn't worth it, Missy!" Krystal shouted. "C'mon back!"

A deputy wearing a harness with a thick rope clutched by firefighters was inching onto the bridge, stepping slowly on one tie after another, attempting to talk to Melissa and hopefully rescue her.

Melissa had the bearing of a cornered animal, looking at the deputy and violently shaking her head. The crowd was silent as the deputy stepped on a railroad tie closer to Melissa, only a half-dozen ties away. They all watched as Melissa shook her head no one final time. They all watched as she jumped and kicked her feet and waved her arms. They all watched as the girl's body hurtled toward the water and rocks a hundred feet below, black hair fluttering behind her.

Clad in sneakers, a polo shirt, and blue jeans, Rick Stonecipher was clearly not paying attention during Melissa's funeral, gazing off into the sunlight pouring through the window of the packed Church of the Brotherhood. Maybe he was thinking about his little sister, who had met the same fate. Maybe he was thinking about nothing. Debbie, in a somber black dress, stood by his side dabbing her eyes with a Kleenex like all the other ladies. Rick clamped on to Debbie's hand at some point during the service and smiled briefly, before getting distracted again by the sun, the window, and his own thoughts.

Debbie had no clue what Rick thought about.

He was generally considered the cutest guy left in town and many of the girls were in awe of Debbie for landing him. He was rawboned, six foot one, with a tan and tight muscles from working outside all summer landscaping. He had short-cropped brown hair and a goatee he stroked when laughing, which he was quick to do. He was a volunteer firefighter for Brotherhood Township and drove the engine each summer during the Fourth of July parade, waving at all the elderly folks lined up at the curb in motorized scooters and lawn chairs. No candy was thrown, as was the custom in parades at neighboring towns. There weren't any children.

Rick also was a favorite at the local tavern, where he was known for holding his liquor and helping drunk friends stay out of trouble. But his most important quality was that the mumps left him sterile and therefore not a flight risk like all the other men.

Everyone in town loved Rick Stonecipher.

Everyone except Debbie.

Frankly, he wasn't very interesting. She likened him to an overgrown puppy, oblivious to the world at large, unlike Debbie, who kept up with the news and even had a friend in Laos she met over the internet, a young woman named Pha Vong. The two chatted online weekly, comparing their daily activities and talking about life in general. It seemed so strange to Debbie that her best friend lived on the other side of the giant earth in a very different country, but still had the same concerns as she did about health, money, and love. She was the only one she'd told about Rick.

"He just wants to mow lawns, drink beer, and watch sports," she typed.

"It sounds like Rick is no good."

But like a child in possession of the toy everyone wants, Debbie didn't want to give Rick up. In her mind, she amplified his tender side. She remembered his face at the funeral for his little sister, Renee. He had openly wept. Even as kids, Debbie knew he had a thing for her, but it wasn't until she saw this display of emotion that she even considered Rick Stonecipher. He courted her with his simple nature, saying he would always protect her. She fell into his arms while they were both grieving for Renee. She liked the way he was in bed, when they didn't have to talk, just touch each other. When he inherited a dilapidated five-bedroom house at the edge of town—the Stoneciphers had once been high up in the church—he invited Debbie to come live with him. They settled into a routine. She kept looking for the sensitivity he'd shown for Renee, but she never saw it again. When she told him about Melissa, all he said was "Wow."

Now at Melissa's funeral, Debbie looked at him staring off into the sun and realized how dense he really was. After the ceremony and luncheon, they went to the house they shared and had sex, which ended with Debbie naked, fetal, and weeping hysterically. Rick had gone into the bathroom to clean up and returned to find her shuddering.

"Hey, hey now, kitten," he said, sitting on the bed and touching her arm. "What's wrong, baby? What's wrong? I know, poor Melissa. Poor kid."

Debbie wasn't concerned with Melissa. She was concentrating on a feeling she had at the funeral that linked her own eventual death with all the deaths of those in the room and how a person could only do so much in a life before that happened. But what to do with a life? One by one, Debbie rejected every idea of how to live besides being a mother and having a family. She didn't feel free from some burden, like Krystal said. She felt like she was trapped in something she didn't understand. Life needed a purpose, and the only purpose she could fathom was having a family. She wanted a baby with the same hunger she woke up with in the mornings before her mind could even form words. They had closed off most of Rick's big house. The rooms sat empty, doors closed, full of dust. She wished she could fill them with life, with children. She suddenly realized that was all she wanted. It took Melissa's death and funeral to bring it into focus.

Was she really going to work at the EZ Mart for the next forty or fifty years and hang out at the Brotherhood Tavern with Rick? The thought made her more miserable than thinking about Melissa dropping through the sky.

Rick stroked her upper arm until she grasped his wrist and turned over on her back. Debbie stared up into his face. He smiled.

"Hey now, kitten. It's all right," he said. "Melissa's gone on to a better place."

"It's not Melissa. I mean, it is, but it's also . . ."

Debbie trailed off and turned her face to stare at the darkened television on the dresser. She never got deep with Rick like she did with Pha Vong, who knew all about the women in Brotherhood.

"Come on, kitten. Tell me what's wrong so I can fix it."

"It's going to sound stupid. But I just sometimes wish so much I could have a baby. I just want to be a mother. That's all I ever wanted."

Debbie felt Rick go lax behind her. He stopped stroking her arm. She assumed it was out of dismissiveness, that he wasn't paying attention and perhaps was now picking something out of his toenail. She rolled over on her back and pulled the sheets tight up to her chin in the same motion and was surprised to see Rick sitting on the edge of the bed looking aggrieved.

"I wish all you girls could have all the babies you want," he said seriously. "I wish everyone could be happy and no one would ever jump off that goddamn bridge again. You promise me you'll never try that, right, kitten?"

"I promise," Debbie said, her eyes welling with more tears. She reached out and touched Rick's naked thigh.

"I already lost my sister," he said. "I can't go losing another girl I love."

Debbie was moved. Every negative thing she'd thought about Rick disappeared. She pulled him into the bed and they had sex all over again. He was different this time, more determined, ferocious; not like a puppy, more like a wolf.

The weather cooled. Summer was ending. The salmon run was on, bringing droves of fishermen into the area. The EZ Mart was bustling for a few weeks, until all the salmon were caught or died off after spawning in Bear River. By the time of their natural deaths, the fish turned black and were more than a foot long. Their corpses bobbed in stagnant pools at the edge of the river and dotted the banks. The smell was terrific, as it was every year. Debbie, wearing a hooded sweatshirt with a plastic name badge pinned to it, rang up tanks of gas, cases of beer, and packs of hot dogs for the fishermen. It was the one time of year the gas station turned a profit. Then October came and Brotherhood was empty again.

On a stormy, overcast autumn day Debbie stood behind the counter of the EZ Mart looking at the hairstyles in a *Glamour* magazine when Rick's pickup truck tore into the parking lot. Debbie hated the way Rick drove; too fast, always attempting harrowing passes on the rural two-lane LaFleur Highway.

She was annoyed with Rick until he came inside. His face looked different, either excited or distressed, she couldn't be sure which. Something was happening. Debbie assumed another girl was on the bridge. Her hands on the shiny pages of the magazine went numb.

"What is it?" she asked.

"Come out to the truck with me."

"Just tell me now. What's going on?"

"I've got something to show you," he said.

A frantic smile flashed on his face.

"C'mon."

Debbie followed Rick out to the truck, and he hustled to open the passenger door. A newborn baby was strapped into a car seat, wrapped in a blanket, wearing a little cap, asleep.

Debbie's face went from shocked to excited to horrified all in a matter of seconds.

"I got us a baby," Rick said.

She yearned to pick up the baby, hold it against her chest, and feel its head on her neck, but the baby wasn't hers and she knew its smiling face meant trouble. She also knew babies weren't supposed to be riding in the front seat of a truck like this.

"What did you do?"

"Doesn't matter. It's ours. We can keep him. We can raise him and be happy. We can leave town tonight. In fact, we should leave town tonight. Right now maybe." Rick looked around nervously, but there were no other cars on the highway. A boom of thunder sounded and it started to rain. The baby boy in the carrier woke up and started crying.

"This is insane," Debbie said. "Take him back. I don't even want to know where you got him, just take him back."

They stood at the open door of the pickup truck getting drenched.

"But isn't this what you want?" Rick said, confused.

Debbie stared at him severely. She wasn't angry because of what he had done. She was angry that a part of her wanted to reach into that carrier, pull that beautiful baby out, and hold him forever. The part of her that said, Yeah, we could get away with it. We deserve that baby. But Debbie knew there was a mother somewhere.

"Not like this," she said. "This is wrong, Rick. It's very, very wrong."

Rick's manic smile faded.

"I thought you'd be happy," he said. "This is legit. It's ours."

The baby continued to wail as the intensity of the rain increased.

"Take him back," she said. "Get in the truck and take him back to wherever you got him. I don't want to know where or how. Just do it now."

Rick looked crestfallen. Debbie marched inside, sobs forming deep in her throat. She wanted to console the poor baby, but knew if she touched him, it would be painful to let go. She didn't look back, just heard the slamming of the passenger door, the opening and closing of the driver's side door, and the truck tearing out of the lot.

Debbie locked the EZ Mart door behind her, pulled the hood of her sweatshirt over her head, and crouched behind the counter to sob for a few minutes before composing herself, reopening the store, and propping herself next to the register. She opened a magazine.

The speed limit along LaFleur Highway toward Bear River from Brotherhood is fifty-five miles per hour. There are no passing lanes in either direction for the entire twenty-four miles from the small village to the larger town. While paved, the road was crumbling in many areas and the Bear County Road Commission received a handful of complaints each year. Crews performed the minimal patching to keep the road from breaking apart altogether. The stretch wasn't traveled often enough to warrant a larger investment.

A Michigan State Police sergeant told Debbie that Rick was going at least eighty-five miles per hour in the pouring rain on a particularly bumpy part of the road when he attempted to pass a Sonata going a few miles under the speed limit. The Sonata was driven by an elderly couple from Brotherhood whom Debbie knew, Dick and Maryann MacArthur, who routinely went to Bear River so Maryann could shop at the yarn store. At that same moment, none other than Howdy Denver in his obnoxiously yellow Lexus SUV was headed toward Brotherhood in the opposing lane. Rick tried to brake and swerve behind the Sonata, but it was too late. He was going too fast. The pickup flipped and rolled three times before striking a tree and bursting into flames.

"I'm sorry for your loss," the state police sergeant said to her over the phone. "Was the baby yours?"

Debbie had no response. She stood in the bedroom of the big, spooky house she shared with Rick, her cell phone to her ear, feeling like she was splintering. It was three o'clock in the morning and she had been up all night worried because he hadn't come home.

"Ma'am?" the sergeant said. "Are you OK? Should we send someone over there?"

"No," Debbie blurted. "I'm fine."

"Losing a child is a terrible thing," the sergeant said.

"You're not from Bear County, are you, officer?"

"Well, no. I was transferred from a post near Detroit last week."

"The baby was not mine," she said. "We don't have any children."

There was a pause on the other end of the phone.

"Well, all the same, I am sorry for your loss."

It took detectives a couple more days to piece together what happened. Each of those days was excruciating for Debbie, who had resolved not to tell anyone about the baby, but the police were not satisfied. Several different officers came to question Debbie, who told them everything except for Rick's brief stop at the gas station and their conversation in the rain.

"You didn't know anything about the baby?"

"No, sir. I worked my shift and went home. When Rick didn't show up, I assumed he was at the bar. That wasn't unusual. Then I got the call from you guys. I don't have a clue what he was up to."

They likely knew she was lying—she could feel it—but there was no way for them to disprove her story. One detective tried scaring her by looking up at the security camera over the counter and saying that Howdy Denver would happily supply them with all the surveillance footage from that day.

"Go ahead," Debbie said. "The cameras are fake. Howdy won't spring for real ones."

Debbie tried to prepare herself for questions, especially after it was discovered the baby boy in the car was the same newborn reported missing to Bear River City Police earlier that same day. The mother was seventeen-year-old Trisha Frenough, a second cousin to the Stoneciphers, who Rick routinely railed against because she ran with the druggie crowd. They were the kids who smoked weed and shot methadone—and heroin when they could get it—into the veins near their knuckles to avoid track marks. The father of the baby, Trent, was in the county lockup pending a litany of charges for breaking into the large homes on the Hill, overlooking the big lake. It was rumored Trisha had accompanied Trent while pregnant on several of the jobs and would soon be implicated.

Debbie immediately understood Rick's reasoning. With both parents possibly serving prison sentences, the baby would surely have a better life with them. Exactly how Rick snatched the baby wasn't entirely clear, though it appeared he didn't have to go to any great lengths. Trisha told police she remembered seeing her cousin that day. That, yes, he came to the squalid apartment she temporarily shared with several others in Bear River's shabbiest neighborhood. She had smoked massive amounts of marijuana and hashish and drank a pint of vodka mixed with Mountain Dew. She went to take a nap. The baby was gone when she woke up.

It's what Rick did after he had the baby that confounded police. Why, for instance, was he headed *back* to Bear River from Brotherhood? The detectives were sharp, Debbie discovered.

"Are you sure he didn't bring the baby back here to you and then you told him to take it back?" the sergeant asked.

Debbie had confidence from telling the same lie over and over again.

She lied so much it felt true.

A week after Rick's funeral, Debbie stood behind the counter unable to concentrate on the *In Touch* magazine splayed before her. She had been trembling for days. Her nails were chewed down, some bloody. Whenever she tried focusing on what she was doing in the present, her mind wandered to the end of the road, beyond the fenced-off land with the scrub trees where the chemical plant had been, to the trail out to the High Bridge and what it would feel like to float through the air until crashing into the tops of the trees or smacking into the rocks along the river.

She told Pha Vong about it.

"Death is the easiest thing on earth. I think you should seek help immediately" was the summation of Pha Vong's reply.

The bell over the door jingled and a slim girl with a sallow face and stringy blond hair came in. Debbie recognized her as Rick's cousin Trisha, who had refused to come to his ceremony and, in fact, planned a memorial for the baby at the same time to test the loyalty of family members. It was widely known that Bear County prosecutors were preparing charges against her for the break-ins. The warrant could come down any day and she'd go to jail.

Trisha carried the strong smell of cigarettes and cheap hairspray into the store. She came up and placed her palms down on the glass lottery ticket case built into the counter. Debbie could see the marks on the young girl's hands, where she had shot up with a syringe. They had never spoken before, but Debbie knew she had a tendency for violent outbursts. Debbie slipped her cell phone off the counter and held it in her back pocket, ready to dial 911.

Trisha glared at Debbie over the counter. Debbie couldn't tell if the girl was going to scream or break down in tears.

"I don't have much to say to you," Trisha said. "All's I can say is don't even think about jumping off that bridge."

Debbie was still touching the cell phone in her back pocket, but at the mention of the bridge she put both hands on the counter and looked off at the chip rack while the image of Melissa's twirling black hair and wheeling arms passed through her mind.

"You deserve more of a punishment than that."

Debbie nodded.

"Now give me some money."

"What?"

"I said give me some money. From the register. Everything that's in there."

Debbie paused, then did the only thing she could, Howdy Denver be damned. She popped open the register, took out a hundred dollars, and set it on the counter. Trisha grabbed the cash and scurried out the door without saying another word. A truck sped away from the gas station. Debbie stood right where she was. She closed the magazine and looked out the window, staring into the glassy eyes of the stuffed deer in the taxidermy shop across the street. She didn't look away. She dared not move.

The Skull House

Lillie Korpela collected skulls.

One morning in early winter, the slim and strong eighty-five-year-old woman crossed the land between the farmhouse and outbuildings to the edge of her property and walked into the woods. She moved steadily but slowly, wearing a fleece-lined red woolen coat she'd bought in Bear River a few years back. Her long hair, the color of corn silk, was mashed inside a black fleece hat that wrapped warmly around her ears and fastened under her chin with a Velcro strap. She walked toward Swanson Creek, which fed into Bear River.

Lillie carried a burlap sack, three finely sharpened knives of varying sizes for any skinning that needed to be done in the field, the walking stick she had carved from a handsome oak branch, and a hacksaw for any beheadings. In a backpack, she carried a first aid kit, flashlight, compass, tarp, rope, matches, a can of beans, a can opener, and a blanket. She'd hauled the emergency backpack around for years and had never needed any of the items inside.

Lillie moved through the cold forest, the sky white and deep with potential snow, the first of the season. Fallen leaves crunched under her footfalls. This time of year, there were always deer carcasses from careless hunters who injured the animals with a bullet or arrow, but never tracked them. She'd found many deer with arrows poking out of their sides down by the creek. Now she scanned the ground and saw nothing but stumps, leaves, branches, and tree limbs.

Lillie's knees began to ache from arthritis. She leaned more on the walking stick with every step. The pain in her knees had become so bad that she hadn't been out in October or November. She usually avoided deer hunting season anyway. This walk might be the last before the heavy snow came. Lillie planned a short trip down to the creek, then home before 3 p.m., when one of her favorite movies, Alfred Hitchcock's *Rear Window*, was on TV. She'd seen the movie as many times as she'd walked this path in the woods, and also never tired of it.

As she approached Swanson Hill, a flash of black high up on the incline caught her eye. The thought that it might be a dead bear came in an instant. Bear skulls were the most sacred. When she was little, her grandfather, an immigrant from Finland, told her that when a bear died it went back to the stars and was reincarnated and returned to walk the earth once more. Bears were plentiful in the days of the natives. Lillie heard all the stories as a child, how the woods teemed with them until a mad four-hundred-pound beast devoured the famed French Jesuit priest Father Gabriel Pierre LaFleur alongside the mighty Bear River and the remaining animals were hunted with a vengeance by the arriving white men. She knew about the lumbermen who followed and clear-cut much of the timber until the land was worthless and abandoned to the government, whose only recourse was to turn it into federal forest and let the trees grow again. She imagined bears running out of the woods and back in. When she was young and started collecting skulls, she'd stumble across a dead bear at least once a year during her daily treks. As more retirees and tourists flocked north to set up permanent homes, continued development of the land in the area made the creatures scarce. Lillie was lucky to find a bear carcass every five or six years.

It had been even longer, probably about a decade, when she saw the flash of black on Swanson Hill. Even though she had avoided the hill in as many years because it was too dangerous, Lillie began laboriously scaling it. She had to make sure.

She stopped to rest not a third of the way up, shimmying out of her pack and settling in on the ground, happy to be relieved of its weight. The black patch wasn't visible from where she sat down in the leaves next to some saplings. She clutched her sore knees to her chest and massaged them. Maybe Karen was right, Lillie was far too old to be hiking in the woods by herself.

Karen was technically Lillie's employee at the Skull House but had in fact become something of her caretaker. Karen had grown up in Sampo, where most girls got pregnant at sixteen and lived off government aid, or left for college and never returned. Karen did neither. She started hanging out at the Skull House when she was in high school, back when she wore all-black clothes and gobbed on layers of black makeup. Lillie was frightened of the big girl with a silver chain going from a piercing in her nose to one in her ear. Lillie told her if she took the earring out, she could have a job taking admission money. Despite her shocking look, Karen was very shy and sweet. She removed the piercings and thrived in the job; now thirty, she'd worked for Lillie in some capacity for almost fifteen years. Lillie had taught her to walk the woods. She taught her how to collect and clean the skulls.

Karen lost weight and got strong from hiking so much. She learned bookkeeping and other skills related to running the small business. Even though she remained living with her parents, who ran a motel at the edge of the village, she became something of a daughter to Lillie, who stipulated in her will that Karen would inherit the Skull House.

In the last few years, Karen was reluctant to let Lillie go into the woods alone.

"Just let me know and I'll come with you," she would say.

Lillie didn't need anyone telling her what to do, even if it did make sense now as she sat on the slope of the hill rubbing her knees. The first few flakes of snow shook down from the sky. She could either continue up the hill toward what she hoped was a dead bear and take its head, or she could turn around and go home, watch her movie, and have Karen bring over dinner. Lillie didn't ponder it long. She hoisted the pack up on her back and started trudging up the hill toward the black patch, convinced more than ever that it was a dead bear.

She hadn't taken more than five steps when both knees buckled. Lillie fell backwards. There were no trees to grab for balance. Everything was awhirl. Her head hit the ground and she tumbled down the hill. She was worried one of the knives on her waist would jostle loose and stab her in the side or that the hacksaw lashed to the pack would cut her, but neither happened. She came to a rest at the base of the hill, the pain in her right side immediate and shocking. Unable to move, she took stock: the hot rush of blood on her head, the likely broken hip. She didn't cry. She lay on her back and stared at the whiteness of the sky and the flakes rocking gently toward her.

Lillie had been disappearing deep into the federal forest behind her family's old dairy farm in northern Michigan's Bear County for seventy years, trudging through knee-high snow in the winter to find the remains of animals that had starved to death. In the summer, the waxy green woods were a hot riot of mosquitoes and flies. She would brave the heat and bugs to find deer, raccoon, and porcupine carcasses decomposing in the steamy swamps and drag them back to the farmhouse to clean.

It started when Lillie was eighteen and checked out a book on osteology from the Sampo branch of the library. The process required ammonia, bleach, peroxide, a sharp paring knife, forceps, dissecting scissors, a paintbrush, and rubber gloves. Over the years, the farm's dairy operations had died down and the family subsisted by selling off parcels, so her dad gave her permission to take over a shed no longer needed to store equipment. Lillie turned it into a laboratory for skeleton preparation. She bought a large cast-iron pot for boiling and dug a fire pit outside the shed's doors. She immersed herself in the process: possums, raccoons, minks, and beavers. Anything she could find.

Lillie would remove the outer skin and fur of the skull until just the red meaty flesh was showing. Then she would put the skull in cold soda water and let it soak before putting it on the fire and bringing it to a bubbling boil. She learned that larger skulls of deer took longer than the small skull of a squirrel. When the flesh on the back of the head started to fall away from the bone, the skull had been boiled sufficiently.

She would run water into the pot, cooling it gradually—otherwise the skulls would crack—and would then use the paring knife to scrape off the remaining bits of flesh, ripping out the eyes and throwing them in the fire where they would hiss. The ligaments holding the jaw were cut, the two pieces separated and rejoined with twine.

She would remove the brain with forceps through the foramen magnum, the large hole at the back of the skull. Sometimes she had to fill the skull with water and shake it vigorously for the brain to come loose, before soaking it in solutions and setting it in the sunshine to bleach.

Lillie Korpela had repeated this process thousands of times, beginning when she was a teenager during World War II. The fear and sadness stemming from the war drove her into the woods where she'd played with her two brothers, Alex and Waino, both lost overseas. By the 1960s, Lillie had acquired thousands of skulls, all crowding the shelves of the outbuildings on the old dairy farm. When her parents died, leaving her alone on the property, Lillie constructed a house out of them.

The Skull House wasn't very big, only about six-hundred square feet, built in the style of a rustic pioneer cabin. For every layer of brick there was a layer of skulls embedded in concrete. The roof had standard shingles, with several rows of animal skulls. When it rained, the water gushed through the eyelets and mouths of the various creatures as it ran off the gutters.

There was a small porch adorned with more skulls; two bear skulls stood on top of the posts in places of honor. Inside the house was a hearth big enough for her cast-iron pot and a giant sink for cleaning off the animals, and there was a small, well-ventilated room off to the side with an exhaust fan for the chemicals. It was everything Lillie had wanted while preparing skulls in the makeshift shed of her youth.

People were bewildered by the Skull House, which was visible from the road. Cars would slow to a crawl while husbands and wives gaped out the window. Children pointed and laughed. While some could never accept such a monstrosity—one local minister called the Skull House a "demon-influenced blight on the wholesome, healthy populace of Bear County"—public tide eventually changed in Lillie's favor. People were curious. Lillie started charging admission and giving tours and demonstrations.

She ran the house by herself for years, making a modest income. There was a spike in business when it was featured in *The Guinness Book of World Records* in the 1970s. She started getting requests from magazines and television shows. *Ripley's Believe It or Not!* came and filmed a segment. In the '80s, a crew from Hollywood arrived and used it as a location in a horror film. Lillie thought the movie was tacky; she preferred classic cinema, her other passion in life.

By the 1990s, the neighbors who had shunned her were dead and the Skull House had become an institution, featured in state and national travel guides. There was even a sign on US 31 a few miles out of town that read "Come see the world-famous Skull House!"

Through all of it, Lillie still foraged in the woods for skulls, though she only got out a few times a year now. She found that collecting and cleaning skulls was so comforting, so soothing, it had become a necessity for living.

Lillie knew very well she could die at the bottom of Swanson Hill with a broken hip and a possible concussion if she didn't move. She slipped out of her pack and slithered painfully away to unzip it. The first aid kit contained painkillers she'd been prescribed for arthritis and she swallowed three of them dry, continuing to rummage through the bag as her side burned, the pain electric. She pulled out the tarp, blanket, and a large Ziploc bag with matches and an emergency fuel stick, then realized she couldn't stand up, so she stuffed everything into the pack and zipped it back up.

She lay on her back, staring at the white sky until the painkillers kicked in and dulled the screaming on her right side.

There was a large pine stump amid fallen trees twenty excruciating yards away. If she crawled to them, she could fashion a tent with the tarp and use the branches to start a fire. If she was to survive the night, she had to have heat and some sort of shelter from the snow.

Lillie rolled onto her stomach and gripped her pack. She used her arms to pull herself across the forest floor toward the stump, grunting through the pain. She had to rest for a moment when she was about halfway there, but then continued dragging herself through the leaves and twigs. Her breathing was deep. Once she got there, she unzipped the pack again and took out the matches and fire stick. There were plenty of dead branches to burn within reach. She snapped and piled them on top of the fire stick, lit it quickly with a match. A small fire began crackling.

The tarp was draped over the stump and anchored by branches and dirt. She crawled to the loose end and weighted it down with her pack, and in one last burst of energy and pain, she rolled under the tarp with her blanket, a can of beans, a can opener, and the remaining painkillers. It was only afternoon, but she was ready for the night. After the rush of activity, she listened to the fire. She listened to the natural rhythm of the woods. Her chest rose and fell. Still alive. The snowflakes tapped the blue tarp overhead. The fire shot up curls of black and gray smoke. If she didn't move, she was quite comfortable.

Lillie didn't know if she wanted to be found.

Dusk came early and brought more snow, frenzied and swarming like bugs in the sky. She continued feeding branches to the fire while an inch of snow accumulated around her. The snow would provide insulation.

She opened the beans and drank some straight from the can. Just a little bit satisfied her hunger. She didn't think about what was going to happen to her. She was happy to be warm, to have the beans.

It was soon pitch-black and the woods became wrapped in mystery. Lillie didn't know them any longer. The sounds had changed. She listened carefully, more alert now than before. She knew that not finishing the beans was a bad idea. They would attract animals. She took one last sip and threw the can, trying not to jar her hip.

It was a stupid idea. The can only made it ten feet and now she couldn't sleep. She waited for a visit from critters as the clouds moved on and the snow was replaced by stars. In the moonlight, Lillie saw a raccoon waddle to the can. She had encountered numerous coons in the past, but never while she was completely incapacitated. It ravenously ate the beans, scuttling the can around in the dirt. Then another coon came up and they screeched at each other. This is what she was afraid of, that the animals would fight and end up on top of her and she wouldn't be able to defend herself. She gripped a large flashlight in one hand and a walking stick in the other as the animals clawed and screamed at each other a few feet away. They eventually settled down once the beans were gone. One took the can and wandered off, and the ground around Lillie was peaceful again. Still, she clutched the flashlight and the walking stick.

Dawn broke cold and painfully. It was a raw morning in every way. The branches creaked into frozen positions. Lillie woke from a haze of restless pain and light slumber, the fire down to embers. She didn't have the strength to stoke it back to life.

She swallowed the last of the painkillers and lay under the tarp, not knowing her next move. Her leg hurt too much. Still, she didn't panic.

Lillie had never been afraid of dying. She welcomed it in every living moment, conscious of it with every breath. Long ago she had decided that she needed to love death just as much as she loved life. Otherwise, she would go crazy. She knew it was one of the reasons she surrounded herself with skulls. She didn't believe in an afterlife but didn't disbelieve, either. It wasn't knowledge human beings needed to have.

She revisited these thoughts. She thought about the way the muscles wrapped the bones in her father's neck when she would see it from the back seat of their old Ford. She thought about the clean sweaty smell of her brothers when they returned from the woods. She thought about her mother's laugh, which they rarely heard but when they did it was high-pitched and startling. It made everyone in the family laugh too.

Then she heard rustling and thought maybe critters were returning for more beans.

"Lillie? Is that you? Oh my God."

It was Karen. Lillie saw her approaching with a Bear County sheriff's deputy who was pulling the radio microphone from his shoulder, pressing a button and mumbling into it.

Karen ran to Lillie and knelt next to the tarp. "I was so worried," she said frantically. "Are you OK? Please tell me you're OK."

"There's a bear at the top of the hill," Lillie said. "Go see if it's a bear."

"That's not important right now," Karen said. "Can you move?"

"I think I broke my hip."

"Ambulance is on the way," the deputy said.

It took an hour and a half to get Lillie out of the woods. The paramedics had to park the ambulance at the Skull House and walk a stretcher out to Swanson Hill. The pain screamed when they lifted her on the stretcher, but then one of the paramedics, a young woman wearing a ball cap, primed her arm with a cotton swab and stuck in the needle.

"You'll be feeling better soon," she said.

The other paramedic was a young man wearing the same type of cap. They got on either side of the stretcher and walked Lillie out of the forest. Karen and the deputy followed alongside.

Lillie looked up at the sky and the gnarled tree limbs as she bobbed up and down thinking, This is what it's like to be dragged out of the woods.

They took her to the hospital, where a doctor confirmed the broken hip. Nurses pumped her full of narcotics and bland food. They turned on the television. Karen said she would check in the next day and left. Lillie fell asleep. It was pleasant enough until the fever set in.

She had a disturbing dream about the bear on Swanson Hill. She was lying on the forest floor again, terrified and unable to move as the bear ambled toward her. She thought it was going to rip her up, but instead it lay next to her on the forest ground, nuzzling her body. Together they were warm. She could read its thoughts. It was a male; he had died on top of the hill after a long, happy life, but he couldn't go to the stars and be reincarnated and come back to walk the earth unless he became part of the Skull House.

"You know about the house?" Lillie asked him.

"We all know about the house," the bear said.

Lillie wept tears of joy and promised she would come back for him. As soon as she could move.

Lillie woke up sweaty and delirious, the dream images of the bear circulating in her thoughts. A nurse came and took her temperature. It was 103 degrees. Lillie didn't care about the fever or that her whole body ached. She had to get that bear from Swanson Hill.

She waited until Karen came the next morning. "You have to get the bear's head," she told her. "I know it's up there."

"You've got a bad fever, Lillie," Karen said. "Try and get some sleep. There probably never was a bear."

"You promise you'll check, though?" Lillie said. "I'm just asking this one thing."

"Fine," Karen said. "I'll let you know tomorrow."

Lillie reached out and grabbed her arm. She beckoned her closer. "I want you to bring me his head," she whispered. "I want to see for myself. The bear wants to walk the earth again."

Lillie's strange dreams about the bear continued. She clutched a raft in open water, which she guessed was Lake Michigan, the only large body of water she had ever seen. The bear was behind her on a different raft, trying to catch up. In another dream, she was locked in a room on the second floor of an old house that felt like a hotel. The room was completely empty. There was nowhere to hide. The bear was on the other side of the door, trying to get in. He wasn't clawing or making any noise, but she was intently aware of his presence.

She woke in a feverish fit to see Karen standing shrouded in shadows and beeping machines. It was the middle of the night and only the hallway lights of the Bear County Medical Center were kept on.

Karen had a large backpack with her.

"Is that it?" Lillie asked.

Karen took a few steps toward Lillie's bed, unzipped the backpack, and pulled out a magnificent, severed bear head. She had to hold it with both hands, it was so big and heavy.

"It was right where you told me to find it, on the top of Swanson Hill," Karen said.

"How is it?" Lillie said.

"It's perfect."

Lillie felt a wave of relief, and then a wave of joy. She lay back on the pillow and closed her eyes, happy that she could clean the flesh off the skull and put it in the house so the bear could go up to the stars and back down to earth.

The fever broke the next morning. Lillie woke up in the bright hospital room with only mild sensations of the dreams from the previous two days. The nurse brought her some orange juice, which she drank while reading the *Bear River Dauntless*. She was midway through a story about an upcoming community theater production of *Fiddler on the Roof* when she felt the bear.

Lillie shuddered with panic. She couldn't remember what was real or not. Had she been on a raft? In an old hotel room? Had Karen been in the hospital room with the severed head? She wasn't sure of anything, and she didn't want to reveal to the doctors, nurses, and especially Karen that she didn't remember. The rest of the morning was spent fretting over the potentially embarrassing things she had said to people in her feverish fit.

Karen came to visit in the afternoon. She was bright, smiling, and carrying a stack of new magazines.

"Jeez, you look a lot better," she said, pulling a chair up to Lillie's bedside and setting the magazines on the table. "You looked like hell yesterday."

"I feel better," Lillie said. She desperately wanted to ask about the crazy things she may have said, but waited, hoping Karen would offer it up on her own. And after a few minutes of chitchat, Karen did.

"You had a heck of a fever," she said. "You were saying some weird stuff."

"Like what?" Lillie asked.

"About how you needed that bear's head, about how it wouldn't be able to come back to life if I didn't find it. You were so sure it was there."

Lillie paused for a long time. "Was it?" she asked finally.

"No," Karen said. "Like I said yesterday, it was a garbage bag filled with old clothes. I brought it here to show you because I knew you wouldn't believe me." She looked concerned. "Don't you remember?"

"Yes, of course," Lillie said.

Lillie propped herself up in bed and smiled at her friend through the embarrassment of not remembering. Karen didn't seem to notice, preoccupied instead with the remote control in her hand. She flipped through various menus to a channel with classic movies where *Vertigo* was just starting.

"You like this one, right?" Karen asked.

Lillie settled back in bed as the awkwardness was glossed over. Lillie had seen the movie a dozen times before but thought it was a perfect afternoon to watch it with Karen, who had never seen many of the movies Lillie loved. The room was light and airy with winter sun shining through the big window as Jimmy Stewart hopped around on a rooftop. They could talk about the movie and forget about the bear on top of the hill. Lillie wouldn't have to worry about any bear's soul that day. The animals knew how to find their own way back to earth with or without her.

Bonecutters

Todd Bonecutter began acting out his dreams, making them true. Last night he dreamed about a video game machine filled with oil, the kind that lubes machines and cars, making them slick inside. Todd was nineteen and liked both cars and video games. He hated to do it, but he took his Xbox, went to the garage, and grabbed a can of Pennzoil from a dusty shelf. He knew his grandmother was watching him from the kitchen window, the nag. She could see him across the small yard strewn with dog shit from Terminator, their German shepherd—solid brown deposits sunk heatedly in the snow.

"What are you doing, Todd? Did you get my lottery tickets yet?" she yelled through the screen.

"I'm busy, Grandma!" he yelled back in his crackling, adolescent voice. He was still going through puberty at nineteen. Having dead parents never allowed you to grow up.

Todd slammed the garage door. Now she couldn't see. She would shuffle off to the kitchen table to enter mail-in sweepstakes and scarf OxyContin. "For my back pain," she always said, plunking them in her mouth and swallowing. Her back seemed to hurt at least seven times a day.

Todd hoisted the Xbox onto the workbench where his father used to carve duck decoys in his rare sober moments, and tilted it on its side. He took the oil can and began pouring. The black liquid enveloped the entire machine.

He'd saved three months working at Bud's Suds Car Wash out on the highway to afford that Xbox before Bud let him go because business was no good, and now here he was, destroying it. But he had to. He was compelled to act out dreams. He had recently climbed the tree outside his elementary school, smacked rocks with a baseball bat in the field next to the cardboard factory, and spent a half hour underneath his front porch in the snow with Terminator. He felt so relieved acting out these parts of his dreams from the past few weeks that he needed to keep going.

His buddy Ryan would have something to say about it, for sure. Ryan was down at college in Chicago and used to brag about screwing girls, but now boasted that he was an existentialist. Todd thought he was being lame when he talked about stuff like that. He wanted to play video games instead.

Now they couldn't. The machinery was downright ruined.

But watching the black oil run over the console was the only satisfying thing Todd had felt since the last time. It matched up with the feeling he had during his dream.

Warm.

In a different place altogether.

The door flew open and his grandmother came kicking into the garage. She was angry, her giant brown leather purse in tow. Her hair wasn't yet gray. She was only in her fifties.

"Where's my checkbook!" she screamed. "You took it, didn't you! Trying to write yourself checks like your brother, eh? And my medicine is gone."

She meant the Oxys Dr. Norwick gave her.

"I never touched your checkbook. It was probably Denise," he said.

His sister-in-law had a gambling problem. She and his older brother would be out at the Indian casino at the edge of town for days when they were riding high at the blackjack table, then come back to the house at Ninth and Elm asking Grandma for money when they were down. When Todd was done playing the Xbox he just destroyed, he used to hide it under his bed so Denise and Roy wouldn't take it, try to sell it at the pawn shop even though it was more profitable in Bear County to fence stuff to friends and acquaintances.

"What the hell did you do to your game thing!" she cried, seeing the destroyed console.

"It's mine. I can do what I want with it."

"But it was three hundred bucks," she said. He regretted telling her how much it had cost, though he had done so with pride back when he bought it.

"So what? It's mine."

"You always were a dumbass, Todd. You and your brother," she said. "If you see him or Denise, you tell 'em I'm coming for them. They can't get away with stealing my checks no more."

She looked at the oiled Xbox on the workbench, shook her head, and left. He heard the Cutlass firing up in the driveway, the crackle of its tires on the gravel. She was probably headed to the casino. She'd sit in front of the slot machines and gamble away the hundred-dollar pension check that was meant to keep them afloat.

Screw 'em, thought Todd Bonecutter. All of them: his grandma, his brother, and his sister-in-law, the only family he had left in the world. There was an older sister too, but he barely knew her. Jill Bonecutter had fled town years earlier to join a punk rock band. Wisely, she never returned.

That night he dreamed he attacked his grandmother with a screwdriver in the stairwell of the collapsing frame house. He felt the tool sink slowly into her chest, the warmth of the blood on his fingers. He felt terrible the day after that dream and cursed his brain for having it. What he most wanted to see in his sleep were hot chicks. Sometimes, he'd dream about screwing movie stars and wake up with soggy boxers. It didn't always have to be a star, though. Sometimes all it took was Lauren, the waitress at Big Don's Pizza Shop. He did not know how to go about re-creating these dreams. Afterward, he'd sneak his sticky boxers into the washing machine and get it running in the wee hours of the morning. He'd made the mistake of leaving stained underwear in the laundry once and never heard the end of it from his grandma.

Todd ignored the dream about stepping up to his grandma with the screwdriver. He didn't try to sneak up behind her, didn't try to act it out. It made him feel incomplete the next day, but he was determined not to be as dumb as the rest of his family.

For years the Bonecutters had been the bane of Bear County: a rap sheet stretching from Lake Michigan to the county line at Hiller Road. Prosecutors for the past four decades would attest to this. While it was just Todd, his grandma, and brother living in town, other Bonecutters—aunts, uncles, cousins, and sometimes no known relation at all, just a shared last name—were spread throughout the county. They built plywood additions onto their trailers in the forest. They drank cheap whiskey in rented rooms in the county's smaller towns away from the big lake. They worked infrequently plowing snow, digging ditches, and washing dishes. They were arrested for poaching deer, drunk and disorderly, domestic assault, and once (Larry Bonecutter, 1974) for attempted murder.

No Bonecutter had ever done much good and Todd felt he was the first in the family to realize this. Shortly after his parents' death—their ice shanty sank on the little lake with both of them drunk inside when he was twelve—a psychologist told him he matured quicker than most kids. Now, at nineteen, with adulthood upon him, he was determined to do something good, no matter how brief and insignificant life was, like his buddy Ryan said.

He knew there was a difference in the ways people used the word "dream." There was the kind like when you go to sleep and see weird pictures in your dark brain, the dreams he'd been trying to understand by making them real. Then there was the Follow Your Dream poster taped on the cinder block wall in his high school with a happy guy and girl, riding hand-in-hand down a rainbow in a roller coaster car toward a bright future. At the end of the rainbow was a real nice house edged with a fence with little stick figures of kids playing in the yard. The thought of having a family and a house made Todd hopeful.

He wanted to be the first Bonecutter to follow that rainbow to a peaceful life. He just didn't know where to start. There were no jobs to be had at the paper mill or salt plant. And all the good-looking girls ignored him.

So, while many citizens in the town of Bear River and the surrounding environs of Bear County thought the Bonecutters were parasites, Todd felt it was his hometown that was nibbling on him from the outside in.

If he could only get out, he'd find that rainbow.

But there was his stupid last name that seemed to permanently assign him to the basements and backyards of Bear County. He had to be around for his grandma, to take care of the family house purchased by great-grandpa Merriman Bonecutter, the last reputable soul in the lineage, who'd worked in the lumber trade in the 1920s and made enough to buy the house in the city outright. Terminator needed food, water, and his daily run on the beach. When his brother wasn't drinking and tearing up the town with Denise, they had a decent drywall business going. Who would be there to mud and tape?

He never wanted to dream about them the way he did about his dead parents, who appeared as ghostly, waterlogged versions of their former selves. Their flesh slid off their bones like something straight out of the zombie movies he and his brother rented from the grocery store when they were kids. Most times, though, they would be trying to grab him and take him someplace he didn't want to go.

"It's very normal to be having such dreams," the psychologist from the county health department told him when he was twelve. "You've suffered a terrible trauma. They will go away."

They didn't. For seven years, his dead parents terrified him while he slept. Todd didn't understand why. His parents weren't very nice to him or his siblings in real life. They would leave them for weeks at a time with his grandma while they went off on benders. They were unemployable, absentee alcoholics.

Two nights after he was let go from Bud's Suds, he had a vivid dream where they tried to lure him into the dumpster behind Lester's Bait and Beer. The lid was down, but their heads were pushing it up just enough so he could see their blue-gray eyes, stringy hair, and sagging skin. Both extended their arms out of the green dumpster and beckoned Todd closer with their index fingers.

They didn't speak. They never spoke, just moaned.

In the dream, Todd took off his shoes and whipped them at the dumpster. After he did that, he woke up in his basement bedroom to Terminator's barking and whining. The shepherd was circling the furnace just outside of the room, wanting to go outside.

Todd dressed, let him out, then rode his bike up to Lester's, still in a trance. Lester's Bait and Beer was actually the main full-service tavern in town. It occupied the bottom floor of a three-story brick building on Main Street along the river. Boaters could cruise up and dock their boat and come inside and grab a beer and lunch, gas up, and even get some bait. Todd used to find his parents in the bar all the time when he was a kid. He remembered the creaky wooden floors, the brass rail running along the bar, the smell of peanuts and beer. The walls were covered with mounted fish, huge lake trout and salmon frozen in action poses.

Todd went around to the back of the building by the river and stood in the same position facing the dumpster as he had in the dream. The lid was down, and he expected it to lift and reveal the bloated corpses of his dead parents. It didn't. Todd removed his Nike LeBron Zoom Soldier III high-tops (he never scrimped on sneakers) and whipped them both at the dumpster—again, like the dream. Hearing the rubber soles bounce off the side of the metal brought him the most joy and relief he'd felt in seven years.

It was as if joining the two worlds gave him a sense of control. Once he started reenacting parts of his dreams, the bloated, zombie versions of his parents ceased to appear.

He'd only seen skyscrapers in movies, but one night he dreamed about kissing the side of a building that disappeared into the clouds. The building was flanked by an infinite empty beach. The water was a sludgy purple. Todd was afraid his parents would emerge out of the dark water and grab him as he crawled down the beach on his hands and knees after kissing the building, but they never did. For some reason his legs didn't work. As the thick waves oozed up and receded, Todd was forced to try walking on his hands to avoid being touched by the rubbery water.

There were no buildings higher than four stories in Bear River, so Todd had to hold off on acting out that part. He left Terminator at home because it was only 10 degrees, went down to the lake, and tried doing handstands. It was freezing out. The large banks of snow behind him made the beach feel lunar. Floes bobbed in the surf. He wore thick gloves and couldn't stay upright for more than a few seconds before flopping over in the cold, snowy sand.

It made him feel better. But still, he wanted to get at that giant building.

When he got home he knew something was wrong, because his grandma wasn't screaming at him when he walked in. Todd knew she was home; he had seen the rusted Cutlass in the driveway. Todd thumbed the two dollars she'd given him and swore at himself. He'd forgotten the lottery tickets she asked for when he left an hour earlier.

His grandma was motionless on the kitchen floor, curled up in a fetal position, Terminator licking blood off her face. There was more blood on the floor. A can of beans bubbled in a saucepan on the range. Todd pulled Terminator away and called 911.

Following the ambulance in the Cutlass to the hospital at the edge of town near the casino, Todd became solemn. Driving

behind the flashing lights and blaring sirens, he felt more dutiful than he had in a long time, as if by showing up at her side
despite how terrible she'd always been, he was making some sort of
sacrifice. He suddenly missed her and started thinking about the
nice moments between them, like when they watched reality TV
and made fun of the contestants. Or when his parents disappeared
on a binge and his grandma took them to Big Don's. She'd buy
them pizza and put a pile of quarters on the table so Todd and his
brother could play Pac-Man.

Police still didn't know who'd beaten his grandma, but Todd
Bonecutter had his suspicions, even if he wouldn't allow them to
take full shape on the drive down the highway to the hospital.

"Her brain is dead, Todd. The machines are keeping her alive.
There's nothing to be done," Dr. Norwick said. "She's gone."

They stood in the gleaming bright hallway.

"Do I have to, like, give you permission to turn off the
machines?" Todd asked. He felt smelly and dirty in the pristine
hospital environment, as if the doctor was dressed in scrubs and
gloves for protection from his insulated flannel that reeked of cigarette smoke, and his scruffy beard, which did too.

"She's already been pronounced dead. We don't need consent,"
he said. Norwick was a boring-looking guy in his forties. He was
smaller than Todd, who wasn't very big himself. Todd didn't like
that he prescribed his grandma pain pills she didn't need. "I'm
sorry," the doctor said, and walked away. Todd suddenly felt like he
was in an elevator at the top of the building that disappeared into
the clouds and it was suddenly released, its wires snapped, free falling. He went into the lobby and took a seat on a couch to get steady.

That's where the state trooper found him and told him what
happened: his brother and Denise had cracked his grandma
repeatedly on the skull with a metal broomstick when she wouldn't
give them money. They stole her checkbook and OxyContin and
went out to have a blast at the casino, where tribal police busted
them for trying to forge her name. They were so stupid they had

already confessed everything and were sitting in county jail, their buzzes wearing off.

That dutiful feeling he felt on the way to the hospital was gone by the time he started the Cutlass for home. He began to see the beating as a way to release him. His grandma was dead and his brother was in jail. For the first time in his life, Todd Bonecutter could do whatever he wanted.

Would Chicago be a new start for Todd, or would he end up preemptively dead like his parents or in jail like his brother? If he became the first in his family to strike out of Bear County in generations, would he find a kick-ass job, a hot chick, and live happily ever after in the house under the rainbow?

That night he got a call from Ryan, who was in town but leaving the next day for the Windy City. They got good and drunk in Todd's garage, rocketing back can after can from a thirty pack of Milwaukee's Best.

"We're all going to die, and when we die nothing happens. It's like we were never alive. Nothing matters, dude," Ryan told him. "Existence precedes essence."

They had been talking about his grandma.

"It seems like there's more," Todd said. "Or why would we be thinking and shit?"

"Just a fluke," Ryan said. Then he saw the oiled-up console on a shelf over the workbench. "What's that?"

"My Xbox. I drained a can of Pennzoil on it," Todd said.

"Why?"

"I don't know. I'm fucking mental," Todd said. "I had a dream about it, so I did it. I keep acting out my dreams. Like, any part of them I can."

"Why?"

Todd hadn't told anyone about the dreams since the psychologist guy when he was twelve.

"I don't know. I just feel like it, I guess."

"That's actually pretty interesting. Like spilling your subconscious out into reality. A strange tactic of Freudian wish fulfillment. What kinds of things have you done?"

Ryan was smiling, interested. Now that he was going to college in the big city, he wore black T-shirts with the names of strange bands printed on them and thick-framed glasses, which made Todd feel like Ryan was smarter than the other kids they grew up with in Bear River.

"Well, I don't dream every night, or don't remember them. And they have to be real vivid. Last week I dreamed I was underwater with a bunch of pictures from history books floating by my face—Hitler, John F. Kennedy, and Madonna. So, when I woke up I found pictures of them, cut them out, and took them into the bathtub. I looked at them with my eyes open underwater."

"Freaky."

"Another time it was more simple. I had a weird dream about the lady that works at the gas station. You know, Shirley, or whatever her name is. Nothing gross, or anything. She's, like, our parents' age. In fact, she was friends with my mom. But she's always been nice to me whenever I go in there. She was only in the dream for like a minute. There was all sorts of weird stuff with spiders and tunnels that would be impossible to act out. So, I went in and bought a slushie from her and felt better," Todd said.

"What did you dream about last night?" Ryan asked.

Todd told him about the building that disappeared into the clouds.

"We have one like that in Chicago," Ryan said. "You've got nothing left here. I'm driving back tomorrow. You can stay with me as long as you want. My roommates won't care."

They drank through the night.

In the morning, Todd locked up the house that had been in the Bonecutter family since 1926 and hopped in Ryan's car with Terminator, bags of clothes, dog food, and a water bowl. This would be the first time in years the house had been completely empty.

He and Ryan had stopped drinking but were still pretty sloshed as they drove down the Michigan coast to Chicago, talking about the jobs Todd could apply for and how hot the girls in the city were compared to Bear County. They were still buzzed when they reached Indiana.

When Todd saw the giant buildings from a bridge, he started to feel like he had after pouring the oil on the Xbox, and doing hand-stands on the beach, and looking at Hitler underwater, and buying a slushie from Shirley.

Terminator panted at the skyline from the back seat. They would start a new life together.

Ryan stopped the car in the thick of downtown, pulling the Escort up to the curb next to the tallest building Todd had ever seen. Cars zipped by. All the drivers seemed to be honking their horns.

"Can we even stop here?" Todd asked.

"It's America. Sure. Here's the Sears Tower. Used to be the tallest building in the world. Go and do your thing."

"But all these people. All these cars." Todd's stomach was churning. His hands were shaking, so he compulsively petted Ter-minator, whose eyes alertly patrolled the street out the window, looking back and forth, his ears reacting to every small sound.

"They won't mind," Ryan said. "People are doing nutty shit in this town all day and night."

Todd got out of the car. He couldn't tilt his head back far enough to see up the side of that giant black torpedo. There was a stream of people walking in and out past security guards. Ever since his par-ents' death, Todd had been wary of people in uniforms. He wanted to stay as far away from them as possible. Terminator barked from the car.

Todd was surprised to see that the building didn't start until several floors up from a concrete foundation. He climbed the steps, not knowing what he was going to do, and walked straight at the security guards. It wasn't much like his dream, but it was still satisfying to look into the eyes of a short, Hispanic guard before placing his lips on the glass door and kissing it. It tasted like disinfectant.

The guard's head jerked back in confusion. "What are you doing? Did you just kiss that door?" he said. "Get out of here."

For the week he was in Chicago, Todd drank and smoked a ton of weed with Ryan's college friends. He had no dreams; nothing to act out. He slept narcotically during the day on a foldout while Ryan and his two roommates were at class. It was nothing like he expected. The amount of people and commotion made him nauseous. No progress had been made at starting a new life. He'd been too afraid to call about any of the jobs he found and was snubbed by the one girl he tried talking to at a party. She was getting beer from the keg when they made eye contact and he said hello. She pretended not to see or hear him, grabbed her drink, and walked back to her friends. The city disagreed with Terminator too. Todd took him to a dog park at the end of Ryan's street and he barked and nipped at all the dogs running around the cramped, fenced-in park.

It all freaked him out.

One day, his cell buzzed on the table next to the foldout couch. It was Jim Trumbull, Bear River's gruffest defense attorney. Before buying airtime on local television stations advertising his expertise in slip-and-fall and malpractice suits, Trumbull had been a public defender. He knew the Bonecutters well, having been court-appointed counsel for plenty of them over the years.

"I've been trying to track you down for days, Todd," he said. "Your grandma's alive. Norwick and the hospital almost killed her. They messed up royally."

Trumbull said Todd was poised to sue for at least six figures—if he retained Trumbull as his attorney, of course. Todd didn't understand a lot of the technical stuff, but the money seemed cool if he could really get his hands on it.

Ryan drove him and Terminator back north as soon as classes were over for the day. Todd's grandmother was still in the hospital, where Trumbull was waiting for them. Norwick was nowhere to be seen.

"He's been suspended," Trumbull said.

Dr. McAllister, the pleasant woman about his grandma's age who had taken over, told Todd that his grandma was basically still a vegetable but could slowly recover if given the right therapy.

"She wakes and sleeps but is unresponsive so far. She could make a full recovery, though. I'm convinced."

"Does she have to stay here?" Todd asked.

"She doesn't have to," Dr. McAllister said. "But she is certainly welcome to. If not, we can do outpatient or in-house therapy."

"You don't have to worry about the money," Trumbull said.

"I'm taking her home," Todd said.

The doctor and lawyer both made pleas for Todd to let her stay in the hospital, but he was adamant that she be brought back to Ninth and Elm. It was the right thing to do.

The ambulance brought her home just like it had taken her away. They plopped her in the living room in a hospital bed with machines and tubes all around. Todd got a Whopper Meal from Burger King and ate it on the couch while the machines beeped in the corner. The noises seemed to keep her alive. He ate and watched television, then fell asleep on the couch.

Todd dreamed of climbing up on the hospital bed and molesting his grandmother. It was the first dream he'd had since kissing the building.

It was so real.

He knew he had to act something out or else his parents would return.

But killing or molesting his grandmother was wrong. Still, it seemed to be the natural bent of the Bonecutters; just look at his brother and Denise, sitting in the county jail awaiting trial on charges of armed robbery and assault with intent to do bodily harm. They were trying to say they were so insane, so mentally unstable, that they didn't even know what they were doing.

Todd knew what he was doing. He knew he'd be in Bear County taking care of his grandma for the foreseeable future, and that the Bonecutters had to change, even if it meant going against their nature.

He'd start with his dreams.

Todd tried to think about the kind of dreams normal people have. While he was taking a leak in the bathroom, beeps from the machines and television voices raiding his brain from the living room, he looked down at the box of Kleenex on top of the toilet and thought they'd look very pretty coming down from the roof, wafting to the snow-covered ground.

He grabbed the box, got dressed, and made sure his grandma was still breathing. Outside, he got the ladder out of the garage, extended it to the roof, and climbed up. He stood at the edge and pulled out the tissues from the box one by one and let them float down to the frozen ground, thinking it was about time for the Bonecutters to start having beautiful dreams.

Lucy and the Bear

The little girl wanted to be a bear. Whenever she walked, she imagined her clothes ripping apart as her arms and legs expanded with muscle and sprouted coarse, black hair. She learned to growl like a bear. At night, she pressed her face into the pillow and roared so loud that the back of her throat hurt. Feeling totally free of all worry and energy, she would fall asleep instantly.

No one would mess with Lucy if she were a bear. She would be safe.

Bears came onto her grandparents' property all the time, which was fitting, because they lived in a place called Bear County in Michigan. She had learned to hold up her palm and point to the middle of the pinkie to show where she lived. She thought this was cool for a month, and did it all the time, then didn't think it was cool anymore. Now she thought bears were cool.

It was after she saw the bear a few weeks earlier. The middle of summer, around dusk. She and her grandpa were watching television when it lurched toward the bird feeders in the yard, looking for a snack. They watched it through the sliding glass door until her grandpa yelled, "Hey, bear! Get outta here!" Lucy watched it slowly walk back into the federal woods, miles of which surrounded the property. The bear went back to the swamp where her grandpa told her it lived. It was in no hurry.

A few weeks later, a bear—they figured it was the same one—tore up the houseplants on the patio late at night while Lucy was asleep. Her Grammy was upset. Pa stayed up all night watching TV with his deer hunting rifle across the arms of his chair by the sliding glass door.

Her Grammy and Pa thought the bear was a nuisance, but Lucy loved him. She thought an animal that deserved so much attention, even if it was negative, earned her respect.

Lucy lived with her grandparents now because her parents were, as her schoolmates said, drunks. They called her trash. They made fun of her mom, who was always seen drinking with men at bars—different bars than the one where she used to work. They also made fun of her because her dad was in jail for beating up her mom in the grandstands at the annual Bear County Fair during a moto-cross event. He smacked her so hard he split her lip and bruised her eye. Everyone saw him do it and many of the fathers who had children in Lucy's third-grade class were the ones to jump on her dad and hold him so he wouldn't punch her mother anymore.

He also liked to punch Lucy when he came home stinking and smiling with his eyes weird, but she didn't like to think about that. He never made her bleed, though. She never had to go to the hospital like her mom, where Lucy would visit and spend a lot of time in the gift shop with Pa.

If Lucy were a bear, she would tear her dad to shreds and carry her mother off into the woods behind Pa and Grammy's house and protect her. She would protect Tommy too, even though he was only her half brother. He lived with his mom, who had a good job at the salt factory. They went on trips to the zoo in Detroit and to water parks in Traverse City. Tommy's mom didn't like Lucy's mom, so Lucy was never invited.

Lucy wanted to be a bear but knew she never would be. So, instead, she decided she would make the bear that visited her grandparents' house become her pet and bodyguard. She had seen pictures in a book at the school library where people had trained bears to play with balls and do somersaults and all kinds of other neat things.

Lucy began leaving treats in the backyard so the bear would visit more often. She read in a different book that bears like to eat sweet things like cookies and jelly, which were easy enough to steal from her grandparents' pantry. She even went and found an old collar and leash from Pa's pole barn from when he used to have a dog.

Lucy planned on feeding the bear until it became nice. Then she would collar it and leash it and walk it down to the jail where they would break in and the bear would eat her dad.

Then she would teach it how to play with a ball.

For three nights she was able to sneak out of her grandparents' house and leave the bear a donut covered in syrup. She would wait until her grandparents were asleep, which didn't take long. They were old and crashed out early, her grandma in bed, her grandpa in the chair in front of the television. The deer hunting rifle was leaned against the wall behind the chair in case the bear came on the patio to mess with Grammy's pots of plants.

In nothing but a nightshirt, Lucy would slink from her room at the back end of the small house into the kitchen and grab the donuts (they'd been on sale at the grocery store that week). Then she'd walk quietly past her grandpa's chair, ease the sliding glass door open, and run out on the narrow patio. Her grandpa never noticed.

The summer grass was wet and cold on her bare feet. She ran out past the bird feeder and pole barn to where the property met the woods. Her grandparents lived on several acres in the middle of the forest and the nearest house wasn't visible for a mile.

She left the bear treats on an old tree stump near the pole barn. It felt like leaving cookies for Santa Claus back when she was living with her mom in the apartment on Main Street in Bear River, before her mom lost the job at the bar. Mom said the boss was a jerk and didn't like her, but Lucy knew her mom had been drinking from the bottles she was supposed to be serving the customers. Lucy saw her do it when she went in to visit.

Lucy left the donuts on top of the stump and in the mornings would be overjoyed to see that they were gone. She and the bear were secretly communicating.

Then, after three days, her mom came home sick with a hangover and curled up on the couch like a zombie in front of the TV while Pa sat in the chair with the rifle nearby. For six hours—Lucy counted—her mom sat on the couch drinking Gatorade, eating pizza, and watching reality shows. She said things like "We're going to be a family again!" and "I ain't going back to the way I was before. I feel like a new person!" She hugged and kissed Lucy and said she loved her and they'd have a new life.

Lucy knew her mom was lying the way a boy at school lied about winning a dirt bike jumping competition when he didn't even have a dirt bike. Her mom had said those things before.

Lucy was also upset that she wasn't going to be able to get to the tree stump. When her mom came home to sober up, she didn't sleep. She stayed up all night drinking Gatorade on the couch. Lucy was tired anyway, and even though her mom made her feel uneasy, it felt better to have her around. It was nice to know where she was, that she wasn't off someplace being hurt.

In bed, having almost drifted off to sleep after a very satisfying roar into her pillow, Lucy heard a crash outside, followed by a commotion in the living room. The thought of putting the collar and leash on the bear and leading it to the jail was scary, but it was possible if she was brave enough. Lucy took a deep breath, grabbed the leash and collar from where she hid them under the bed, and ran out of the bedroom. It was time.

In the living room, her mom was standing in front of the TV wearing sweatpants and a T-shirt, her belly spilling out over the waistband, hands up to her mouth, shrieking. Her eyes looked ghostly.

Pa had the rifle and was sliding open the patio door. "Goddamn bear is back!" he screamed.

Lucy was excited. The crashing was coming from outside by the pole barn where she had been leaving the donuts. It meant her new pet was hungry. It meant he would soon be her bodyguard and she could walk down Main Street with her bear in the collar on the leash and no one would mess with her. It meant she'd walk him all the way out by the jail. It meant he'd eat her dad.

"What are you doing with that leash, Lucy?" her mom said.

"I'm catching the bear!" she said. "He just wants donuts."

"You've been leaving donuts out there?"

"The bear's gonna be my pet. We're friends."

Her grandpa was swooping a large flashlight across the property, illuminating a truck and a couple snowmobiles with tarps covering them. "If you've been leaving donuts for this bear," he said, "that explains why he's back." Pa was calm, as usual. He always made Lucy feel safe. But now, heading out into the dark with the flashlight and rifle, he scared her.

There was another loud crash from the darkness.

"He's getting into the pole barn," Pa said. Standing on the patio, he fired a shot in the air. "Get out of here, bear!"

Lucy ran for the patio, but her mother grabbed her and held her close.

"I gotta catch the bear, Mom!" She still clutched the collar and leash.

"You're not going anywhere."

Her grandpa disappeared into the darkness with the gun and flashlight, still hollering at the bear. All Lucy could see was the bobbing beam of the yellow light. She squirmed but couldn't break free from her mom. Lucy could only listen and watch the flashlight. They were agonizing moments for her. She didn't want her grandpa to shoot the bear.

"Please, don't kill it, Pa. Please!"

Her Grammy was up now. She ran out onto the patio in her nightgown and screamed at Pa. "What is it?"

There were three gunshots.

"Goddamn bear! I got it on this tree stump here."

"It's dead?" her grandma yelled.

"Dead as ever. Tried coming at me. Poor thing."

Lucy finally broke free of her mother's arms and ran out to the tree stump. Her mom and grandma followed at a slower pace. Tears came rolling from Lucy's eyes and she felt like her chest would explode, but she made it to where her grandpa stood. The bear was sprawled over the stump where she had been leaving donuts. The flashlight on its face showed blood smeared on its teeth and it had the saddest look in its eyes. It made Lucy cry even harder. She jumped on the bear and screamed, "No!"

She had never touched a bear before and it was more raw and scary than she thought. She felt the heat from its freshly dead body and the coarseness of its coat throughout her own body. She knew it was the strongest thing in the world besides people, and all people did was hurt other people with that strength. It didn't seem fair. The bear just wanted a donut. After it had devoured her dad, she would have taught it to play with a ball in no time.

"Get away from it, Lucy," her mom said. "It's probably got rabies or something."

"You shouldn't be feeding these guys, Lucy," Pa said. "They're dangerous. You could get hurt."

Her grandpa was pulling her off the bear now. Even though its big, dead, hot, scratchy body was the scariest thing she had ever felt, she wanted to hold on to it with all her life.

The Final Voyage

Captain Fred Bjorklund stared at the silver Samsonite emblem swimming on the black suitcase like a beacon in the dark and knew it was time to flee. Age and disease had taken his vigor. He refused to look at his naked body in the mirror anymore. The sag of his underarms and the mushy lumps his muscles had become didn't make any sense. When his wife fell asleep at night, he would do push-ups in the dark. They were weak and feeble—nothing like what he performed in the navy years before—but they built his strength up, something he didn't want his wife to know. It was like he was a convict planning an escape, which in many ways he was.

"Have you finished packing yet, Fred?" his wife yelled from the bathroom.

She knew he could not respond, that he couldn't speak since the stroke, but she never broke the habit of asking questions that needed a response. He just shook his head and stuffed a pair of new leather sandals—sandals he was determined never to wear—into the suitcase.

Lake Michigan commanded the horizon through the window of his bedroom. The salary he'd received piloting freighters earned him a nice little estate on the water indeed. He had spent a better part of his life on the Great Lakes, bodies of fresh water so large they were really inland seas. Throughout the 1950s, '60s, and '70s, Captain Fred Bjorkland carted shipments of iron ore, mined from the Mesabi Plains of Minnesota, from Duluth to the ports of Ohio or Illinois, traveling down Superior and either Huron or Michigan. He'd get going in March, when the sun beat on the ice floes, breaking them apart, and finish up in January, when the waters froze again. Then he'd be back to his home port of Bear River, where he'd grown up learning how to boat.

When he was home, he'd sleep much of the time and watch hockey. He'd basically hibernate his way through the winter like a bear, his head never truly operating at full capacity until he was back on the freighter. In the winter, it was as if his mind and vigor seized up like ice. As he looked at the suitcase on the bed, it was autumn again. The cold depths of the lakes had fused with his bones and heart, he felt, and the hot Arizona sun would surely destroy him.

"Think of everything we can do not being cooped up here," his wife told him.

The snow in Bear County prevented them from leaving the house much of the winter. The piles tall as men cast shadows on the sidewalks and driveways in town. His wife cleaned, cooked, and watched television, and the Captain interrupted her routine when he retired. He felt unwelcome in the house and began hanging out at the bars in town. Then one evening, while propped up on a barstool watching a hockey game at Lester's Bait and Beer, he felt his mind boil. The left side of his body went numb and seized for good.

After he got out of the hospital, talk of Arizona started. He sat in the living room watching the lake more than the television, the left side of his face drooping, unable to ask for a glass of water. Losing the ability to speak was devastating. It made him feel already dead.

The Captain wasn't convinced retirement in the desert was the answer to his problem, but he was afraid to disappoint his wife. His beloved house on the lake was sold. They would pack a carry-on suitcase for tomorrow's flight. Their children would take care of the furniture and the rest of their affairs. They would stay at a resort for a week, then move into a new condo near Phoenix.

The Captain's black Samsonite suitcase had been recently purchased by his son, Will, to replace the old leather satchel he had taken with him on the freighters for decades. It was neatly packed with clothes he had never worn and never would, summer stuff that would expose his spindly, sagging arms and legs in the burning Arizona heat, which the Captain knew rose above a hundred degrees. The shorts and flamboyant, patterned shirts somehow insinuated a festive future.

He grabbed his cane, wobbled over to the door, and closed it. His satchel was hidden underneath the bed, already packed. The Captain snatched it and headed to the window. It was autumn and the cold air rushed in when he opened it. Usually he would be coming in off the water this time of year. When he was younger, he'd stay on the water until the shipping season ended in January, but all the grave misfortunes happened in autumn when corporate bosses tried to squeeze in a few extra trips to make more money, so he'd started docking early.

The Captain pulled a jacket out of the satchel and fumbled his way into it. Using his cane, he scooted a chair over to the window and carefully climbed onto it. Then, with a mighty effort, he tossed the cane and satchel into the yard and boosted himself out. It wasn't too difficult. He hung on to the sill and let himself drop. It was ground floor, but still hard to do for an old man. That's why he had been practicing, sneaking out every night after his push-ups. Throughout the summer, he would walk around town in the wee hours of the morning. He would go down by the lake and check his little aluminum fishing boat in its slip at the Bear River Marina, making sure everything was set. Then he'd walk all the way out to the Protestant cemetery (not to be confused with the Catholic cemetery across the street) and look at the plots he and his wife had purchased years ago. He'd be in bed by the time she woke and would sleep until ten in the morning. She was always happy he was resting.

"Jeez, you sure did sleep in today, didn't you?"

The Captain would stretch out the good side of his face and lips—a smile—and nod.

But this was daytime. He had never gone out the window during the day. And this was no trial run. This was the real thing. The walk down to the boat took about fifteen minutes. He had timed it. His wife wouldn't cause a fuss for fifteen minutes. He would miss her and the wonderful smell of her meals wafting through the house around suppertime. He would miss her embraces and kindness. But she would understand.

He walked through town and down to the marina, where his boat with the outboard was tied up, bobbing in the waves next to a wooden pier. It wasn't the size of the freighters he'd commanded with large crews of men, but with his diminished capacity, it was all he could handle. He had bought the boat after he retired, but before the stroke. For a few years he took it out close to shore on the big lake or up Bear River in the summer for lake trout and salmon; sometimes alone, sometimes with one of his grandchildren, whom he never recognized in public. He couldn't remember any of their names. He had the same trouble with his own children. It was the sacrifice he had to pay for being gone for such long stretches of time. It had been the family joke that even when the Captain was home, he was never really home.

He remembered his oldest, Tom, the best because the Captain was still young when he was born and there's always the excitement of a first child. Then came a daughter, Joy, and another son, Will, all within a span of five years. Whenever he got home, they'd crowd around and politely hug him. He'd always intended on getting them some sort of souvenir from the places he visited, but somehow never got around to it.

The youngest, Grace, was separated from the other three children by almost ten years. He knew her the least. She was conceived in spring, just before he left for the season, and when he returned, it seemed she was ten, then fifteen, then she had disappeared downstate to art school in Detroit, a problematic child his wife worried about late at night. He was hard-pressed to conjure her face in his mind before the stroke, and after, she all but evaporated from his memory.

The Captain slowly crawled into the fishing boat and realized he had misplaced his satchel. He shrugged it off, untied the vessel, and shoved off into cold Lake Michigan. It was then he heard the young woman from the dock. She was blurring with the rest of the shore, but he knew it was the woman from the night before, wrapped in the same baseball hat and dark trench coat. The interaction the previous night had been short but pleasant, he recalled. They stood on the dock and spoke about one of his daughters.

Now the woman was standing on the dock shouting something he couldn't hear.

The Captain had the words in his mind—I'm just going to see my brother up in Frankfort—but couldn't say them. In a few moments, the woman was too far away to hear him even if he could speak like a healthy man. He smiled and waved, hoping that would be enough to send her away. He turned and faced the water. The Captain motored the boat into a chilly October wind blowing in from the west. His brother had been dead for ten years.

Grace watched her father head straight out toward Wisconsin in the fishing boat. She lit a cigarette. It wasn't easy because of the wind. She had to put both the smoke and lighter inside her coat to get a flame. She was wearing one of his old navy-blue trench coats she found in a closet and had her long, dark hair wrapped up into a baseball hat so no one would recognize her. She had considered sunglasses but thought that would be a touch too much.

Out on the wide, gray lake, the boat jerked to the north, but kept going. She felt calm watching him even though she knew he wasn't coming back. The boat got smaller until it was just a pinpoint on the horizon and disappeared behind the Coast Guard station. Grace waited until she could no longer see him before turning around and walking back to the town. She wouldn't call the authorities. She had already made up her mind.

Grace had taken to trailing her father weeks earlier. He had never held much prominence in her life. She barely knew him and realized that was why she was following him, but never allowed it to grow into a full-blown thought. It was the same rationale she used with drugs: don't think about it too much and it isn't a problem. That's the first thing therapists made you do: admit there was a problem.

Grace knew what the biggest problem was: she was sober, living with her brother Will and his family in Bear River, taking it one day at a time, as they say. The biggest problem was simply not being fucked up all the time, walking around bored, deprived of the agents that had accompanied her for the past fifteen years. Now life was stretched out before her like a predictable road. The malaise of working, eating, shitting, and sleeping. Life was so long when you were sober.

When she was still getting hammered, time was turned on its side and spun quickly down a steep hill with thrilling bumps. Sobriety had slowed things down to the speed of life, to the regular beat of a heart, not the heart sent thump-thumping with line after line of cocaine. There you were, sitting in a chair or standing in a room, doing ordinary things with ordinary people like listening to Will and his wife talk about bills and meals and oil changes and shopping.

So boring; so *long*.

Grace would wake up each morning, go out to the shed her brother had helped her convert into a studio, and pretend to paint; though not much was coming these days, she felt compelled to keep regular work hours. She'd sit around looking at European fashion magazines while smoking cigarettes like she did when she was a teenager. Then, around four or five, she'd come back to the house and help with dinner. After dinner, she'd read or watch television with her teenaged nieces and nephews until everyone went to bed.

And it all took so *long*. The sheer length of sober life didn't really feel like it was worth living, though if she went back to what she was doing before, she would hit the fiery depths again, ignite and fizzle.

Grace, almost forty, wasn't proud of her life. Starting in her twenties, she lived in downtown Detroit working as a bartender at a punk rock club where the booze and drugs flowed freely. She tried to sell her paintings on the side—big, crazy abstracts no one really wanted. There were a lot of guys, most more messed up than her.

But then the car crash. She survived. Jorge, her longtime friend, fellow artist, and roommate, did not. They were already blitzed out of their minds, driving down a particularly nasty section of Michigan Avenue in search of more coke at four in the morning when he lost control of the little Civic and crashed into a telephone pole. Grace emerged unscathed, but her best friend was dead from head trauma. After the funeral, she reassessed her situation, moved out of the downtown loft she'd lived in since her Center for Creative Studies days, and headed north to her family, to the town she had fervently tried to escape since she was a young girl.

Grace Bjorklund would detox herself.

Sobering up in Will's house proved comfortable. Unlike their brother, Tom—a pompous cigar-smoking know-it-all who worked for one of the auto companies near Detroit—Will was sympathetic about Grace's condition. He and his wife Sarah both worked for the US Forest Service. They didn't make much money, but they both loved being in the woods. They frequently saw their sister, Joy, who had also stayed in town after marrying the local district court judge, with whom she had three children.

A lot of the time with Will, Sarah, and their two teenaged children was spent preparing meals and watching television, two things Grace hadn't done much of in the last fifteen years. But she had adjusted, and could help in the kitchen now, and even knew the characters on some of the shows. It felt nice to be in the warm glow of their domestic life.

Nighttime, however, she was on her own. The bed in Will's guest room was nice and soft, but without pills or booze, Grace found sleep impossible. She tried waking up early—five, six in the morning—hoping she'd be just too tired for insomnia when night came. It didn't work. She'd be dog-tired at ten, in bed by eleven, asleep by midnight, and wide-awake and eyeballing the ceiling by two o'clock in the morning. Without knowing her dad was doing the same thing on the other side of town, Grace began propping open the window and walking Bear River at night.

One time she was rounding a corner near the lake and nearly smacked into an old man with a cane. She saw the startled face of her father.

"Dad?" she asked.

His expression showed that he did not recognize her. Half his face sagged like it was melting off his skull. He took his cane and whacked Grace on the leg. The blow hurt and she kicked her leg up and grabbed it instinctually while her father continued down the sidewalk. Grace felt compelled to limp behind him to see where he was going, which turned out to be the cemetery.

Grace watched from behind a tree as the old man gazed down at the ground where he and her mother would be buried. It was near her grandparents, all of whom had grown up in this small town on the lake. Grace waited for him to do something ceremonial, like pray, even though she knew he had never been religious. But he didn't. He just stood there.

His nonreligiousness was one of the few things Grace knew about her father. The Captain was always kind to her in a very polite way. He was already in his late forties when she was ten, sixties when she was in her twenties. She felt he was distant, more like a youngish grandfather than a father in the same way her older brother Tom always felt more like an uncle.

"I sometimes feel sorry we had you so late," her mother used to say. Grace was ten years younger than all her other siblings. "But we love you, Grace. Don't forget that."

The first night, Grace followed her father back to her parents' house and watched him climb through his bedroom window, a feat she found amazing for an old man who had suffered a stroke. But the Captain had always been strong. She followed him for the next two weeks. His schedule was the same each night: he would prop the window open and fling himself out into the bushes. He would hobble away from the house with his cane, then down to the lake, to his dock, where he would crawl into the little fishing boat. There he'd sit for about twenty minutes, staring at the water. He would then go to the cemetery, gaze at the plots, then back to the house and climb through the window. The process took two hours.

The night before he went off into the lake, Grace approached him after he climbed into the little fishing boat. Something was different. He had his leather satchel with him this time, which he set down at his feet. "What are you doing?" she asked.

He looked confused. She knew he couldn't hear very well, so she loudly repeated herself until he understood. He smiled and pointed to his mouth like he wanted something to eat, but was, in fact, gesturing that he couldn't speak. Grace was prepared for this. She pulled out a pen and paper and handed it to him. Her mother had said he could still write. He could still form sounds with his mouth, but they sounded animalistic, and he was embarrassed by them.

The Captain took the pen and paper, slowly wrote something, and handed it back to Grace.

I am Capt. Fred Bjorklund. This is my boat. I am preparing for a trip tomorrow. Who are you?

Grace could have said the words out loud, but instead wrote them for her father so she wouldn't have to shout. There was also

something comforting about it: if he had to write to be understood, so would she.

*I am a friend. Are you the same Captain Bjorklund who braved a
great November storm in 1986?*

Her father beamed with pride when he read it and wrote a
response. His body used to be giant and commanding, Grace
remembered. Now he had shrunk so you could see the bones in
his face. His eyes looked the same, however.

How did you know?

I was friends with one of your daughters.

Joy?

Grace.

Grace lives in the city now. She is an artist. She paints beautifully.

Grace nearly wept when she read this. She had no idea her
father even knew what became of her. She never sought any sort of
acceptance from either of her parents about her decisions in life.

I didn't know that.

She doesn't visit. Will you help me out of the boat?

Grace hoisted him out. He motioned for the pad and began
writing.

*I am leaving tomorrow. It is a secret and you can't tell anyone.
But please, tell Grace I will see her soon enough.*

Where are you going?

Her father took the pad, scribbled something, and handed it
back. He hobbled off into the night before Grace could read what
he had written.

*I'm going to visit my brother in Frankfort. Goodbye. It is very
late.*

Mary Bjorklund quickly applied cream to her face
before the mirror in the brightly lit bathroom, only half paying
attention to what she was doing. Mostly she listened through
the wall to make sure Fred was packing. It had been quiet for a

few minutes and she guessed he had gone down for a nap. Mary rubbed the cream deeper into her sturdy face.

Mary had never imagined she would end up in Arizona, but here she was, on her way. She would finally get out of the cold. Her work was done. The children were raised, tuitions paid off, Fred retired. She needed the present and a future, not the past. She would drag Fred down to Arizona whether he liked it or not.

She glanced in the mirror to make sure nothing was too out of place before going out and knocking on Fred's bedroom door. She wanted him alert when the children arrived to take them to the airport. If he didn't have enough time to wake up and get his bearings, he tended to be snappy, especially toward the grandkids, whose names he could never remember.

Mary cocked her ear toward the door and listened. There was no rustling, so she knocked again. "Fred?"

She opened the door and found the room cold and empty. The window facing the front of the house was open, with a chair underneath. Mary shut the window.

"Fred?" she said again.

The screen had been popped out of the window. Mary stuck her head out and saw her husband's worn leather satchel in the bushes. She calmly went through the house to make sure that he was gone, to see if he had really done what she suspected him of doing, before calling first the police, and then her children.

Grace took the long way through the cemetery back to her parents' house. She had sat outside the house all morning, waiting to see if her father really would emerge from the window in daylight. She walked back and forth on the chilly sidewalk across the street all morning. Now Grace didn't know what to expect when she returned. It would have been discovered that her father was missing. She was resolved to say silent and was surprised she wasn't feeling more conflicted about it.

There was a Bear River Police Department car parked along the curb outside the large house overlooking the lake. Will and Sarah's Subaru and Joy's Lincoln were in the driveway. Tom would probably be up from Detroit by dinnertime.

Her family was huddled in the living room, where two uniformed police officers and a detective in a polo shirt and windbreaker were talking to them.

"Your father's gone missing," her mother said.

Grace couldn't help noticing the exasperated strain in her mother's voice. It still didn't affect Grace's decision. She had never been so sure of anything in her whole life.

"You haven't seen him, have you, honey?" her mother asked.

"No," Grace said. "I haven't."

Tom launched into nothing short of a full-scale investigation into the matter.

"What the hell is going on here?" he said. "How could you let this happen, Mom? He was weak! How does he just hop out of a window and disappear? He could barely walk!"

"I told you," Mary said. "I was in the bathroom for five minutes. What could I have done? He was sick, but he isn't an infant, Tom. I can't watch him twenty-four hours a day."

"If that's the kind of care he needed then that's what we should've done. I knew you weren't up to the challenge of taking care of him."

"He'd been planning it for a long time, I think," Will said.

"It's this stupid Arizona thing, isn't it? Why couldn't you let him retire here, where he wanted? Jesus! And what do you mean he was planning it?"

"Tom, don't you get it? Dad is probably dead and he probably wanted it that way," Joy said.

Tom finally retired to the deck with a bottle of scotch and a cigar. He sat out there fuming for hours. The rest of the family drank coffee in the kitchen and living room, waiting for any word from police. None of them slept.

Grace was accustomed to the late hours. She played UNO with her frightened teenaged nieces and nephews and helped keep them calm. She brewed tea and made popcorn. Her secret grew into something more beautiful the longer the night wore on. She realized it was the only gift she had ever given her father.

The Coast Guard found the Captain's body the next morning after the weather cleared. They discovered the capsized fishing boat rocking in the surf a few miles up the coast to the north and the Captain's drowned body washed up on a nearby sandy beach. The authorities put him in a van and drove him to the medical center. Tom took his mother to the hospital to identify the body while the family waited at home.

Mary didn't cry when she saw her husband on the gurney. She merely nodded. Still, Tom clutched her as if she were in hysterics because he didn't know what else to do. They returned to the house in silence.

Mary, Joy, and Grace prepared a lunch. Everyone drank more coffee to combat the fatigue of a sleepless night. No one spoke much while they prepared a meal. Finally, Tom couldn't help it anymore.

"Well anyway, Mom, I know the house is sold, but you can come stay with me after the funeral," he said.

"What do you mean? I'm going to Arizona."

"You can't still be thinking of going down there, can you? After this?"

"Well, of course."

"Yeah, why not?" Will said. "There's no reason she shouldn't go."

"This is a traumatic thing, Will. I don't think Mom's in any shape to be going anywhere, especially a thousand miles away. I thought it was a bad idea to begin with. So did Dad, obviously."

"Why don't you let me decide what shape I'm in?" Mary said. "Besides, everything is all set. I'll just have to get a refund for your father's ticket."

"That's all you can think about now?" Tom said. "Refunding your dead husband's ticket? He's not even in the ground yet, Mom! This is insane! This whole family's crazy!"

"I'm still going and that's the end of it," Mary said.

Tom dropped that line of questioning and began interrogating the family again. He wanted to know everything from the past couple of weeks leading up to the day before. Did anyone notice anything strange about Dad? Was he eating differently? Had he acted oddly at all?

"Jesus, Tom. There's nothing we can do now," Will said. "What's the difference?"

Tom ignored him and turned to Grace. He'd barely spoken to her since he arrived.

"And you?" he said. "Did you know anything about this little plan? Or were you too wasted to notice? You popping the pills again? Snorting lines?"

"Leave her alone, Tom," said Will. "She's clean."

"I don't know anything," Grace said, hunched over chopping an onion, not bothering to look at Tom. "He didn't even know who I was."

Lady of Comfort

Kylie's first visit to Teddy Andropoulos's stone house was simple enough: the old man slugged back a boner pill and they massaged each other's feet on the couch before he felt up her breasts while beating off. Then he paid her $70. Not bad for an hour's work. It was better than stocking shelves at the Dollar-and-a-Half Store in downtown Bear River.

"I'd like you to be my regular lady of comfort," he said before she left.

The term sounded so old-timey and grand that Kylie blushed in the entryway of the house. She was blitzed on blow, grinding her teeth, pupils like full moons, anxious to get out. He even bowed and kissed her hand. She could see that the dark mop on his head was a toupee woven into his existing gray hairs. By then he was wearing a knee-length flower-print kimono and black socks.

"Well, just call me like you did before," she said. "And we'll see if I have time."

It was farmland for miles around the pleasant and pretty stone house. Kylie grew up in a broken-down farmhouse on the other side of Bear County that was neither pleasant nor pretty, escaping to the county seat of Bear River as soon as she dropped out of school at sixteen. She worked menial jobs for a few years and got hooked on drugs while working as a barmaid at Lester's Bait and Beer. Her party habits soon got her fired. A few months later, nineteen and broke, she posted her first ad on Boinkers.com, a classified ad service that delivered escorts to gentlemen all over the world, including the hinterlands of northern Michigan.

Kylie was told she had a cute face, marred only by the crooked teeth her parents could never afford to fix. Her new friend Jazmine (the fellow barmaid at Lester's who got her snorting lines) snapped a few shots of her wearing nothing but undies in a variety of poses that showed off the tattoos on her upper arms and thighs. Kylie smiled in the pictures, but kept her mouth closed so potential customers couldn't see her teeth.

"Guys only care about tits and pussy," Jazmine said. "They ain't looking at anything else."

The only responses she got at first were too far away, in neighboring Manistee and Benzie counties. Teddy, out in Good Soil Township, was the first Bear County local to call her. Jazmine, who'd been making $2,000 a month with her own Boinkers.com page, had explicitly told Kylie phone calls only.

"Cops can't track phone calls like they can texts and emails," she said. "These old guys like to write some dirty ass shit. Cops can pull it off your phone. Remember, it ain't illegal to get paid to come over to just hang out with someone."

Initially, Kylie had been nervous about being with men for money. She'd had her fair share of sex since fifteen, mostly with guys she barely knew, and wasn't exactly thrilled about it anyway.

"It ain't much different than that," Jazmine said. "They stick it in for a little bit and then it's over. You go home paid in full."

Now, walking away from Teddy's farm after that first visit, her body and brain still buzzing, she didn't feel so much ashamed as uplifted by the easy money in her pocket. She had to endure the masturbatory habits of brothers her whole life for free. Getting paid for watching an old man beat off while he tweaked her nipples didn't seem that bad in the scheme of things. She felt like she was pulling a fast one on the world.

Two months later. Kylie was dead asleep on a sofa when the phone vibrated near her head. She felt sick immediately and nearly threw up as she fully entered consciousness. Her mouth still tasted like the vile combination of Faygo Moon Mist and vodka they'd been swilling. She tiptoed over three guys sleeping on the floor, Derek Muskrat and a few of his friends from the Ruins, a low-income tribal housing project by the casino. They were all wearing the same clothes from the night before. Jazmine was asleep in her bedroom with one of the guys, their naked limbs tangled in blankets visible through a crack in the door. A window unit blasted cold air in the dark flat, the blazing sunlight kept out with drawn curtains. The end tables were covered in empty beer cans and liquor bottles, a hunting magazine splayed open with white powder residue on the snout of an elk. They'd snorted all of Derek's stash and hadn't gotten to sleep until nine in the morning.

Kylie checked her phone while she took a pee. It was one in the afternoon. Teddy had called and wanted to see her at the stone house. She'd been out there a half-dozen times now and he was becoming a regular. Even though she wanted to crawl back on the couch and hide under a blanket, she texted back that she'd be there soon. She spent all her cash on drinks and party favors. When she woke up after big nights like that, she sometimes couldn't find herself in the mirror. She wondered why her parents had bothered making her, with her jacked-up teeth and hopeless future. Her face was sallow and sickly. Derek sometimes gave her stuff for free, but that was in the past. Now she had to pay. He would give her another packet of cocaine for what she earned out at Teddy's and that would make her feel better. She took a shower and put on the purple bra and undies that Teddy liked, then stepped over the bodies on the floor and left the apartment, one of three units in an old house on the east end of Bear River.

It was hot outside, but Kylie had the chills. She felt sicker than just a hangover, like she was coming down with the flu. A neighbor's pit bull staked out in a dirt-packed part of the yard barked and strained against his chain as Kylie walked out to the Chevy parked along the curb. She drove out of town, hit the highway, and was soon driving past fields of corn and soybeans. The trees and farmhouses and barns shimmered in the miasmic heat of a cloudless sun. That old smell—animals, dirt, and muck—crept into the car and made her stomach churn, reminding her how much she hated farms.

Kylie noticed a big, multicolored tent that sold fireworks next to the stone house and wondered what that was all about. Before Kylie could even get out of the car, she was hanging out the opened door vomiting. It was definitely more than a hangover. But Kylie figured she'd go in, get Teddy off, and be out of there in an hour.

Teddy was waiting just inside the door, wearing his kimono, with a friendly smile. She could tell he'd been handsome in his youth. He had the black hairpiece, a prominent nose, and dark features—a Greek, which wasn't common in Bear County.

"You made it."

"How are you, Teddy?" Kylie tried a closed-mouth smile but thought she'd puke again. "I didn't know you sold fireworks."

She turned and looked at the tent by the road.

"We all earn our money somehow, right?"

"Does the tent get much business? You probably don't get much traffic out here."

"People who want the good stuff know where to find me."

There were flowers planted in beds all around the house. Kylie didn't know their names, but they were red, yellow, and purple. There were also two apple trees she'd never noticed before. It seemed like a nice place to live in old age.

"Come in."

The stone house was comfortable and clean. Teddy had a big fan that kept the rooms cool. The floors were made of stone too, which felt nice on Kylie's bare feet after she slipped off her sandals.

Teddy sat down on the couch like he usually did, letting his robe slip open so she could see his bare thighs. Kylie started to undress in front of him, but Teddy wasn't smiling or trying to get himself hard like usual. She thought maybe he forgot his boner pill. He put his robe together and leaned forward as Kylie fumbled with her shorts, thinking she was about to be sick again.

"You don't seem like yourself today," he said. "Are you OK?"

"I don't feel well," she said.

"You don't look good. Your face is all flush," he said. Teddy came to her and put the back of his hand to her forehead like her mother used to when she was little. It felt cold like the stone floor. "You're burning up. You have a fever. Come and lie on the couch. I'll get you a wet washcloth and some aspirin."

"No, no, I'm fine. Maybe we should just reschedule. I'll come back again when I'm feeling better."

Teddy put his hand on her back and led her toward the sofa.

"Nonsense," he said. "You shouldn't even be driving."

Teddy left the room and was soon swooping back in with a glass of apple juice, a wet washcloth, a Ziploc bag of ice, and two Advil.

"Lie back on the couch," he said. "You need to get some rest. I'm not letting you go anywhere until you feel better."

Kylie managed a weak smile and sat down on the couch. It felt nice to be taken care of.

"Do you want something more comfortable to wear?"

"Yeah, OK."

He returned with a full set of pajamas—pants and button-up shirt—too big for Kylie but loose in a way that felt comfortable. Teddy left so she could change, which seemed odd to Kylie since he'd seen her naked several times already, then returned with a blanket he set on the couch. Teddy sat down in an armchair. He'd changed into a pair of jeans and a T-shirt.

"Should we watch TV? Do you like *Family Feud*?" Teddy clicked on the television in front of the sofa where Kylie was lying.

"Sure."

Kylie didn't intend on staying the afternoon, or spending the night, but it was nice being away from the frantic party at Jazmine's. A few times she had to hop up and go use the bathroom to throw up, rinse her mouth out with water. Teddy thankfully stayed out of her way. The next thing she knew it was night and she was asleep on his couch. Then the sun was out and it was morning. Teddy was sitting at a table in the kitchen area of the house drinking coffee and looking at his laptop, probably the same computer he used to find Kylie's Boinkers.com ad.

"Do you know what the northern lights are?"

Kylie shook her head. She was groggy, but she'd slept well and the fever had broken.

"No, what's that?" She sat up and leaned on her elbow looking at him.

"The aurora borealis. It's when the sky is filled with streaks of brilliant green light. It's amazing. They say the northern lights should be visible later this summer. Wouldn't that be great to see them?"

"Yeah. I guess. Do you mind if I use your bathroom again?"

"Sure. Feel free to take a bath or a shower. It might help you feel better."

Kylie sat on the edge of the big bathtub and looked at her phone. She had a million messages, mostly from Jazmine, "Where are you? Have you been murdered!? I'm calling the cops if you don't respond to me soon." That type of thing. Kylie told Jazmine she was fine, she'd gotten sick but that she was feeling better and would be home soon.

Kylie took a quick bath and got into the clothes she'd worn over there. She wished she could just teleport from the bathroom to home and not have to face Teddy again. He'd been so nice, but now it felt awkward, especially because she was sober and feeling better. She didn't really know him. But when did you really know someone? She didn't really know Jazmine or Derek or any of the other people she'd been hanging out with. She lived with her parents and siblings till she dropped out of high school and felt she barely knew them. Maybe she didn't even know herself, she thought, looking into the mirror—mouth closed, no makeup, red patches of irritated skin and acne, wet brown hair clumped together. She smiled insanely at herself, admiring the front tooth that stuck straight out of her gums the wrong-ass way.

When she emerged from the bathroom, she felt obligated to ask Teddy, "Do you still want to play with my tits?"

Teddy smiled and shook his head. "I made you breakfast. I want you to tell me about yourself. You come over, but I barely know you."

Kylie sat down to the eggs, toast, and orange juice. He'd also brewed a steaming mug of tea. Jazmine had warned her of this too; guys who turned into stalkers, who wanted to save them, who wanted to buy them things and take them to church after screwing them every which way they could.

"Don't let them *Pretty Woman* you," Jazmine had warned.

"What does that mean?" Kylie had said. One night, they found the old movie with Julia Roberts and Richard Gere. Kylie thought it was romantic, and while she knew she had to stay free and stay tough, she wouldn't mind someone looking out for her.

"Ain't no one gonna save you," Jazmine had said.

And here was Teddy, who didn't look totally unlike Richard Gere, except older with that hairpiece, asking about her life.

"What do you want to know?"

"I want to know about you. Did you grow up in the area?"

Kylie sipped her juice. The old man seemed harmless, but he could be hiding something.

"Yeah, out in the boonies on a place like this. North part of the county."

"Your parents still out there?"

"Probably. I don't know. I left three years ago."

"You finish high school?"

Kylie shook her head and finally took a sip of tea. The hot liquid felt delicious in her mouth and stomach.

"Family help you out?"

She shook her head again. She didn't want to talk about her family.

"I mostly get by tending bar. Then I fell into this kind of work. It's fine. I don't plan on doing it forever."

"It's sad there's no options for young people in this country anymore. The rich are filthy rich and the poor people like us are just scraping by. It's a shame. Do you like music?"

Teddy went away from the table, hunched down in the living room by the couch, and reached underneath an end table. He came up with a black case.

"Yeah, I like music."

She thought he meant like dance or pop music. Before she could say anything else, Teddy was sitting in the armchair unlatching the black case on his lap and pulling out a clarinet. He pieced together the parts without saying a word, licked his lips, and started playing. Kylie opened her mouth in amazement and watched the old man bounce around the room in a comic way, playing old timey music, circling the couch like the pied piper.

"You're pretty good," she said.

"I used to be a professional musician. I even played in the US Marine Corps band during the war."

"You were in a war?"

"Yes. Vietnam."

He played her a couple songs and they laughed and told each other a little more about themselves, but then she remembered what Jazmine said about getting too close. She decided she'd better leave but felt bad because she had not performed any of the agreed-upon sex acts. As she stood by the door, Teddy still reached for his wallet. Kylie tried to stop him.

"You don't have to pay me."

"I insist."

"But I didn't do anything I was supposed to."

"You kept me company. At my age that's worth more than sex, to be honest. You let me take care of you. That made me feel good."

Kylie broke into a big smile, unselfconscious of her teeth for once. Teddy smiled too, his hands behind his back, rocking on his heels. She had never thought about how it felt good taking care of other people. She said goodbye and hurried out the door to the Chevy. She waved to Teddy standing on the front porch in his blue jeans and shirt. She thought about him and his clarinet the whole drive home.

Kylie learned all about Teddy Andropoulos in the ensuing months. He was born and raised right there in Bear County to a Greek family that owned a restaurant in town. When he was young, he escaped to Chicago to pursue his passion for music, playing in a jazz band. Then he was drafted into the Marines during the war. Sometimes Teddy's head hung down and he hid his eyes when he talked about the war. But he always spoke warmly about being in the Marine marching band. Kylie asked if he did anything dangerous.

"Before the band I was in an explosives unit," he said, but he wouldn't tell her anything else. After the war, he returned to Chicago, got married, and had kids. He had an ex-wife and three grown daughters there. He didn't speak about them much and there weren't any pictures of them in the house, which he kept meticulously clean for an old bachelor. He'd divorced around the time of his mother's death and moved back up to her old stone house in Bear County. He was a master in the art of black powder, blasting caps, and dynamite. He helped neighbors blow out stumps. He got licensed by the state and put up the fireworks tent by the road. For the past twenty years, he was Bear County's exclusive dealer of cherry bombs, firecrackers, and bottle rockets, even back when some of them were illegal.

Teddy's sexual proclivities remained the same. He required boner pills and liked her to undress and tease him a little while he jerked off. He never took off either his toupee or his kimono, which she learned he got overseas. She once asked him why he never wanted full-on sex with her, something she'd only done a handful of times with other guys since first posting her Boinkers.com ad.

"Well," he said, "I'm a gentleman."

A few times after he finished, he started crying and asked that Kylie leave the room. She complied and didn't ask him about it. She understood that he was damaged because she was damaged too, and she knew enough not to meddle in someone else's sorrows without an invitation.

Mostly he treated her like a queen, always referring to her with a wink as his "lady of comfort." He paid her so well she didn't have to take on any other customers. She took her ad off Boinkers.com. They began eating dinner together. He'd play the clarinet and she'd dance around the living room in her undies. She started spending the night. A few times later in the summer they climbed a small hill behind his house hoping to see the northern lights, but it was always a bust. It was still pleasant sitting on a blanket watching the night sky with Teddy. It reminded Kylie of how she and her first boyfriend, a lazy-eyed farm boy from down the road, used to watch the night sky from her barn after her parents passed out. With no ambient light, Teddy and Kylie lay on their backs underneath all the stars and talked about silly things.

"You're getting too close to that old pervert," Jazmine said.

Kylie didn't care. He was sweet. Her only complaint when it got to be October was that it was too cold in the stone house. Teddy refused to hook up his propane furnace. Instead, he built fires each night that made Kylie's clothes smell.

"We used to live out here with just a fireplace," he told her.

"But Teddy, I'm freezing," she said.

It was true. Her skin broke out in goose pimples every time she disrobed.

"OK," he said one night. "I'll get it hooked up as soon as I can. I usually have a guy come. He's out of town, but I guess I can do it myself."

"Thanks, Teddy," Kylie said.

One fall day when she got to the stone house, Teddy was drinking whiskey from a Mason jar. It was November now, with short days and long nights. Teddy never usually drank, but he was so excited because the aurora borealis would be visible that night. Kylie didn't want to ruin the mood.

"I think it's real this time," he said.

Kylie stayed wrapped up in her coat. If he was drinking whiskey and excited by the northern lights, then she might not have to put on her usual show. When it got dark, they went out to the hill behind the house and sure enough the sky was glowing with an increasingly vibrant shade of green.

"Isn't it beautiful?"

It was the strangest, most lovely sight Kylie had ever seen. She let her thoughts waver up there with the green and purple streaks in the sky and felt that she was in the middle of some kind of magic.

"Yes, it is very beautiful."

"I have something I want to give you."

Teddy was fumbling in the pockets of his brown Carhartt coat. He was sitting on the blanket next to Kylie, who had her knees tucked up to her chest. She couldn't imagine what was in his pocket. He was drunk and unpredictable. He finally found what he was looking for.

"Hold out your hand."

"This is weird, Teddy."

She thought of Richard Gere in the movie presenting Julia Roberts with a box of jewelry. She was letting him *Pretty Woman* her.

"Just do it."

Kylie held out her hand and Teddy placed something cold in it. She could see just enough with the green light in the sky: some kind of medal with purple ribbon and George Washington's face on it.

"What is it?" she asked.

"I don't have many years left. I want to start making sure the right things go to the right people."

"OK. But what is it?"

"It's my Purple Heart. I want you to have it."

Kylie knew it was something military people got for bravery.

"Did you do something good to get it?"

"They said I did something good, but it didn't feel very good."

"What did you do?"

"I blew up a bunch of people. In the official version of the story, I only blew up bad people. But I know there were innocent people."

Teddy scooted over and laid his head down in her lap. He was starting to sob. She stuck the Purple Heart in her coat pocket.

"What do you mean?"

"I had no choice. I swear I had no choice."

Kylie had never seen a man his age cry like this before.

"When did this happen?"

"In the war. But you can't look it up. It never officially happened, which is why it messes with my head. A lot of things that happened over there never officially happened and a lot of things that didn't happen did officially happen. Everyone was creating their own reality. There's no way to really know someone else's reality. I say something happened but you say it didn't happen. And here we are. Not knowing if anything is really happening."

Kylie smoothed his forehead with her fingertips. In the green light, she could see the whites of his eyes were going yellow, like yolk from an egg had seeped in.

"It's OK," she said. "I understand. So you accidently blew up innocent people. But it was war, right? You were just doing what you were told."

"They gave me a medal for it. Everyone thought I was some hero. My wife and daughters still do. But I couldn't go on like that. I asked to be transferred to the military band."

Kylie let her fingertips trace the wrinkles on Teddy's forehead and cheeks.

"If you don't think you deserved the medal, why did you keep it?"

"Because I want to remember. I need to remember what happened. I don't want to bury it."

"Why do you want *me* to have it?"

"You have to promise to never give it to my family. I never want it destroyed. But I never want it celebrated. And those are my wishes."

There was nothing more to say about it as the green light filled the sky.

"Isn't it beautiful?"

Kylie didn't say anything, just nodded in agreement.

A few nights later, Kylie went out on a wicked coke binge with Jazmine, Derek Muskrat, and his friends. The next morning, they sat at the Chit Chat Grille still tweaking, no sleep, sipping orange juice, when one of the old timers at the counter started yakking with the waitress.

"Well, old Teddy Andropoulos finally blew himself up last night. Tried hooking up his propane himself. Don't know why. He knew better."

"You know his family used to own this place," the other old guy said.

Kylie dropped her fork on her plate and left Jazmine sitting at the booth alone. She drove straight out to the stone house, which was surrounded by fire trucks, cop cars, and yellow tape. She parked down the dirt road and ran to the edge of the tape, where she was stopped by a Bear County sheriff's deputy. She could only glimpse the debris of the exploded house, stones and wood piled in heaps around Teddy's car.

"You know him or something?" asked the deputy.

"He was my boyfriend," she said.

"Well, you still have to stay back. Fire marshal will probably want to talk to you, so don't go far."

It was then, standing at the yellow tape on the edge of Teddy's destroyed house, that Kylie realized how deeply she felt for him. She missed everything about him suddenly: the kimono, the dark socks, the toupee. The dinners they had together. His clarinet. The stories he told and the way he had made her feel safe and comfortable and cared for. She still had the Purple Heart in her pocket. She ran her thumb over it while standing at the yellow tape looking at the big pile of stones and wept harder than she ever had before. He was buried somewhere in all those stones. It would take the authorities all day to find his body. She couldn't imagine her world without him.

Jazmine told her not to, but Kylie insisted on going to the funeral. She had no other dress-up clothes besides the too-tight skirts she wore while meeting up with men, so she went and found a black dress from the secondhand shop in Bear River. Her hands were shaking as she put on makeup.

The ceremony was held at Tark's Funeral Home in downtown Bear River. Kylie knew it would be a viewing with a religious service at the end. A Greek Orthodox priest was coming all the way from Traverse City. Teddy was well known in the county, but not enough to have a big funeral. As soon as Kylie walked in, she knew it was mostly family. Four women sat in the front row by the casket, all skinny with dark hair, wearing nice clothes. She assumed they were his ex-wife and daughters.

Kylie put her head down and marched to Teddy. She could feel the stares from the women in black.

Despite the blast, the authorities had pulled his body from the rubble relatively undisturbed. It was an open casket. He looked well, Kylie thought, though the funeral parlor had stitched his hairpiece on in an awkward way and forced an unnatural smile on his face.

She started to weep. She wanted to touch his face but was scared. She didn't notice one of Teddy's daughters, a woman of about forty, come up next to her.

"I know who you are," the woman said. "The police told us about you."

Kylie kept her mouth closed and looked down at her black strappy shoes. She'd gotten them from the secondhand store too.

"We've been through all of dad's stuff that was in the rubble," the woman whispered. "And things are missing. Money. A watch. His Purple Heart from the war. Do you know where any of those things are?"

The Purple Heart was in the small purse Kylie was carrying. She had thought about placing it in the casket with Teddy but decided that would be the wrong gesture. She wasn't sure of anything that day.

"I don't know where those things are. Probably lost in the explosion."

"Are you sure my dad didn't give you anything that should belong to the family?"

Kylie finally looked the woman in the eyes and shrugged.

"I'm sorry, I don't know anything else."

The woman scoffed and crossed her arms.

"Well, the family would appreciate it if you paid your respects and left."

Kylie opened her mouth, allowing her bad tooth to slip out past her lips, and said, "I'm not going anywhere."

She ignored the glaring women and walked slowly to the back of the room, picked a seat in the last row and sat down. She set the purse in her lap and waited for the service to start.

Compensation

Jimmy Blizzard ran out of pills.

It was fall, a few days before Thanksgiving, and he should have been whooping it up out at deer camp with all his friends. Instead, he wrapped his hand in bandages and left his Fourth Street apartment for the doctor's office. His heart was beating about a million times per minute and the goo dripping down into his throat from his clogged sinuses forced him to hawk loogies out the front window of his pickup. After checking in with the front desk, he writhed in an uncomfortable green chair next to a table with old magazines. He'd lost his index finger in some machinery at the cardboard plant a few months earlier, but his hand didn't hurt much anymore. Now he hurt everywhere else. He felt feverish and squeamish deep in his gut. The lack of pills had something to do with it, he knew, and if he wrapped his hand before seeing the doctor, her sympathies might turn in his favor. She might prescribe him more Oxys.

His stomach had the squeezes, like he needed to rush to the bathroom at any moment. It felt like he had swallowed a snake, the kind he used to catch alongside Bear River with his best friend, Pete Bell. The snake was angry, twisting around in his gut. He clutched his stomach with his good hand and hoped it would pass.

The doctor would make him better. She would give him a slip of paper that he'd take to the drugstore, where they would slide an orange bottle across the glass counter. He would immediately take three. The snake in his gut would stop moving. Brenda and her new husband, Al Ulster. His injury. The money he needed to pay back. All of it would go away.

The waiting room served four other doctors' offices in a complex across the street from the Bear County Medical Center, where the surgeon had failed to reattach his finger after the accident. No one visited him in the hospital. Brenda and Al had taken the kids to a theme park in Al's new motor home that week, and Jimmy's own parents had moved down to Kentucky. He didn't have anyone in town to look after him except Pete, who was currently out at the annual deer camp with the rest of their old gang from high school. Pete pleaded with Jimmy to come along, that it might help get him out of his funk, but Jimmy's mind was on pills.

"We're only a half hour away in Sampo," Pete had said. "Come out if you change your mind."

Jimmy didn't need anything from his friends. The only person who could fix him was the surgeon who had worked on his hand, Dr. Reese, a lovely woman about Jimmy's age, early to mid-thirties, from one of the big cities downstate—Detroit, Flint, or Grand Rapids. Jimmy didn't know how the attractive surgeon came to be in Bear River. All he knew was that she still had his index finger somewhere, probably in a jar back at the hospital, and that she could give him more Oxys.

He thought about the promise of more pills while clutching his gut. He hadn't even glanced at the magazines on the table next to him, or the four old people and the one very small child with his mom in the waiting room. That's who belonged at the doctors, the very young and old. Just as the kid started screaming and the mother yelled something back at him, Jimmy felt a hot trickle seep in the bottom of his blue jeans. It shocked him. His body was revolting. The snake was making its way out. He shit himself just a little, but enough to panic. He was humiliated even if no one noticed. He didn't know what to do. A nurse came out one of the doors.

"James Blizzard?"

He raised his bandaged hand like he was in grade school.

"Yeah, that's me. Can I use the bathroom first, please?"

Jimmy was having a hard time even before he got hooked on Oxys. Brenda left him and took their kids, Miley and Ricky, to live with Al Ulster, a prominent attorney in town. Brenda didn't know anything about the law until she took a job as a secretary in Al's office. She talked about how Al was so funny and smart. Jimmy just figured she liked her job a lot. Then one day she came to Jimmy and said she was sleeping with Al, who was also married, and that they were in love. Brenda was still a good-looking woman, in her mid-thirties, with long blond hair and bright blue eyes. She and Jimmy had been together since the eighth grade. He loved her like a wife and a sister and a mother all combined. Brenda told Jimmy that she still loved him too, but it was a tired kind of love. She said sometimes people just wear out on each other and need something new because life is very long.

"But I've never wanted anything else but you," Jimmy told her.

And it was true. He was heartbroken. He cried on and off for days after she left. When the kids weren't visiting, he spent his weekends wandering the woods outside of town. He started hanging out at the bars downtown with some of the younger guys from the cardboard plant. He stayed out too late one night, drinking shot after shot of Jäger at the bar. The next morning, he was still basically drunk and let his hand slip in some machinery. Lopped his index finger clean off. He thought he would die when he looked down at the fleshy red gash where his finger had been. But coworkers came to his aid, tied a tourniquet around his wrist, retrieved the finger, and helped him to the ambulance.

While he was recovering, his wages and doctor's bills were taken care of by workman's compensation. He was so high for a month he didn't realize Human Resources had made a mistake and both the cardboard company and the insurance company were paying him. He'd never had Oxys before. They not only took away the pain but brought him such peace and joy that he never wanted to feel any other way. He walked his dog all over town, enjoying the fresh air blowing in off Lake Michigan. He kept his pill bottle in his pocket. The rattle of the little white tablets against the orange plastic made him shiver with excitement because that meant he could prolong the feeling. For the first time in his life, Jimmy felt like he belonged in the world.

Then he got a phone call from a woman in Corporate who sounded like she was accusing him of orchestrating a scam. He felt guilty even though he didn't do anything on purpose. Jimmy was scared and stuttered on the phone with the woman, apologizing and saying he didn't know how it had happened. He finally checked his bank account and saw something had gotten screwed up, but he truly had not noticed. And in his Oxy haze, he was spending more money than usual. Now he would have to pay it back and he didn't know how. The HR woman told him his wages would be garnished until he came up with the money.

The money stuff was easy to ignore while he still had his Oxy supply, but now he had run out. When he called the doctor's office, the woman told him they couldn't fill a narcotic prescription unless he came in for an evaluation. So he dressed up his fingerless hand and came down, shaking, sweating, his stomach heaving. And here he was, cleaning himself up the best he could in the bathroom after shitting himself, the snake still writhing around in him. He felt it in his brain now, nibbling at his eyeballs from behind while he looked at himself in the mirror—flannel shirt, sunken cheeks, scraggly beard, messy hair. He balled up his plaid boxer shorts, wrapped them in a wad of paper towel, and threw them in the garbage can. He still smelled and had a big wet stain in the ass of his jeans. But there was nothing he could do. He felt like crying and screaming. Everything felt overly stuffed in his body and about to burst unless he got more pills. Even the air touching his face felt wrong. This plan had to work.

He made sure to sit on the examination table's disposable paper when he got into the room. There was a knock at the door and Dr. Reese came in—trim, tall, curly brown hair, cute little nose. Jimmy immediately knew he had made a mistake. She didn't smile. She was busy, looking at a chart.

"What's the trouble, Jimmy?"

"I ran out of my pain medication."

There was an awkward pause. She looked at the chart, then caught his eyes in an indifferent way. Jimmy knew in that moment Dr. Reese would not be his savior.

"We're a few months out from the surgery now. I think ibuprofen should be sufficient. You can get those over the counter. Let's see the hand."

Jimmy's heart sank and his stomach rumbled as he held up the bandaged hand. Dr. Reese sat down in a chair, rolled it over to the table, and began unwrapping the bandage. Jimmy hadn't been touched by anyone in weeks and it felt good to have someone else's fingertips on his skin. She had a big diamond wedding ring and nice, smooth skin. Her body seemed like an appropriate fit for the world, unlike Jimmy's. Someone like her could exist peacefully without the pills, but he could not. Couldn't she see he was pulsing, seething, twisting right before her eyes? Why can't she see? Why won't she help? She peeled away the layers of gauze and bandages Jimmy had clumsily and unnecessarily applied hours earlier. He looked away. All he saw in his mind was the blood-spurting gash from when the machine took off his finger. He could even smell the floor of the cardboard factory and hear the shouts of his coworkers.

Dr. Reese's face was pinched as she investigated.

"It looks great," she said.

The redness and swelling on the hand were gone. It was a perfectly normal hand besides the missing finger, the space where it had been healed and scarred over now. Jimmy finally looked at it.

"I don't feel great. I feel terrible."

"You know, those pills are very habit-forming," she said. "I should have taken you off them a week ago. Do you have diarrhea?"

He nodded.

"Fever? Shaking? Trembling? Flu-like symptoms?"

"Yes."

"You're going through withdrawal."

"Does that mean I get more?"

The doctor let go of Jimmy's hand and rolled back to the chart on the counter, away from him.

"No. I'm sorry. But your hand looks good. As good as it can. You shouldn't be in any more real pain."

Jimmy felt a fury rising in him as he began to wrap his hand. He felt it welling deep in the bottom of his gut and didn't know if he wanted to scream in anger or cry and fall into her arms.

"But I don't feel good," he said.

"Drink a lot of water, take vitamins, take a long walk. You should feel fine in a couple of days."

Jimmy didn't know what else to say. He was never good at getting in people's faces to get what he wanted.

"Are you sure you can't give me just a couple more? I'm still in a lot of pain. I feel terrible."

"I could refer you to an addiction specialist or a local twelve-step program."

The snake was in his arm now and it wanted to strangle this woman and force her to write the prescription. The pills would bring him the relief he required and she was the only thing standing in his way. He'd never go to some sad-ass twelve-step meeting in the basement of the church. A few of the sober guys at the plant were always talking about meetings and their Higher Power. It sounded boring to Jimmy. People just lying to themselves.

"No thanks."

"OK, I'm going to write you a prescription for some vitamins. Get some rest. Anything else?"

She was in a rush. There was so much more he had to say. He wanted to tell her how lonely he was, how he missed his children, how he didn't know if he could pay back the money to the cardboard company.

Still, he said, "Uh, no."

"Call my office if you need anything."

And then she was gone.

Jimmy politely picked up the prescription for the vitamins from a girl in blue scrubs behind the desk as he checked out, then threw it in a public wastebasket in the parking lot.

When he got back to his apartment, he stripped, threw the soiled blue jeans in a garbage bag, and took a long hot shower, scrubbing himself clean. He took the garbage bag out to the bin in the alley and smoked a cigarette. Then he went up and played two hours of Xbox before the snake worked its way into his legs and he couldn't sit still anymore. He unlocked his gun safe and pulled out his deer hunting rifle and shoved it into his bag. His hands were shaking.

The air was crisp and cool. He threw the gun bag in the back of the truck cab and hopped in the driver's seat. It was only a half hour out to deer camp in Sampo. The boys would be rifling back beers and bullshitting in the cabin. His sinuses were still dripping a thick goo in his throat, so he stopped and bought an energy drink, which made his heartbeat even more frenzied. As he drove through Bear River, past Main Street and the dead bucks hanging up outside Lester's Bait and Beer—four deer with nice-looking racks—Jimmy got to thinking about how he was acting like a child. He'd drive out to deer camp and meet up with Pete and the gang. He'd buy a bottle of schnapps on the way. He'd get good and drunk like he used to back when they were in high school. Why couldn't life be more like that anymore?

We were young. We were raging. We were happy.

But Jimmy didn't make it out of town. The snake was in his ears now and it felt like his whole head would burst from the pressure. Pete and his friends wouldn't make him feel better. Nothing would make him feel better except more pills. It was the doctor's fault. If he just had his pills he'd feel normal by now. He loved the two pills he took in the morning. He loved them more than anything. He'd wake up early, before sunrise, excited to be stoned at daybreak. It got him out of bed at five or six in the morning. He spent some of the best mornings of his life on two pills just sitting in his apartment watching ants crawl on his windowsill. He sat out on the front porch watching leaves flutter in the wind with pure rapture. The touch of a blanket on his skin was a delight. By ten or eleven, he'd be coming down from that initial high and either break a pill in half or pop another full one to keep the high intact through the afternoon, when he'd do the same, trying to maintain the feeling as long as possible. The more pills he took, the more he itched everywhere. That was the only drawback. The itching and the constipation. He went a full week without taking a shit, but he didn't care. He barely needed to eat. The pills gave him everything. In the evening, he'd drink two or three beers on top of the pills and it would send him into a state of pure oblivion. Once you experience it, you are changed forever. You can't go back to coffee and work and chitchat. While stoned, he stared dumbly at his television, nodding off every so often, all fear snuffed out, all feelings and desires snuffed out, all bad things snuffed out; no red gash in his hand, no heart in his chest, no brain in his head, nothing but the bright inner light from the pills. He wanted this bright nothingness. He wanted to exist in this state of bliss forever. Without it he would die. His frenzied brain was churning. He had an idea where he could get more pills. A year earlier, Brenda had her gallbladder removed. Jimmy watched the kids while she recovered. He hadn't thought of it then, because what did it matter in those pre-pill days, but she must have gotten some painkillers at that time. They would be at Al's house.

Jimmy parked in the driveway right behind the expensive motor home. Al lived in a big brick colonial with white shutters on the nice side of town. Oak trees on either side of the house were hanging on to their orange-and-brown leaves. Ricky and Miley both had new bikes standing upright on their kickstands in the path leading up to the house. It made Jimmy think of his own apartment—three claustrophobic rooms he never bothered to dust or scrub.

Jimmy pulled the deer rifle out of the back of the truck and went up to the door. He inserted a trembling middle finger into the trigger guard, which he had loaded with just one bullet. He didn't want to hurt anyone. He just wanted three minutes in Brenda's medicine cabinet to see if she had any leftover pills. And if there were no pills, he just wanted someone to listen. The gun would help with that. He wanted someone to know his pain. He wanted another human being to understand how the snake was twisting inside him, how he couldn't stop thinking about the gash on his hand that still throbbed even though the skin had healed. He wanted someone to touch him, maybe let him cry a little and tell him things would be OK.

Everyone was home. It was getting dark, almost dinnertime. The door was unlocked. Jimmy stormed in and yelled for his kids like he did when he came to pick them up for the weekend.

"Ricky! Miley!"

There was a TV on somewhere. Jimmy stood in the tight space of the landing near a coat rack. It was too small to swing the rifle. He moved into the dining room and stopped when he heard the scuttle of humans.

"Where are you kids!"

"Jimmy?" It was Al's voice off to the left in the family room. Ricky appeared on the staircase. His hair was shaggy in a way Jimmy did not like. His son, thirteen, had a big mouth and big biceps. "Dad! What are you doing?" he screamed when he saw the rifle. Jimmy stopped. He saw two flashing figures ahead in the kitchen: Brenda and Miley. His daughter, eleven, looked so much like Brenda—the blond hair, the blue eyes, the pointy chin—that Jimmy couldn't be in the same room with her for long. He sensed them all approaching. They were terrified. He tried to picture what they saw: Jimmy coming in with a gun, wild-eyed, shivering, barely existing in the world, the pressure on his ears too much to even hear anything.

"Goddamnit, Jimmy, why do you have a gun?" Al said.

Al had been sitting on the couch in the family room watching a hockey game on a giant flat-screen TV. He wore different kinds of clothes than Jimmy—corduroys, a sweater, a fleece vest. He didn't like snowmobiles or hunt deer. He came lunging into the dining room, where Jimmy stood with the rifle.

"Don't be stupid, Jimmy," Brenda said. She had her hands on Miley's shoulders, standing where the hallway met the dining room.

It felt like Al and Brenda were closing in on him.

Jimmy brought the rifle butt to his chin and swiveled it over to Al, who was framed by the giant screen that made the hockey players on it look like they were in the room. Jimmy couldn't afford such a big TV.

"Don't be crazy, Jimmy," Al said. "We can work this out."

"Put your arms in the air, Al," he said.

Jimmy was slightly satisfied to see the hands go up. Both Ricky and Miley were bawling, which made him feel terrible. "Everyone shut up and let me think!" he cried.

"Goddamnit, Jimmy. You know this isn't going to end well," Brenda said.

"What do you want, Jimmy?" Al asked.

"Pills."

"What?" Brenda said.

"Didn't they give you some pills when you got your gallbladder out?"

"I . . . I don't have any pills, Jimmy."

"You did! I saw them," he cried.

"I flushed the rest so the kids wouldn't mess with them."

The pressure was unbearable. His heart was beating in his ears so loudly Jimmy thought he'd collapse. He moved the gun all around the room, confused. He didn't know what he was even doing. He turned his direction to Al, whose mouth was hanging open.

"Then here's the deal, Al. I'll sell you my kids. That should be fair. You love 'em so much. I'll sell them for six thousand bucks."

That was roughly what he owed the cardboard company.

"You took my wife. You took my kids. You took my finger. Where's my compensation?"

"I'm calling the police, Jimmy. Now put that gun down before you really hurt someone," Brenda said.

She knew Jimmy wouldn't shoot anyone. This infuriated him.

"Yeah?" he said. "No one's gonna get hurt, eh? How about this?"

Jimmy brought the tip of the rifle down, aimed at his foot, and pulled the trigger. His body erupted with burning pain. It was like the cardboard factory all over again. The flash of emergency. He saw the entire world as a blood-pumping wound, the snake slithering to get out. Jimmy was brought back to earth by the screaming. Ricky and Miley were both crying. Al took a step toward him and stopped. Brenda was gasping.

"What did you do!" she screamed.

"I don't know," he cried. He started to sob himself.

"Drop the gun, Jimmy! Put it down!" Al said, inching toward him with his arms out.

Jimmy dropped the rifle, which hit the carpet and settled softly on its side. He fell to his knees and slid the gun toward the family room. His blue jeans were covered in blood now. The pain was next-level, but it had erased the nausea. The sobbing was making it bearable, deep sobs bubbling up from that place inside the pills had sealed off. Without the pills it was wide open. Jimmy sat there, clutching his knees to his chest, bleeding on the white rug underneath the dining room table. Now he smiled and sobbed at the same time. He felt a great sense of relief. The pressure, the snake, everything was all gone, draining out through the wound in his foot. Al grabbed the rifle and was on his cell phone calling 911. Brenda had both kids in her arms, tucked close to her body. They were trying not to look at him from across the dining room. Blood seeped out his right foot and onto the floor. Jimmy looked at Brenda and the crying kids and smiled meekly. Dr. Reese would have to refill his prescription now, even if he was in the county jail. The pills would last him at least another two months. Maybe three.

Rich Girl Blues

She met Lainey for brunch at their usual Wicker Park joint after yet another scandalous night that took them all over Chicago. Jessie Powers had a thick hangover and ordered a Bloody Mary. She was resolved to drink all the hard drinks, think all the hard thoughts. Large sunglasses with fire-red frames blocked half her face. She hadn't bothered to put on makeup before leaving her condo.

She and Lainey, her best friend, had only been apart a few hours, having accompanied each other to the Empty Bottle for Trevor's show and then a party back at his place in Logan Square. It ended poorly, with Jessie and Trevor fighting about their respective bad attitudes. Trevor then took to the couch with an acoustic guitar and made up a song about Jessie for everyone hanging out drinking beers and toking blunts.

"I call it 'The Rich Girl Blues,'" he shouted.

The song, a standard blues riff, soon had the entire apartment rolling with laughter.

She's got too much money for drugs, too much money
  for booze
She's got what I call the rich girl blues
And she's so high, oh yeah, she's so high
That she'll never come down
Alive

Jessie fake-laughed along like she was in on the joke, then promptly made out with Trevor's bass player, Chad, who had some downright hellish halitosis. She impulsively kissed him on the walk-up porch behind the brick apartment building where a bunch of people stood smoking in the summer heat. Trevor saw their faces locked when he came out.

"Whores!" he screamed.

That's when Jessie and Lainey left and went dancing at a club. Jessie barely remembered getting home but was glad to see she was alone when she woke up. The guilt and shame were crushing. Now reunited, she and Lainey stood at the curb outside the restaurant smoking cigarettes, ashing into a sewer drain, gossiping about the night.

But Jessie was having a hard time concentrating on the conversation. Yes, she was feeling low, but it wasn't just Trevor. Or the song. Or the guy with bad breath. It was something indescribably sad that sometimes hit her on Sunday mornings when she and Lainey caught up over brunch. It was as if all the days and nights of idle chatter concerning their mindless amusements reached their point of reckoning and always fell short of adding up to anything.

The girls went back into the restaurant, where their food was waiting. Jessie had a mushroom and spinach frittata and freshly squeezed mango juice. She ate ravenously when hungover.

"I dunno," she said between forkfuls. "I mean, don't you think there's something more to life than all of this? Like, we just keep forging endlessly on into the future doing the same stuff, an endless pattern, an endless loop."

Lainey sighed.

"I hate when you get all emo-existentialist on Sundays."

Lainey also hid behind large shades. She was ashamed of her nose and the muffin-top flab that hung over her leggings. Lainey was not as well off, the daughter of a doctor who was the son of a factory worker. Nouveau riche, as some of Jessie's meaner, older friends would call her. But she was Jessie's heart and soul. They'd known each other since freshman year at DePaul, where they both graduated several years ago, and had each other's backs ever since.

"What do you have on you?" Jessie asked.

Lainey knew exactly what she meant and began digging through her purse, coming out with an orange prescription bottle of Oxys and setting it on the table.

"Sweet," Jessie said, unscrewing the childproof lid and dropping two into her hand, then swallowing them down with the first sip of a second Bloody Mary. "We should go to the movies later."

Lainey began looking up listings on her phone. While they were discussing what to see, a girl appeared in Jessie's periphery wearing cutoffs and a T-shirt, with her hair pulled back, much like what Lainey and Jessie wore, but not quite as lazy Sunday chic.

Jessie thought the girl would pass their table and go to the bathroom at the back of the restaurant, but she didn't. Jessie understood the vapidity of instantly judging people on their looks and their clothes, but it was always her immediate response. This girl had a peasant face. Stringy blond hair. Cheesy vintage T-shirt from Hot Topic. She was also fumingly mad.

"Are you Trevor's girlfriend?"

Jessie now recognized the girl as someone from the party last night.

"Um, yeah. Kinda. What's up?"

The girl reached across the table, grabbed the Bloody Mary, and dumped the frothy contents on Jessie's head. The slimy red tomato juice dripped down her neck. The other early afternoon brunchers stopped eating and gawked.

The girl cussed at Jessie, called her a nasty name.

"You made out with my boyfriend last night," she said.

Jessie panicked. Her mind raced to make sense of it as she wiped the red slime from her stinging eyes.

"That's crazy," Jessie said. "What are you talking about?"

"Chad," she said. "Everyone saw you kissing him."

Jessie's eyes darted around. Near the entrance, waiting for a table, was sullen Chad, the dude with bad breath. He dared not make eye contact with any of them.

"Chad?" Jessie said to the girl.

"Yes," she said. She was sobbing. "How could you do something like that?"

Jessie began squeezing the Bloody Mary out of her hair. It had spilled all down her shirt, onto her shorts and bare legs. She'd never thought about Chad beyond being a tool in her revenge against Trevor and his stupid song.

"I'm really sorry," Jessie said.

"You rich girls think you can do whatever you want," was the girl's reply. She called Jessie another nasty name and stomped off in a huff. She and Chad left the restaurant.

Lainey was giggling. She flagged down a passing waitress.

"Can we get a towel and another Bloody Mary, please?"

"I need to change my life," was the recurring mantra in Jessie's mind in the cab. She ignored the driver, an African guy talking on an earpiece in a language she didn't understand, and instead sought refuge in her phone, looking up drug and alcohol rehabilitation centers, yoga studios and career counseling. In the five-minute ride to her condo, Jessie had it all figured out. She would refuse handouts from her family, get a job, stop drinking, pay her own way, buy a dog, and quit smoking.

Then her brother Ben called. She groaned, let it go to voicemail, paid the cabbie, then groaned again as the phone buzzed and lit up a second time as she walked into her condo and dumped her purse on the sofa.

"What do you want, Ben? I need to jump in the shower. I have a Bloody Mary in my hair."

"What?"

"Don't worry about it."

"We need to talk," he said. "Why aren't you responding? I sent you like four texts last night."

Jessie vaguely remembered the phone vibrating, the missed call alerts. She grabbed a towel from the bathroom and patted her wet hair as she slumped down onto the couch.

"Sorry. It's been weird."

"It's going to be worse soon if we don't talk."

"Is it Dad?"

"No. It's the Money."

The Money was mythical, epic, a large mysterious mass of pleasure and pain earned generations ago by their great-great-grandfather, Overbrook Powers, a northern Michigan lumberman.

"What's the problem now?" Jessie asked.

There had been worried conversations about the Money going back as far as Jessie could remember. While it afforded the succeeding generations of Powers great wealth, it also haunted the family ever since Overbrook clear-cut thousands of acres of white pine in Bear County starting after the Civil War.

"The problem is that it's gone," Ben said.

"What do you mean?" Jessie said.

The Money was believed to be as deep as the ocean. Jessie had grown up with the faith that the Money was inexhaustible. She believed in it more than any god.

"I messed up," Ben said. "And Dad's not replying to any messages. The Money is gone. I lost it. Well, our part of the Money, at least."

"What did you do?"

Jessie lit a cigarette and kicked her feet up on the coffee table as a second painkiller kicked in, thrusting her down into a pleasure pit of opiate love that drowned out the most piercing anxieties.

"The latest venture of mine didn't pan out," he said.

"What venture? What did you do with our money, Ben?"

Their father, Bill Powers, had inherited a dying business in the 1980s. He'd spent most of his career closing down factories, firing hundreds, downsizing to nearly nothing. He was a depressive who spent his time hunting birds, trout fishing, and brooding at Wild Acres, the family cabin in Michigan, the last stand of virgin pine Overbrook Powers left in Bear County. Meanwhile, their mother was living in California with her new husband.

Jessie and Ben mostly blamed their father for problems with the Money. Ben was supposed to be turning it around, though. He'd gone to business school and had big ideas. Jessie had majored in English literature with the belief she would never be responsible for having to earn a real living.

"That investment with Rick didn't pan out." Rick was their step-father in California. "That was all of it."

"I thought it was a sure thing," Jessie said.

"So did I."

"Did you talk to Mom?"

"I did. And you know what she said?"

"Tough luck?"

"Pretty much."

"She just wants us to go crawling to California. To live with cheese-dick Rick in their big cheese-dick house so she can control our lives."

"They probably stuck our cash in something Rick knew would tank."

Jessie and Ben didn't have much fondness for their perennially tanned, platitude-spewing stepfather who swooped in when their father was suffering his worst bout of depression after miscalculating how difficult it was to pull a shotgun trigger with his toe.

When it came time for college, Ben went off to New York, where he remained, and Jessie to Chicago. Neither visited California much.

"So, what do we do?" Jessie asked.

"Well, I have an idea."

"That's what you said when you talked me into trusting Rick with an investment."

"This is different."

"What now?"

"Great Aunt Maureen still has millions. No kids. No heirs. Me, you, and the cousins have got to be the only people listed in her will. As far as I know, she lives up in a retirement home. Barely spends any money at all. Doesn't leave town."

"Are you talking film noir now?"

Jessie joked because she had fond memories of her aunt and didn't know how else to respond.

"We're not gonna bump her off, Jess. But if you could go up there and ask for an advance on the inheritance, we'd be set until nature takes its course. Think about it. She's the only one left up there. Besides Dad, I guess. But who knows what he's up to."

This nearly brought tears to Jessie's eyes. Her beloved Grandpa Jackie and Grandma Eddie had both died within the last five years. Jessie and Ben had spent most of their summers with them up on the Hill in Bear River while their dad lived in solitude at Wild Acres. Jackie had been a song and dance man on the USO circuit and would teach Jessie the routines in the parlor, the scratchy records skipping as little Jessie leapt around. Grandma Eddie smoked, wore sundresses, and made cheese balls, deviled eggs, and finger sandwiches for the kids. They'd do puzzles, play games, and take walks down to the beach for ice cream sundaes. Grandpa Jackie had a head for music, not business, and was also to blame for the current financial misfortunes of the Powers family, something neither Jessie nor Ben cared to dwell on.

Jessie missed both of her grandparents terribly, especially in the summer. They'd died within a few years of each other, the big house sold to a couple from San Francisco who turned it into a bed-and-breakfast, the profits of which Ben used to pay off some debts—or so he said. Jessie could never be sure what her brother did, but still she trusted him to manage her share of the Money.

"So the idea is that we go up there, take her out to an early dinner and ask for money?" Jessie asked.

"Something like that," Ben said. "Except I was thinking maybe you could go? I mean, you are her favorite. You used to go visit her all the time. And I don't want to have to get back on a plane."

Ben had recently been vacationing in Australia with his girlfriend.

"Asking for money feels, well, kinda sleazy," Jessie said.

"Humble yourself, sweet sister. Unless you want to start pounding the pavement for an occupation, I think you should make a fast break for Bear River. The Pickle Princess won't let us down. Remember, she's family."

Jessie needed to escape Chicago anyway. The tawdry escapades were much more interesting when she was in her twenties. They made her feel interesting and glamorous then. If this was five years ago, she and Lainey would have spent hours recounting Trevor's dumb song, the scandalous make-out session with Chad, and the Bloody Mary dumped on her head with perverse humor. What was funny at twenty-five was slowly becoming pathetic by thirty. The scandals were becoming rote, mechanical and forced.

Jessie was sick of trying to behave poorly to cut the image of a badass. She was tired. A trip to Bear County would do her good. When she finished packing, Jessie pulled the car out of her parking garage and hit the road. While inching her way out of the city, she pondered how best to navigate this inheritance business with her great aunt.

For the better part of her life, Aunt Maureen was known as the Pickle Princess. As a young man, Archibald Powers—Jessie's great-grandfather—was faced with a bottomed-out lumber business. He turned to pickle manufacturing and hired an advertising man out of Chicago who used six-year-old Maureen as the new pickle company's mascot. They dressed her up like a green wood sprite with a wooden sword and put her on a giant pickle like it was a horse. The image was plastered on thousands of pickle jars across America. The new pickle line was a great success at first, and Aunt Maureen went on grocery store tours across the country, delighting customers by sitting near a display of pickle jars and singing the jingle:

> *Powers Pickles are the greatest pickles that will get ya out of any pickle.*
> *Don't be fickle; give your tummy a tickle with Powers Famous Pickles.*

As far as Jessie knew, it was the only thing her Aunt Maureen had ever done in life. She never married, never had any kids, and not until recently did she move out of the old mansion. She'd had various issues throughout her life and had once been studied by a famous doctor because she couldn't stop sleepwalking, something that still got her into trouble at the nursing home. And she was the only person left in the family who had any sizable chunk of the Money.

Jessie had five hours on the road to dwell on how she hadn't done much in her life either, that she was perhaps on the same spinster path as her aunt. When she got to Bear County, the hazy sun was still a lemon drop dissolving in the hot gray sky. Jessie went straight to her family's old Victorian mansion on the Hill, the grandest neighborhood in Bear River, built on a bluff overlooking Lake Michigan. The house, now a bed-and-breakfast, was once the biggest single-family residence in town. Jessie used to visit her family there every summer, including Aunt Maureen, who in adulthood was bookish and reclusive. She was content with spending her days reading books from the mansion's library.

Jessie joined her in the library when she was old enough. They would eat saltines, drink pop, and do crossword puzzles on long summer afternoons. Aunt Maureen was losing her eyesight, and would have Jessie read to her. Jessie remembered the imposing heft of the volumes: *Middlemarch, Little Dorrit, Tess of the D'Urbervilles*. On rainy afternoons, while Ben played Nintendo, Jessie was immersed in the lives of the sprawling families in the novels, the noble characters trying to find their fortunes among wicked old uncles, complicated marital arrangements, and an unforgiving social and class system that stifled the individual. She identified.

Jessie wrote about these themes in essays during her unremarkable tenure as an English major at DePaul. She never got better than a 3.0 grade point average. When she mentioned graduate school to a favorite professor, he looked surprised and said, "Um, yeah, I guess that's a possibility?"

It was then Jessie knew she'd never be a great producer or scholar of literature. Instead, like Aunt Maureen, she could be that elusive creature, the *serious reader*, and gave up on scholarly pursuits. She learned it was fun to spend money. It was fun to go to parties. Why not? She could be a ruined socialite like in a Fitzgerald story. What else was there in life? Maybe it was for the best that Jessie ended up a spinster in a drafty old room filled with drafty old nineteenth-century novels like her aunt. At this point, it didn't sound half bad.

Jessie had her fill of the memories provoked by the mansion in the fading sunshine and hit the road. Aunt Maureen was in her seventies now, and lived in a nursing home on the edge of town. She probably had enough money to live in a big house with a staff of aides attending to her, but she disliked that kind of lifestyle, preferring to do things regular, non-rich people did. She liked the company in the nursing home. It wasn't a bad place. She could come and go as she pleased in her red Cadillac. The nursing home was close to the Bear River Library, where Aunt Maureen had been on the board for years. She spent much of her time visiting with old friends at the library and reading. And the doctors found the right pharmaceutical mixture to control her sleepwalking after she tried attacking a fellow patient.

Jessie had never talked about the Money with Aunt Maureen, or anyone else in her family besides Ben, really. It was considered bad form to bring up financial matters. But here she was. Jessie the Beggar. She got to the nursing home and sat in the parking lot for a few minutes, summoning the courage to go inside and shake down her old aunt for money.

Jessie went in and asked the nurse—a large man with a goatee and glasses—if he could show her which room Maureen Powers was in.

"She hasn't been here the last couple days," he said. "Nothing serious. She's just visiting family."

Jessie was surprised.

"What family?" she said.

"I don't know. People come and go as they please. She left a message with the desk that she would be staying with a nephew or something. At a cabin in the woods."

Jessie sighed deeply. "OK, thanks."

She really didn't want to pull her father into all of this. She was hoping to avoid seeing him altogether.

Jessie drove toward Wild Acres. As the last two members of the once mighty Powers family still living in Bear County, Aunt Maureen and her father checked in on one another occasionally, one recluse keeping a distant eye on the other. It was a difficult situation with her father, who was always a difficult man.

Jessie had not seen him since her grandfather's funeral. He showed up looking morose and uncomfortable in a dark suit that smelled like mothballs. He'd lived at the hunting cabin on Wild Acres since the family business went under and his divorce from Jessie's mother, fishing for trout on the Little Bear River in the summer and hunting in the woods in the fall.

"I'm happiest out here with the dogs," he told Jessie, referring to his two English setters.

Jessie loved her father. He wasn't mean or cruel. And she knew he loved her. But he could never love anyone or anything more than his sorrow, even his children or his dogs. Jessie had figured that out a long time ago.

There was no road to the cabin. She took the two-track to where it stopped at a little clearing where her Aunt Maureen's red Cadillac was parked, leaving her car alongside it and following the trail on foot for a mile and a half. This was a young forest, part of the land Overbrook Powers clear-cut in the nineteenth century. Some of the stumps of the huge virgin white pines were visible through the smaller, young aspens. The stumps were so huge it would take three people holding hands to circle them. These types of massive trees soon came into view. During his frenzy to cut the forest, Overbrook had decided to preserve a thousand acres of the virgin pine that made him rich. The pines were tall as skyscrapers, unbendable in the wind blowing in off the lake. When Jessie was inside those huge trees, she felt like she entered a new world of shade and cool breezes. This is what the world felt like before humans arrived. A soft wind blew through the green leaves. She soon arrived at the A-frame cabin in the woods.

Jessie saw her elderly aunt sitting on the front porch looking at a magazine, a spindly pile of bones in a rocking chair. Jessie walked closer, where the uncut grass was long and matted under her feet. Her aunt was wearing a white, fuzzy long-sleeved sweatshirt and a pair of beige polyester pants despite the heat.

"Aunt Maureen?" she said, her voice low enough not to startle the old woman.

Her aunt set down the magazine, a confused expression on her wrinkled face.

"Hello? Who's there?" she shouted.

Jessie felt like an intruder. "It's me, Aunt Maureen," she said. "It's Jessie."

"Jessie? What are you doing here, honey?"

It was a very good question, one Jessie couldn't immediately answer.

"You shouldn't be here," Aunt Maureen said, rising slowly from the rocker and stepping closer to her. This made Jessie feel even more dizzy and uncomfortable. The Oxys had worn off around Indiana. She wished for a shot of vodka. Anything.

"I guess I don't know what I'm doing here," Jessie finally said.

Her aunt, whom she'd never seen angry or upset, was now both.

"I guess I need help," Jessie blurted.

She couldn't hold it in any longer, the sadness she felt earlier that morning at brunch unloosed. She started sobbing right there on the matted grass next to an old Weber grill. Aunt Maureen's face relaxed. She came down the steps to where Jessie stood weeping and wrapped thin arms around her, smoothing her back. Her voice was reassuring.

"Are you here for money, dear?"

Jessie pulled away from the embrace and looked around, embarrassed. Of course Aunt Maureen knew. Why else would Jessie be there if not for the Money? She could do nothing but force a smile, look down at the ground and nod. Like a little girl.

"You should have just called. You shouldn't have come here," Aunt Maureen repeated. "Your father is sick. I'm helping him get better."

Jessie didn't understand. Her confusion stunted the tears.

"What's wrong with Dad?" she asked.

Aunt Maureen released Jessie from the embrace, but kept Jessie's hands in her own.

"Well, I'll be frank, honey. Your father is sitting in an armchair in that cabin with a Winchester shotgun. He's been this way for a couple of days. He hasn't said a word."

Jessie felt dislocated from her body. She took a step back.

"What do you mean? What happened?"

"One of the setters died."

"His dog?" Jessie asked.

Aunt Maureen nodded.

"Yes. Roscoe, the poor thing. I think there's more going on, but it started with the dog."

Jessie started nervously pacing.

"I don't understand," she said. "What's he doing? He's not, like, holding you hostage or anything, right?"

"No, my goodness, no, honey," she said. "In fact, I think he'd much rather me leave him alone. But we've been through this before. We're the only ones left up here. We take care of each other."

"I still don't understand," Jessie said.

"He means to kill himself," Aunt Maureen said bluntly.

Jessie was shocked and embarrassed that she didn't immediately understand this.

"You shouldn't have come here, honey," Aunt Maureen said again.

Jessie panicked. "Well, we have to stop him!"

"Oh, I've tried, honey. But this will pass. He's been in this spot before. We always just wait it out."

"Has he been taking his meds?" Jessie asked.

Aunt Maureen shook her head.

"That's the problem. I wasn't here, of course. Roscoe ran off and accidentally drowned in the creek. Poor dog. But since I got here, I've been sneaking the meds in his beans. Crushing them up so he doesn't know."

Jessie always knew her family was slightly off-kilter, but this was a new dimension of weirdness.

"And this has happened before?" she asked.

Her aunt took a breath and nodded.

"I've known men like him before," she said solemnly. "Couldn't face the world after the darkness gets to them. They just need patience."

"Well why has no one called Ben or me? We're his kids!"

"He specifically asked that I never get you involved. He doesn't want anyone to see him like this. He's ashamed. And that can make it worse."

"We should call the police. Or a doctor. Or whoever," she said, reaching in the back pocket of her cutoff blue jean shorts for her phone. But it wasn't there. She'd forgotten it in the car.

"That's not a good idea. It would only make it worse."

"This is crazy," Jessie said. "If this is happening again, he needs help."

When Jessie was a baby, her father lost the company and sunk into the deepest of depressions. During a family vacation at Wild Acres, he went into the woods with his shotgun, sat on a stump, put the barrel to his head and tried pulling the trigger with the bare big toe on his right foot, but he only succeeded in nicking the top of his left ear with some of the pellets. Years of treatment, medications, and recovery followed. He healed to the point where doctors trusted him with a shotgun again. Bird hunting had been one of his true loves in life, after all. He was supposed to be supervised with weapons, however.

"Well, I'm going in to see him," Jessie said.

She moved toward the door, but Aunt Maureen raised her bony hand.

"That's not a good idea," she said. "I have everything under control. He'll be fine in a day or two if he eats his beans. Then you can come back and see him. He wouldn't want you to see him like this. It could make him worse. Trust me, I've seen your father like this before. If you walk in there right now, there's no telling what he might do."

In a strange way, what Aunt Maureen was saying made sense. This realization must have shown on her face because her aunt continued in a softer tone.

"Go back to town. Stay the night at the LaFleur Inn downtown. Can you at least afford a room there?"

Jessie nodded.

"Good. We can talk about money later. If your dad is doing better, I can tell him you're here and maybe you can see him. He just needs to be prepared. But a shock like this won't do him any good right now."

Jessie and her aunt had read *Jane Eyre* together. They'd never negotiated hostage situations. It made Jessie feel lost and scared.

"It will be OK, honey," her aunt said. "Trust me. These unpleasant things happen."

"Should I at least call the doctor when I get to town?" Jessie said.

"It's too dangerous," Aunt Maureen said. "This is the best way. A couple days and he'll be fine. Maybe even tomorrow. He might go to sleep and wake up better."

"But what if he doesn't? What if he shoots himself? Or shoots you?"

"Honey, I took the shells out of the gun the first night I showed up," her aunt said. "He doesn't know, of course. Or maybe he does but doesn't care. We've been through this before. Come back tomorrow. And in the meantime, don't mention it to anyone. He'd be so ashamed."

Jessie walked back to her car, first through the towering virgin pines, then past the huge stumps in the newer forest. She didn't pay any attention to the wind blowing through the green leaves now. Her phone had been bombed with messages in her absence. She distractedly skimmed over several messages from Lainey about the interminable Chicago scandals. Trevor had left a half-dozen pleading and pathetic messages begging her to come over that night.

She only got one text from her brother, "You talk to Aunt M. about the Money?"

She wanted to text back: "She already knew. We're so pathetic that she already knew," but she didn't. She drove back out the unnamed two-track onto LaFleur Highway and onto US 31 into the town of Bear River in silence.

The Nudists

Shelly Bowman had to save her mother from the nudists.

One summer day Shelly's father informed her that Margery Bowman, best known for her pies and pot roasts, had run off to "some sex camp" on the shores of Lake Michigan south of Bear River.

"She's not the same woman she used to be," Dad said. He was sitting in his armchair watching the news in the living room. He seemingly hadn't left the chair since retiring from the Junction Fruit Canning plant five years ago. "She's been, well, disagreeable. They can keep her as far as I'm concerned."

Even though Shelly had a million other things she needed to be doing—an eight-month-old refusing to nurse and the Open Carry potluck picnic—she left Baby Bobby with her husband, hopped in her shiny Ford pickup, and hit the road for the cross-county drive to Captain Al's Nudist Resort. She didn't have much of a plan beyond showing up and pleading, "Mom, please come home. Please."

Shelly represented the least populated, most rural district on the Bear County Commission, encompassing her barely-there hometown of Junction (the fruit canning plant, a depleted downtown, and little else) in the southeastern part of the county, forty miles from the lake. To get to Captain Al's—which Shelly had heard rumors about since she was little—she drove due west till she hit the water, then north along the coast, through a few small towns and hamlets, opening the window and letting the lake air rush in while pondering her dilemma.

Shelly didn't really get along with her parents. They had reared their only child in a quiet, traditional way that amounted to making sure no one was judging them in the same way they were judging others. Her mother was upset when Shelly didn't like wearing dresses as a little girl and preferred going out to cut wood with her dad. It was her mother's domestic acquiescence that inspired Shelly to get into politics. She wanted to forge a new, more modern way for Republican women based on equality and economics. But somehow Margery Bowman had lost it entirely and was hanging out with a bunch of naked liberals at the beach. As Shelly thought it through in the pickup truck, she couldn't help but shake her head a few times in disbelief. It made no sense.

But this was the only way Shelly could think of to save both her mother and her reelection campaign, not to mention pursuing her dreams to the state house, the US House, and eventually the Senate. Who knew how far she could go? If the *Bear River Dauntless* caught on that her mother was frolicking naked on Captain Al's beach with a bunch of bikers and hippies, Shelly would be out after one term, back to managing the late shift at the fruit canning plant. Her supporters—mostly farmers, retirees, and canning plant employees—would be shocked and disappointed. The far right wing in her own party would certainly make use of rumors that her sixty-three-year-old mother was fornicating with long-hairs next to a bonfire.

She specifically thought of Merv Marl, the main right-wing hothead who was running against her in the primary next month. For the past few years, Merv had been showing up to county commission meetings clad in a cowboy hat and a soaring eagle belt buckle.

He'd wait until public comment to rail against the evils of government. His flamboyant efforts were ignored at first, but now people were starting to listen.

Shelly fumbled with her phone to look at directions, not remembering the name of the turnoff. Out the window she saw nothing except a smattering of old farms and pole barns framed by the lush summer tree line.

Shelly had looked up Captain Al's on the internet the night before while her husband, Darrell, stood behind her desk holding Baby Bobby. Darrell had gone to school downstate and worked in IT at the Bear County government offices where they had met. He only moved out to the remote Junction area when he married Shelly, whose family had been there a hundred years. Now he rarely left Junction, only going to the Bear County administration offices a few times a month for meetings. Working mostly from home meant he could take care of the baby, a role he enjoyed. Darrell claimed not to care about politics, but Shelly secretly suspected he had been converted into a Democrat during his time in college. He laughed when Shelly pulled up the poorly designed web page with its light blue background and gaudy red lettering: "Captain Al's Nudist Resort." The site featured a dozen low-quality pictures shot from so far away you couldn't even make out a nipple. People in their sixties and seventies doing a variety of activities in the buff: water skiing, volleyball, Putt-Putt golf.

"I wouldn't think to do that stuff with clothes *on*," Darrell said.

"Being naked frees you from your inhibitions in a variety of ways," Shelly said mockingly.

Captain Al's slogan was written in large lettering on the top of the page: "Reveal the real you."

Shelly wasn't sure how she felt about it yet. Darrell and a few boyfriends in high school were the only people to see her naked, besides the doctor, her mother, and of course Baby Bobby, who was going through a phase where it felt like he would take neither bottle nor boob. The poor boy kept Shelly and Darrell up all night crying inconsolably, lying on Shelly's chest, shaking his little head when presented with her breast. By three thirty in the morning, when Baby Bobby finally latched on, Shelly would be near tears herself. Besides intimate family moments like this, Shelly felt bodies should be kept private to maintain some sort of boundaries between one another; still, she didn't really care what anyone did as long as it didn't hurt other people. But people were being hurt here. *She* was hurting. Her mother knew Shelly was in the public eye and that taking off to Captain Al's could have a disastrous effect on her reputation. Shelly never felt her mother fully supported her political career in the first place—and now this.

A roadside sign displaying an unclothed pirate with a strategically placed sword came into view. The pirate had flowing black hair, a hat, a mustache, and a pointy goatee. His left hand was holding the sword over his groin area while his right arm pointed down a dirt road on the other side of US 31.

"In search of hidden booty? Captain Al's Nudist Resort, this way," the sign read.

Shelly pulled off the road onto the gravel shoulder so her truck was directly in front of the sign, unable to turn in. Not yet. She wondered briefly about the origin of the pirate theme. In the brief research she conducted, it seemed most resorts played up an earthy, hippie vibe. Be one with nature. That sort of thing. But Captain Al's was different. Pirates were lawless. Nudists were lawless. Margery Bowman, who tended house and greeted visitors with a plastic smile for thirty years, was now in the hands of these pirates. Her mother, in fact, *was* one of these lawless pirates.

Shelly noticed another billboard a hundred feet away that had a simple slogan painted in white on a black backdrop: "Unmarried sex = sin." Underneath, it read "Sponsored by the Republican Women of Bear County." Shelly was a member of the group herself and remembered voting to put up the sign even though she and Darrell had plenty of sex before they got married. Being in politics meant doing such things.

A motorcycle suddenly came roaring up, driven by a gray-haired biker with a woman on back, her arms wrapped around his body. The bike turned into Captain Al's. Shelly imagined them playing badminton together without clothes on.

It took her five minutes to muster the courage to drive in. Lake Michigan came into view, then a sand-covered parking lot with a dozen or so cars, trucks, and motorcycles next to the grassy dunes that led to the beach. Shelly parked and walked to a trail that was blocked by a gate. A shirtless man with shoulder-length hair, probably around Shelly's age—mid-thirties—was sitting in a booth, reading. Shelly slung her purse over her shoulder and hugged it tightly with her right arm as if she expected the man to leap out and try snatching it. Instead, he set down the book—a faded paperback entitled *Paradise Lost*—and smiled widely.

Shelly didn't trust his smile. She thought it suggested he was excited at the prospect of seeing her naked. But all he said was, "Welcome to Captain Al's! I'm Dave. How can I help you?"

Shelly was close enough to the booth to see the man only wore a fanny pack. Luckily, he was sitting in a way where Shelly couldn't see anything down below. She took a step back so she wouldn't be tempted to look down farther.

"I'm wondering if I could just go in and find my mother," she said.

"That's cool," Dave said, with the strung-out ambivalence of a new-wave hippie pothead. "But you still have to pay admission and sign our contract." He reached for some paperwork in the booth.

"Is it OK if I keep my clothes on?" Shelly asked.

"No clothes here," he said. "Captain Al's rules. But you can wear a bathing suit."

"Listen, I just really want to talk to my mom. I'm going to be out of here in a few minutes."

"I'm sorry," he said. He unzipped his fanny pack, pulled out a Snickers, unwrapped it and started gnawing. He was definitely stoned. "Those are the rules."

"I don't have a bathing suit," she said.

"Underwear works too."

"And what happens if I refuse?"

"Can't let you in. Cause any trouble, call the cops. They don't like us much here, but it's still private property."

Shelly pondered her options. She could leave with her dignity intact and brave the unknowable in the primaries and the election. Or she could suck it up, strip down to her undies, go in and grab her mom, and be out in ten minutes.

"OK, how much is it?" she asked.

"Thirty bucks for a day. Price goes down to twenty if you're gonna stay the night at one of the campgrounds. Only five bucks a day if you stay more than a week."

"Thirty bucks? That's a lot. I'm only going to be in there ten minutes."

"Ten seconds, ten hours, still thirty bucks, unless you stay the night. That's when it gets rockin' around here anyway."

"I just want my mother," Shelly said, digging in her purse for her wallet.

She should be at the Open Carry picnic, she thought, scooping ambrosia salad onto a plate. Shelly was ambivalent about guns—she owned one old shotgun to scare away coyotes on her property—but the Open Carry vote is what helped her coast to victory four years ago and now she was missing the big event. She should be flirting with the old guys strapped with Glocks and .45s, who would smile and flirt back and tell her she was in the safest place on the planet.

Dave took the money she slid over the counter and produced some papers for her to sign. He highlighted the contract as she took a pen and scanned them.

"No cell phones. No pictures. Captain Al's isn't responsible for any lost, damaged items," Dave mumbled through a mouthful of candy bar. "The regular BS."

Shelly went to her truck, opened the driver's side door and used it as a shield for her body. She looked around but didn't see anyone, then took a deep breath and started disrobing. She was wearing a pair of khaki shorts, flip-flops, and a cream-colored short-sleeve blouse. She kept scanning the beach and parking lot to see if anyone was looking as she shimmied out of her shorts, tossing them on the driver's seat. She was horrified to realize she was wearing mismatched underwear: blue panties and a white bra. And while she had been blessed with good metabolism and never had to crash diet or go to kickboxing classes like some of her friends to keep weight off, she'd had Baby Bobby less than a year ago.

Ten minutes and it will be over, she told herself.

She slid her feet back in the sandals and put all her clothes in the truck. She locked the door and realized she had no place to put her keys. She wished for a fanny pack.

Dave looked up from his book and opened the gate when she returned.

"Have fun," he said. "My shift ends at seven. Find me out by the beach if you wanna hang."

His head was angled in such a way that Shelly thought he was staring at her breasts over the rim of the book, but she couldn't be sure.

"Like I said, I'll be leaving in ten minutes."

"I've heard that before," Dave said.

Shelly found a sandy trail, a cool breeze from the lake rushing over her bare skin. She didn't feel liberated. If anything, she felt trapped.

Shelly's stomach rose with the frightful anticipation of seeing the nudists. She heard voices before she saw anyone. Then she heard a clanging noise. As she crested a small dune, she saw a group of nudists playing a game of horseshoes, three people grouped near one stake, three by the other. She would have to pass right by them. Shelly tried not to leer and instinctively hugged her arms over her breasts. She looked to see if one was her mother.

"Yo-ho!" one of the men cried. "Welcome to Captain Al's."

"Yo-ho!" one of the women cried.

"Yo-ho!" they all cried in unison.

Someone tossed a horseshoe and it thudded into the sand. They were all drinking from bottles of beer. A few of them were smoking. She tried not staring at their bodies while scanning the faces in the group. Shelly didn't see her mother and pressed on toward the main campground.

Pop-up campers and tents stood in various sites beneath pine trees near fire pits. Shelly began to see so many naked people that it stopped shocking her. They were going about their daily activities, albeit in the buff: washing out cups, stoking fires, grilling up hamburgers for lunch.

Shelly found her mother sitting in a lawn chair eating a hot dog under the awning of an old camper. She was easy to spot, with her spiky gray hair and the way she held the bun with two hands. Her mother, who had been trim like Shelly when she was younger but filled out in her older age, was sunk in the lawn chair in a very relaxed way, legs crossed, large breasts spilling off her chest. She took a bite of the hot dog and a squirt of mustard dripped on the slope of her right breast just above the nipple; she reached for a paper towel and was dabbing it off as Shelly walked up. Shelly stood there, leaning her weight on one leg, not knowing what to do with her arms. Her mother looked up with a perplexed expression.

"Shelly?" she said finally. "Is that you? Oh my goodness! What are you doing here?" She set down the plate on a table beside her and finished wiping off her chest with the paper towel, which she balled up and clenched the whole time they spoke.

"I'm bringing you home," Shelly said.

A man bounded out of the camper. He was tall and not particularly handsome, long hair, billy-goat beard, a large penis dangling out of a thatch of graying pubic hair. Shelly felt her stomach churn and remembered her own seminakedness.

"Please, Mom. We need to go."

"Honey, this is Jerry," she said. "Jerry, this is my daughter."

"Oh, great to meet you," he said, hopping over and extending his hand.

Shelly again hugged herself and ignored him.

"We can talk about all of this in the car on the way home," Shelly said. "But please, we have to leave. I am extremely uncomfortable. We really need to go, Mom."

Her mom went lax. The chair creaked as she reclined into it.

"I'm not going anywhere," she said.

Jerry just stood there with his hands on his hip, penis hanging like a taunt. He was trying to smile.

"I'm not sure what you're trying to prove here, Mom," she said. "But you're really hurting my feelings. And Dad's."

Her mother scoffed.

"Your father has been taking advantage of me for years," she said. "You don't understand how suffocating that man is."

Shelly did. She understood how suffocating and needy all men were, even her husband, who wasn't nearly as bad as her father.

"Take up a hobby," Shelly said.

Jerry had been eagerly waiting for a chance to jump in the conversation.

"You're just brainwashed into conventions," he said. "Your mother is learning to release her wild spirit into the world."

Jerry spread his arms when he said "world," like he was releasing his own spirit at that very moment.

"That's a load of bull crap," Shelly said. "This is all just an excuse for people to screw. There need to be rules."

"This isn't about sex," he said.

"Not now, Jerry," her mom said.

"But she's just like the rest of them!" he cried.

"Well, if you can't come home for Dad, think about me," Shelly said.

Her mother snorted, picked the hot dog up off the plate, and took a nibble. "I know what this is about," she said. "You're afraid for your political career. You're afraid that if it comes out that your mom is here, you'll lose your primary."

Shelly shifted her feet, feeling exactly the way her mom wanted her to feel: selfish.

"Is that so bad?" she said. "I want to make a difference."

"I wanted to make a difference in my life too," her mother said. "You were always braver than me, but I can be brave too. You have to respect that. And if people won't elect you for your talents and who you are, then who needs them? Who cares what I'm doing, or what anyone here is doing? It's just a body, Shelly. Look. We all have one. Look at me. They're just tits."

Shelly hustled out of there as quickly as possible and put her clothes back on next to her truck. It felt comforting to be covered again. She'd go back to Junction alone. Shelly couldn't force her mother to leave, after all. She could only hope none of her political foes caught on before the primary.

Those hopes were immediately dashed.

Waiting out at the entrance of Captain Al's was none other than Merv Marl, his ancient, beige Ford LTD parked in front of the pirate sign. He was leaning against the sedan with a camera slung around his neck, wearing his cowboy hat.

Shelly craned her head out of the window of her truck. Merv brought the camera up to his eye and started snapping pictures as she turned her pickup onto US 31. Shelly thought about stopping to give Merv a piece of her mind but punched the gas and sped off feeling defeated. In her rearview mirror, Shelly saw Merv give a pleasant wave.

Shelly took Baby Bobby to visit her father, who was sitting in his armchair watching the History Channel. He'd been living off canned meats, SpaghettiOs, and pinto beans. Shelly saw the evidence in the kitchen when she passed through, a dozen cans meticulously emptied, stripped, and cleaned next to the sink.

He made funny faces at Baby Bobby, who crawled around on the floor in front of the television. A documentary about Hitler's secret gold was playing at a very high volume. He did not bring up her missing mother, so Shelly had to.

"Have you heard from Mom?"

"She called," he said. "She told me about your visit."

"And is she coming home?"

Her dad didn't want to talk about it. Instead, he put his hands up like antlers and made a funny face for Bobby, who kept crawling over to the armchair and trying to pull himself up on the footrest, then falling on his butt.

"I think if you went up there maybe she'd come home," Shelly said. "Seeing you would make a difference."

Her dad's face got serious.

"There's no way I'm going up there to chase after your mom with a bunch of freaks. If she comes home, fine. She knows where to find me. It will get cold soon enough. She'll have to be back by winter."

Shelly finally got Baby Bobby to take a bottle. He lay on her stomach in bed clutching it when the evening news out of Traverse City came on. Darrell was in bed next to her with a laptop propped on his chest, working on some new features for the Bear County website. The next segment caught her eye, so she turned up the volume. On the screen was her official county commission portrait. In the picture, Shelly was smiling politely, her brown hair loosely tied behind her head to keep it off her shoulders, wearing a blouse and jacket she had for functions and pictures. She sat up straighter in bed to see the TV and forgot about Baby Bobby for a moment. When the guys at the Open Carry picnic and the women at the pro-life bake sales asked why she got into politics, Shelly explained she wanted to be a good steward of their tax money and help get things done. Her main political aim was keeping things fair, she said. She didn't admit that she also liked the attention.

This was not the kind of attention she sought, however.

The local news was having a field day with the story. "Why was politician visiting nudist resort?" "Commissioner unclothed?" "The naked truth about Bear County commissioner." The press, as usual, only had half the story. They had Merv's pictures of her driving out of the camp and a lot of speculation. After the newscaster introduced the segment, the broadcast cut to an on-camera interview with Dave, who confirmed Shelly had paid to come in, though he didn't know what she did while inside or when she left.

"I dunno, seemed like any other chick that comes through here," he said.

Thanks Dave, Shelly thought.

They cut to a quick interview with Merv standing outside his dumpy farmhouse. Like Shelly, he lived in rural Bear County outside of Junction.

"This just isn't the type of behavior we want from our leaders. I am clearly the more decent, moral candidate. Check out my campaign blog for more information."

Darrell punched a few keys on his laptop.

"He's been following you other places," he said, pointing at his screen. "Look at his blog. Here's a picture of you and Baby Bobby at the grocery store."

It showed a frustrated Shelly trying to strap crying Bobby into his car seat, a look of panic on her face that could easily be misconstrued as anger. Shelly remembered the day well—Baby Bobby had a screaming fit in the produce section, and she had to drag him out of there. She felt numb knowing Merv was in the parking lot snapping shots. On the blog, he wrote, "How can Shelly Bowman take care of her constituents when she can't even take care of her own baby?"

Back on the TV screen, Captain Al himself appeared on camera, relishing the free publicity. He was big, bearded, and tan everywhere. The news blurred out his crotch on the telecast as he extolled the virtues of nakedness and his resort.

"I think all politicians should spend a day here. It would make them more honest," he said.

The shot cut back to the news anchor, a generically handsome dark-haired man in a suit with his hands pressed on the desk.

"Commissioner Bowman declined to comment when reached by phone," he said.

It was true. Shelly had declined to comment for any of the stories. She knew the right thing to do was to sit down with one of these reporters, explain what was happening, crack a few jokes to keep it light, and say she wanted to focus on the real issues. People responded to honesty. But she also felt it was no one's business and wasn't going to dignify it with a response. Just as the news cut to a different story, Baby Bobby dropped his bottle, which rolled on the floor. Before he could start crying, Shelly gave his tummy a tickle and planted a kiss on his soft head. Baby Bobby giggled.

Shelly took back roads past the creek to get to Merv Marl's place. Merv's father, Drake Marl, once operated a chicken farm before getting mixed up in local politics. He was the Bear County drain commissioner for many years until being appointed the main administrator. Drake Marl was well known and beloved for his pleasant nature and sharpness with the budget. No one knew what happened with his only son Merv, who never married, never had a steady job, and lived by himself at the now defunct chicken farm that he was selling off parcel by parcel to survive while living inside the collapsing house. What was once a prosperous farm was now a junkyard, tall grass and wildflowers growing up between the dozen broken-down old cars and tractors. Shelly parked her truck next to his LTD. In front of the barn, on cinder blocks, no tires, was a cargo van painted like an American flag, red and white stripes on the side, blue with white stars on the front end, and "1776–1976" emblazoned on the side in old-timey letters. The van was painted during the bicentennial celebration, before Shelly was even born. Shelly remembered Merv's father, who had been dead for years now, and then Merv himself, driving the van in Junction's Fourth of July parade when she was a little girl in the 1990s.

Shelly cautiously made her way to the door. The boards on the front porch creaked and bowed under her weight and Shelly feared she'd fall through. When she knocked, it sounded like about a thousand dogs started barking inside. Merv appeared at the door, a flurry of canines scratching the hardwood floor behind him, barking and circling. He wasn't wearing his cowboy hat, which normally covered a bald dome. A handgun strapped to his hip shifted around while he ate a sandwich. A few of the dogs were leaping up to try and get a nibble.

"How can I help you, Commissioner Bowman?"

He didn't open the door, and spoke through the screen with his mouth full.

"Hey, Merv. I want to talk about this blog of yours."

"The Framers had the foresight to enshrine freedom of speech into our great Constitution," Merv said. He took another bite and smiled, then broke off a few pieces of crust and let them fall to the floor. The dogs started fighting for the scraps, snarling and sniping at each other.

"Why are you following me around?"

"I'm trying to keep you honest, Commissioner."

He took another bite. Shelly lost his eyes in the screen, but she could tell he was afraid to look at her. She sensed he was secretly afraid of people, maybe women in particular.

"I don't care if you have pictures of me," she said. "I don't care about the nudist resort. We can let the voters decide if they really care about that. But stop using pictures of my baby. I'd appreciate it if you could take those off your blog."

"It's just politics," Merv said. "Get out if you can't play the game."

"I remember your father, Merv. He was a good man. He never had to stoop to this kind of politics. Creeping around, stalking a young mother and her baby. Would he approve of this?"

Merv stopped chewing and took one last swallow, then broke up the rest of the sandwich and let it drop to the floor for the dogs. He looked down at his boots.

"I'm not proud of the blog, to be honest, but I really need to win this primary," he said. "No one in this county respects me or what my family has done."

Shelly breathed deep and half smiled at him.

"I get it, Merv. Your father was a great man. You have a legacy to continue here in Bear County. But this election doesn't need to get personal. Just leave my baby out of it, please. I'll promise to be civil if you do."

Merv scratched his head and nodded.

"Will you back off?" Shelly asked.

There were only two dogs on either side of Merv now, mutts that looked to be somewhere between shepherds and labs, sitting nicely while he stroked their heads.

"Yeah," he said. "I promise."

Shelly got plenty of calls in the wake of all the news coverage, even from the head of the Michigan Republican Party. She ignored them, wanting to hide under as many layers of clothing as she could and never show her face again. But that wouldn't work. There was a commission meeting in a week.

"Just skip it," Darrell said. "What's the worst that could happen? Say you're going on vacation."

"It's a cop-out. It's suspicious. I'm going to have to face this. I just wish I had more time."

The morning of the meeting, Shelly hoped a plan would present itself. She went to the far back of her property with a chainsaw to hack up tree limbs and branches to think it through. Darrell was no good at this kind of work. He was a computer guy and left the upkeep of the land to Shelly, who enjoyed the physical labor. It helped her think. America was lost, she decided while ripping through a maple tree. *She* was lost. Someone needed to save the country from the left-wingers like Jerry, letting his dick swing in the wind and doing whatever he wanted, and the right-wingers like Merv, armed at home alone and doing whatever *he* wanted. It wasn't easy persisting in this eternal contradiction, this conflict and tension that would never end, with no solution in sight. How could she really say what she wanted at the meeting? She would have to keep being polite and hold everything in, which made her think of her mother outside Jerry's camper, her breasts hanging out, eating a hot dog.

She dragged the chopped-up wood over to the pole barn, then went inside where Darrell was bouncing Baby Bobby in his arms. The baby was just up from his nap and happy, but would be hungry soon. Shelly took a quick shower and climbed into bed with Darrell, who was now intently watching *Battlestar Galactica*. Still in her robe, she pulled Bobby onto her chest and tried to get him to take a nipple, but he stamped his little fists on her breastbone, punching her throat. Shelly reached for a bottle.

"You figure out what you're going to say at the meeting tonight?" Darrell asked.

"I wish I could just say it like it is: that everyone is crazy. I'm probably crazy too, but at least I'm honest enough to admit it."

Darrell laughed and stroked her arm. "People aren't interested in the truth," he said. "You know that."

Even though it was a scorching summer day, Shelly wore a long-sleeved turtleneck and pants to the meeting. A half-dozen reporters were waiting outside the Bear County administration building in downtown Bear River when she arrived, some from Traverse City and others from as far away as Detroit, so she took a side entrance. Her Republican colleagues, folks she called friends, wouldn't make eye contact with her in the back room, so she decided to sit in the chambers.

As soon as she walked out, a flurry of cameras flashed and reporters started shouting questions.

"Did you have sex while you were there?"

"Are rumors that you participated in an orgy true?"

"Is your husband also a nudist?"

"Will you raise your baby in the nudist lifestyle?"

Shelly buried her face in the agenda packet and didn't say a word. On the agenda were the usual issues: drains, a report from the sheriff, road salt for the winter. The rest of the commission eventually came in and took their seats. Shelly was burning with embarrassment. The cameras made it more intense. The head commissioner, Rod Daniels, a longtime Republican, took his seat.

"All right, all right," he shouted. "Everyone settle down. We'll have time at the end of the meeting for public comment, but for now we have an agenda to get through. I'd appreciate it if the members of the press would please be respectful and save their questions and picture-taking until we're done."

The crowd settled into their seats. In the back row, Shelly could see the top of Merv's cowboy hat. She wondered if he was going to honor their truce. For the next forty-five minutes, Daniels led the commission through the mundane agenda. All the votes were unanimous.

Then the meeting was opened for public comment. The mood in the room shifted. The photographers lifted the cameras from their laps and the reporters got ready to record. An elderly, gray-haired woman took the podium first, so short she could barely reach the microphone.

"I'm a Christian woman," she said. "A woman's body is a gift from God, something to be cherished. And I just don't know what's going on with this country. I'm talking about this woman over here who I've seen on the news." She pointed a finger at Shelly. "The one who can't keep her clothes on. I'd like to know what she has to say for herself. That's all. I just want her to explain."

Shelly felt the hot light of attention on her, the clicking of the news cameras, the glares from the public. She leaned forward so her lips were close to the microphone and her voice came out too loud. "I'm not going to comment on that situation," she said.

The crowd bristled, craving drama. A second woman, in her thirties like Shelly, took the podium and gave her name and where she lived. She wore a tank top that revealed tattoos on her arms and a ball cap with a ponytail coming out the back.

"I just want to say I don't think it's anyone's business what Miss Bowman was doing over at Captain Al's. I'm sure you all have shameful things you do too. But that's not why I'm here tonight. I'd like to ask the commission what they plan to do about dangerous cell phone towers. I've read several stories on the internet about how these towers emit radiation that cause cancer. What are we doing about these towers?"

While the woman was speaking about radiation, Shelly watched Merv rise from his seat and line up to speak. As the woman finished her comments and sat down, Merv moved over to the podium. Shelly tried to catch his eye, to maybe get a hint at what he was about to say, but he wouldn't look at her.

"I'd like to start by talking about my own mother," he said into the microphone. "Many of you remember her. She was a fine woman, a wife, mother, church leader, and champion pie maker. She had the type of morals we should all aspire to. I don't know what's happening with this new generation of women, but it's an abomination. And there is no greater example of this than our own Commissioner Shelly Bowman."

Shelly looked down at her agenda packet and pretended to read a page.

"Now let's address the eight-hundred-pound gorilla in here," Merv continued. "What everyone wants to know is what Commissioner Bowman, after talking so much about family values in the past, was doing at Captain Al's?"

Shelly shuffled the pages before her nonsensically.

"This is not the type of behavior we want out of our elected officials," Merv said.

There were a couple of grumbles of agreement in the room.

"I'd like you to explain yourself, ma'am," Merv said. "What were you doing there?"

"I am curious why you were stalking me," she said.

Merv flashed a smile.

"The last thing this county, this state, and this republic needs are more whoremongers in office. Who knows what despicable, lewd activities Mrs. Bowman was doing there? With a husband and a baby at home. This is filthy behavior and it needs to end. Like the other fine woman who got up here said, a woman's body is sacred. It's one of the most sacred things in this world."

Shelly felt all the words spoken against her writhing around inside. She felt the turtleneck squeezing her throat. She felt her mother staring at her even though she wasn't in the room. She felt herself standing up. She felt her fingers clutch the hem of the turtleneck. She felt her arms lifting her shirt. She felt the cold on her bare stomach. She felt the shirt go over her bra. She felt the hot cameras on her. She felt the flush of anger rising in her.

"They're just tits, Merv," she heard herself say. "Get over it."

The crowd gasped. The shutters clicked. The cameras rolled.

Shelly bolted from the meeting, got into her pickup, and turned on the radio to drown out her thoughts. Her cell phone was buzzing and lighting up every few moments. She tossed it on the floor. What had she done? She couldn't explain it to herself. All she could picture was Merv saying the word "filthy" and it made her want to do it all over again. Shelly decided it was worth it even if she was never elected again and spent the rest of her life in Junction.

Baby Bobby was asleep when she got home. Darrell was watching the six o'clock news in the living room, a bemused smile on his face.

"Well, you showed them," he said with a laugh, pointing at the TV with the remote.

"It was impulsive," she said. "I couldn't help myself."

She glimpsed herself on the television, an endless loop of her flashing America. Her chest was blurred out like Captain Al's crotch, even though she had a bra on.

"Well, the news is getting a real kick out of it, that's for sure," Darrell said.

"And what do you think?"

"Me?" Darrell said. "I think you did what you needed to do." He opened his arms with a smile, beckoning her next to him on the couch. "Come watch."

On the night of the primary, Shelly stayed glued to the computer at home, watching the unofficial election results come in on the county clerk's website. She and Darrell were taking turns refreshing the site while the other took care of the baby. She had been invited to numerous GOP watch parties in Bear River, but Baby Bobby wasn't taking the bottle and Shelly wanted to stay with him.

The early results looked promising. Shelly had a lead on Merv.

"You shouldn't be surprised," Darrell said. "Look at all the publicity you've gotten. You're a star!"

Shelly demurred, rolling her eyes, but Darrell was right. After the commission meeting where she lifted her shirt, Shelly had done numerous media interviews where she explained what happened with her mom. She also shared her honest thoughts about how she was scared the radicals on both ends of the spectrum were the biggest threat to America. Her interviews were everywhere. Even the head of the Women's Republican Party contacted her to talk about a possible run for state senate in two years.

"You've become quite the sensation," the woman said.

By midnight, after hours of refreshing the election results page, it became clear that Shelly had solidly beat Merv Marl. Darrell broke out a bottle of sparkling wine and toasted her in the living room while Baby Bobby slept in his crib down the hall, sated after Shelly finally coaxed him into eating.

"Do you think Merv will call to concede?" Darrell asked.

Shelly looked down at her phone on the table.

"Not in a million years."

A few weeks later, Shelly and Darrell brought Baby Bobby to her parents' house for dinner. Her mother had finally come home and replanted herself beside her husband, back in a floral blouse and khaki capris, fussing with a pot roast in the oven. After dinner, Shelly helped her clean up in the kitchen while Darrell and the baby stayed in the living room with her father, who was sitting in his armchair, yelling for Margery to bring him more pie. The women ignored him.

"He's lucky I came back," her mother said with a jolly air. She seemed cheerful and rejuvenated, smiling and humming while she loaded up the dishwasher. Shelly wiped down the table and counters.

"Why did you come back?"

"Oh, I had my fun," her mom said.

"What about Jerry?"

"He went home to his kids in Battle Creek," she said. "It would have never worked out. He was a little too out-there for me. Besides, this is where I belong. This is my life."

After they got home that night, Shelly lay in bed with Baby Bobby. She was trying to get him to breastfeed when Captain Al popped up on the evening news being led away in handcuffs from the nudist resort, a blur hovering over his crotch. It turned out the Captain hadn't been paying taxes for years. All the publicity from Shelly had prompted investigators to crack the books.

Captain Al was undaunted.

"This is America!" he shouted into a news camera. "I'll be back! I'll be back, America!"

Shelly couldn't help but laugh. And maybe it was her laughter that finally did it. As her body was shaking, Baby Bobby squirmed up toward her neck and clamped down on her nipple and started suckling. Shelly winced with pain, but rubbed his soft head as she continued to laugh.

The Hermit

Karl Haglund woke before dawn to start plowing. As a three-day snowstorm continued to dump a foot and a half across Bear County in northern Michigan—from Bear River, to Brotherhood, to Sampo, to Junction—he climbed in his blue pickup with the blade affixed to the front and hit the city streets of Bear River well before municipal crews could get to them. Sometimes he saw the city plow drivers just starting their rounds after he'd been at it for hours. He'd give a slight wave. Karl never sought payment. City officials, many of whom were kids when the "Crazy Karl" rumors spread throughout the county, knew better than to try and stop him.

The storm started on a Thursday night in late January. Solid clouds of snow rolled in off Lake Michigan for hours. Karl didn't remember a storm like it since he was a kid. The snow meant Lars—the son of a cousin and his only living relative—Lars's wife, Ellen, and their two kids would be home all day because the schools and the entire town shut down. Karl could manage civilization when he was left alone in his little propane-heated room attached to the garage, but he couldn't handle hours of commotion. The kids had a Ping-Pong table in the garage and made a bunch of noise all day.

The light pop of the ball against the paddles, music, and young people's conversation was enough to make him cringe in his little room. He desired the solitude he'd sought out since he was a young man. So he left his room, fired up the truck, and took to the streets with the plow. He could plow for hours. The rhythmic scraping of the blade on pavement was soothing. He never turned on the radio, just looked at and listened to his memories. He'd grown up in town, then escaped for fifty years, and then was forced to return when his diabetes made it too dangerous to live on his own.

Karl had kept a place way out at the edge of the national forest with no running water, no electricity, no modern appliances, nothing but holy silence. He dug a well, made his own candles, and hunted for food. His beloved cabin was humble but comfortable. During storms like this, he'd rock in a chair by the fire for days chewing on venison jerky, reading old newspapers, and napping. As he got older, Lars checked up on him more and more. Last winter, Lars found Karl passed out on the cabin floor, his head precariously close to the lit fireplace. His beard was singed and it smelled like a raccoon's ass.

"I'm sorry, Uncle Karl, but you can't live here anymore," Lars had said. "You have to come live in town with Ellen and me so we can keep an eye on you."

Karl was fearful of people, but equally afraid of death, so he didn't fight it. He refused to sell his cabin or any of the land, however, foolishly hoping he would be able to move back when he was healthy enough. He knew better. Karl wasn't as crazy as the kids made him out to be. That had been an act to keep them off his property. Early on, he realized his choice of solitude attracted attention. Kids from all over the county would come to snoop on Crazy Karl's cabin, sometimes even stealing a saw or hatchet on a dare. So Karl started to put on a show for them. He made a suit of stitched-together rabbit furs he'd don whenever he sensed their approach. He'd go wild-eyed and start chanting nonsense, stalking around his cabin like a maniac, screaming at the sky.

It worked. He was left alone until his health failed. Karl knew he couldn't scare disease off with a rabbit costume and a bit of howling.

The first city plows made their way out of the DPW building on Water Street around four a.m. Karl had already been at it for an hour. The snow was relentless, making the sky glow a porcelain white, furiously covering his windshield. His wipers swished back and forth hypnotically. Karl needed a break. Most old fellas headed down to the Chit Chat Grille for coffee, but Karl hated listening to his contemporaries spew their embellishments and lies, so he went to the Wesco gas station for a Styrofoam cup of coffee instead. On his way out, a headline on the front page of the *Bear River Dauntless* in the news box caught his eye: "Maureen Powers, Former Pickle Company Mascot, Reported Missing from Nursing Home."

Karl knew where she was headed. The article, accompanied by a recent picture of Maureen at the retirement home, smiling, confirmed his fears:

> *Maureen Powers, 78, was reported missing from a Bear River retirement facility Thursday morning.*
>
> *She was last seen by employees in her room at 7 a.m. She is believed to have left the facility in a Cadillac DeVille.*
>
> *The public should be aware Powers is in the early stages of dementia and has a history of sleepwalking, according to police.*
>
> *Powers is described as 5 foot 5 inches tall, slim build, gray shoulder-length hair, last seen wearing a red robe and blue pajamas.*
>
> *As a girl, Powers was the mascot for her family's company, Powers Pickles. A picture of 6-year-old Powers was featured on pickle jars nationwide. At the*

company's peak of popularity, she traveled the country
as the company's spokesperson.
    Bear River police are asking the public to call
the department if they know anything about her
whereabouts.

Karl first met Maureen when they were teenagers, shortly before he built his cabin in the woods. His path to solitude was not straight or determined. Instead, it was an accumulation of small decisions. Desire mixed with circumstance. In short: it just happened. Karl grew up in town an only child, a desperately shy boy who blushed crimson when called on in class. His father was a house painter, stern and deeply pious. His mother was a tall, pretty woman, always busy in the kitchen, smiling and singing songs for little Karl. When he later smelled alcohol, he thought of his mother and realized that in his memories she was drunk. There were precious few memories because she disappeared when Karl was five, left his father for another man and moved away. It completely broke his father. Karl was left on his own. As he grew older, he escaped into the woods with his fishing rod and .22 rifle to wander for days, learning the old Indian trails and how to hunt game and pick berries. This was how Man was meant to live, he decided when he was thirteen or fourteen—alone in the woods away from the confusion of the town and other people.

One summer when he was a teenager, Karl and his father painted the Powerses' mansion up on the Hill. Karl was moving furniture in a room, carrying a rather heavy chair, when he saw a slim girl around his age coming down the stairs with a book tucked under her arm. When their eyes met, Karl dropped the chair with a bang, causing her to look at him. Redness filled his face. Her eyes and smile felt so familiar. He was charmed.

The girl kept walking outside where she took a seat under an apple tree and opened her book. She plucked an apple, wiped it on her sleeve, and started to read and munch. Karl couldn't help but catch a glimpse of her whenever he went out to the truck to fetch something for his father. One day, she called him over to where she was reading and asked who he was.

He introduced himself, stammering out his name while holding two paint buckets.

"Why are you so scared?"

He felt all the muscles in his neck seize up, like his head would come rolling off his shoulders.

"I'm not scared, ma'am. I think I know who you are. You're the pickle girl."

She laughed and he felt he would fall over. But her familiar eyes and smile were calming. His neck muscles relaxed.

"That was a long time ago. It feels like another lifetime," the girl said.

They talked until Karl's father called him inside, but the brief conversation left him tingling all that night into the next day. The girl wanted to talk to him again. They talked every day he worked at the house. She sought him out and he learned she liked it when he sought her out. Karl wasn't sure what was happening. He kept finding reasons to go back out to the work truck and find the girl, who one day called him over to a hidden spot next to the house's brick chimney. He had never been this close to a girl before. She pulled him to her body. Her face a few inches away looked different, more beautiful, her dreamy eyes almost closed, mouth slowly opening. They kissed right there between the chimney and a rose bush. When he pulled away, he felt his body rushing up into the clouds above.

They kept their love a secret. For the next few weeks, after the painting was done, they would meet at the park or down by the riverside. Karl felt more comfortable with her than he had ever felt with anyone else. Then one day she showed up to the beach where they had agreed to meet, Lake Michigan stretching out to the sky, and she was weeping. She was sick, she said, and had to leave town.

"For how long?"

"I don't know," she said. "A long time."

"What is wrong? You seem healthy to me."

Her haunted eyes held some secret she couldn't disclose. She told him she was sorry, but it had to be this way. Karl was broken and went into the woods and screamed at the treetops. He decided he would never be foolish enough to risk such humiliation. In two years, he saved enough from painting houses with his father to buy his own plot of land out at the edge of the national forest. He built his own cabin and learned how to be self-sufficient. Years passed. He meditated on his solitude. He never went in for his dad's religion, but decided the silence of the woods was holy. He was inside Time itself in a way a life filled with mindless distractions would never allow. To become Time meant becoming the wind in the leaves, the rush of the river, the beat of his heart, each intake of breath.

It was an amicable situation: Karl didn't bother the world and the world didn't bother Karl.

Ten years passed since he took to the woods. It was spring. Karl hated to do it, but he needed to go into town to find a book so he wouldn't poison himself again. He was lean and had a beard now. He didn't look people in the eyes. After stopping at the hardware store for some nails, he went to the Bear River Library to see if they had a particular book about mushroom identification. He'd misidentified some fungi the previous spring and gotten terribly sick and didn't want to make that mistake again.

The library was built by the Radke family in the early 1900s, a limestone building with ornately carved statues on the steps and a musty smell and creaky floors inside. Karl loved the library as a boy simply because he loved places where people kept to themselves. He spotted Maureen sitting with a book at a long wooden table in the back of the main reading room. She was thinner in adulthood, her blouse hanging off her bony shoulders like it was on a hanger. Karl was paralyzed and stopped near the welcome desk and froze when the woman asked if she could help him. He was about to turn and leave, but Maureen looked up just at that moment and saw him standing there wringing his hands. She smiled and he couldn't help but smile back before looking down at his boots.

She was like the rush of a river into his life. It couldn't be stopped or contained. They sat at the library table whispering and laughing into each other's ears. It made Karl's neck tingle to feel her breath so close to his face.

"I would like to see your cabin," she said.

The next thing he knew she was sitting in the front seat of his pickup heading back to the woods. The next thing he knew she was touching his face. The next thing he knew they were kissing and laughing and looking into each other's eyes again. These were true moments he never knew could exist again. Maybe that's what made them true. The not knowing. The surprise.

Karl had made a large bed from a couple of oak trees he felled on his property. It was a simple but sturdy frame, covered with bedding Karl trucked back to the cabin from the department store in town. It would become their sanctuary. Karl was shy at first. His head still raced when he touched her. Maureen seemed to let go of her thoughts. It took him several tries to turn off his mind, to fully commit body and soul to the process, to shed his personhood along with his clothes, to do what animals do with each other's bodies. He watched deer and other animals do it in the woods sometimes.

He didn't allow people this close to him, but Maureen was special. One touch led to a thousand. The spring air seeped in through the cracks of the cabin. They made love in the rough-hewn bed again and again. Everything was new.

Spring. "What is it you see in me?" he asked, looking up at the beam and rafters of the cabin. His beard was down to his chest, naked and hairy. He didn't know what to do with his arms after sex until she burrowed into his side, forcing his arm around her. He didn't know how to love a woman. His father never had a chance to love his own mother—or anyone at all. This lack of love in his childhood, Karl decided, was part of the reason why he distrusted people. But Maureen was different. She was in one of his button-up work shirts, her long brown hair loose in the collar.

"You want things to be simple," she said. "I want things to be simple. That's it."

Summer. The buzz of the insects. Hot wood floors. A slice of blue sky Karl could see through a window from the bed. Days of thunderstorms when they never left the bed. The rain dripping off the roof into the cisterns Karl used to water his vegetable garden when it was dry. Maureen slept in a long nightgown. She had brought all her things. She slept on her side with no sheet or blanket. He loved the way the flesh of her legs pressed together. Her skin was sweaty and sticky. Watching her body was like watching a sunset. He could watch it all day. She slept with her mouth open. He always woke early and fixed breakfast—fresh eggs from the chickens strutting around outside the cabin—and boiled water for tea.

They went for long hikes in the woods to pick wild blueberries. Karl knew all the best berry bushes and hoped to get there before the bears did. The summer was in full hot bloom, the bugs and fruit and foliage and birds and animals and earth changing and pulsing with each new day, each rotation around the sun, the ferns wavering in the breeze, and when the sun got to a certain spot in the sky, they noticed something change inside themselves, a slight internal shift of a day lived. They walked to the end of his property and then for miles into the federal forest along Bear River, where sometimes they stopped to fish for trout. They picked a big load of blueberries and sat on the ridge overlooking the river, eating the berries in the waning sunlight. They shared their inner lives with one another, something that was new to Karl. He told her how terrible he felt around other people, how he only felt capable of breathing in quiet, uncomplicated places where nature went about its business without the selfish interests and ambitions of most humans.

When it was her turn, Maureen talked about her troubles sleepwalking and confessed that was why she had rejected him when they were teenagers. It was why she never married. Her parents felt she was too fragile for any kind of relationship and sent her away.

"It started when I was four. My grandparents owned a cherry farm. This was shortly before they switched over to cucumbers and started the pickle company. I would wander off in the middle of the night and pick the cherries from the trees and eat them while I was sleepwalking. I'd wake up to my grandma shaking me. My white nightgown would be covered in red cherry juice. No one knew how to help me. When I got older, around the time I met you, I became violent when I was sleepwalking. I once attacked a servant girl who had been unkind to me. When they finally shook me awake, I was standing over her with my hands around her throat. I will never forget the terrified look on that poor girl's face. My parents were so worried they took me to Switzerland to meet with a very famous doctor. He published a groundbreaking paper about somnambulism that earned him great accolades. Unfortunately, it did little to help me."

The sleepwalking, Maureen explained, had been in remission for the past several years.

"I'm not sure why. The doctors aren't either. They know nothing. But it could start happening again at any time."

Maureen always became melancholy when the sun started dipping below the trees, when the glow of the day started to fade.

"This is the time of day that makes me most sad—but happy at the same time. It's the most bittersweet time of day."

One evening, they sat in the ferns overlooking the rushing Bear River while the sun was setting and Maureen, with a handful of wild blueberries, said, "This is where I want to die."

She read to him from a book called *Tom Jones* about a young man born of low social class striving to become better. Karl had never heard of the book—or any other books that didn't have to do with learning practical things like building a wheelbarrow or avoiding poisonous berries. They'd lie back in the big bed or sit by the fireplace at night and she'd read to him about this person Tom Jones. Fiction didn't make sense to Karl. Why would anyone want to know about someone who wasn't real?

"Sometimes to tell the truth you have to make stuff up," Maureen said.

Karl was surprised when the men and women in the old-timey tights and frock coats and bodices started screwing. Whenever they got to those parts, Maureen would look up from the book and catch Karl's eyes and she would set the book down and they'd kiss in the middle of the cabin and stagger over to the bed and undress. Karl would fall into her warm mouth and body. It was all connected somehow by a moist wetness down there and in her mouth and somehow the black universe. If he was making love to her and kissing her at the same time, he felt entirely wrapped up inside of her and complete.

Fall. One night, Karl woke in the cold to find the bed empty. He bolted up and looked around. Maureen was not in the cabin. He put on his boots and started looking around outside. A cold wind whistled through the woods. He searched the cabin and nearby. He finally found her along the creek curled up in a little ball, her legs pressed together in her nightgown, covered in dead leaves. She already seemed half awake, but he shook her body anyway. She looked at him like she didn't know him at first, like he was a stranger. Then a look of recognition changed her face and she looked terrified.

"I must have been sleepwalking," she said. "I'm sorry."

"I'll take care of you," he said, picking her up like a groom does a bride.

He found her in that same spot sleepwalking two more times that fall.

Thanksgiving. Maureen spent the holiday with family in town and showed up the day after with a camera, a modernistic metal contraption. It reminded Karl that despite the way she'd been living rustically with him, she still had millions of dollars stashed away somewhere.

"What's it for?" Karl asked.

"To capture some of the beauty that we see every day. Don't you think we should be preserving some of these memories of our lives?"

Karl nodded but he was burning with discomfort. Maureen was changing. She had been going into town more and more. She asked him to use the contraption to take her picture inside the cabin. Her smile felt big and disingenuous, like the smile he remembered from the cover of the Powers Pickles labels when she was a girl.

She begged him to let her take his picture. It only happened once. She caught him chopping wood beside the cabin on a gloomy morning just before winter. She showed him the picture: he was standing next to the wood pile in a plaid shirt, naked trees behind him. His mouth was closed tight, his eyes squinted, the axe in his hands. He did not recognize himself. It made him feel disconnected from reality.

Maureen lost interest in the camera after another week. Karl was pleased.

Christmas. Trapped on a train, hurtling southward, more and more people boarding at each station, Karl felt like he was underwater and unable to come up for air. Maureen talked him into taking a trip to Chicago to visit some of her cousins and go shopping downtown. She'd been visiting Chicago since she was the pickle mascot.

"The city is wonderful around the holidays. You need to experience more of the world, Karl," she said. "You don't know you'll hate it until you try."

Karl was trying to be a good sport, but he was skeptical. He had never been to a city beyond his hometown of Bear River, which he thought was too big. Maureen sat next to him writing in a journal, glancing away from it every so often to give him a reassuring smile. He'd agreed to come on the trip because he knew he was losing her. He even agreed to wear a ridiculous stiff new suit that felt like a straitjacket. He smiled back, masking his inner turmoil, sharp and jagged feelings of fear and dread, a new jolt of unpleasantness with every new face he noticed on the train, men and women and children clamoring and crying and making unnecessary noise. Karl imagined a big city like Chicago must be the noisiest place on earth and therefore the opposite of simple and therefore the opposite of pleasant. It astounded him that so many people were afraid of solitude, his natural state of mind, the silence that made life bearable. He thought if he stayed steeped in that silence long enough, some sort of answer would present itself, though he wasn't sure what questions he wanted answered. The mystery of the universe or the mystery of himself? Or were they the same?

He was calmed by the familiar sight of Maureen's face, but felt she was too excited for the trip. He now knew she could never truly disconnect from the world of trains, cars, cities, books, cameras, and noise. He sat with his hands in his lap and closed his eyes and pretended he was in the woods by the river as the train shunted along beneath him until it finally, thankfully, stopped. Karl managed to get off the train and onto the platform. In a dreamlike frenzy, he carried their suitcases into the station.

"Are you OK?" Maureen asked. "Isn't this exciting? Wait until you see the hotel."

He nodded. She was paying for everything. The train. The hotel. The food. She walked fast, excited. He was seeing a new side of her. They walked out into the main room of Union Station and

Karl felt the entire world rushing in through his eyes and mouth and it was too much. It was the biggest room he'd ever been in. He couldn't breathe. He couldn't walk. His mouth was dry. The ceiling was so high it made him dizzy to look up, though even in his narrow vision he saw it was beautiful. He had never been in such a large crowd of people before. They bumped him and jostled each other and checked their watches and picked their noses and shouted and took pictures and laughed. He stopped in the middle of the crowd with both suitcases in his sweaty hands. He was unable to walk another step.

"Are you OK?"

Karl said nothing. His body collapsed in the crowd of people. They kept going, stepping over him while he gasped for breath. Maureen rushed down to help him, but he couldn't see and everything was spinning. They got out of the station and onto the street into a cab, but he collapsed in the city three more times that day—on the sidewalk, in the hotel lobby, and in a restaurant bathroom—and they cut the trip short and left the next morning.

Winter. By January there was a foot of snow outside. Maureen paced the cabin like a caged panther. Karl sat contentedly by the fire looking at a knitting book—he wanted to learn to make his own clothes. Maureen got up and looked through the half-dozen books on the shelf, then sat down. She got up again and went into the kitchen and started clanging around the teapot.

"Is this the only kind of tea we've got?" she said.

"I think so." Karl set the book down on his knee.

Maureen came and sat in a chair and looked out the window at the snow, away from Karl.

"I don't know if I can handle this."

They had a fierce, world-ending argument. Maureen stood in the center of the cabin shouting at him. Karl didn't understand what to do. He started crying and put his hands on his ears and tried to bury his head in the bed.

"I can't reach you. I can't save you. It's not my job to save you," Maureen said.

She told him he was hiding out in the woods because he wasn't brave enough to face the world. When he finally broke through his fear, he became angry with her for the first time. He shouted back at her, saying she was vain and egotistical and just like everyone in the world he was trying to avoid. The shouting made him afraid.

After the fight, Karl withdrew deeper into himself. He wouldn't look at Maureen or speak to her for days. When she announced that she was leaving, he didn't say anything, just nodded and walked out the door into the snow and kept walking with no coat or proper boots all the way down to the frozen river. He shivered under a pine tree for an hour, cursing the white sky, sobbing into his shirtsleeve. He nearly got hypothermia. When he got back to the cabin shivering, Maureen was gone. She never came back.

Karl was heartbroken. The affair was an entire universe for him, a reservoir from which to draw for emotional nourishment and sustenance his entire life. For the better part of a half century, he thought of her when he walked the woods, when he sat alone by the fireplace. She was always with him. He vowed to never let anyone else in.

Outside the gas station, Karl stared at the newspaper headline announcing that Maureen was missing, then climbed into his pickup. It was a wonder that he was the same man as he had been when he loved Maureen. He did the math. Forty years packed into this body and mind. He'd been carting the same body around for that long. He was starting to feel dizzy and would need his insulin soon, but he didn't want to go through the hassle of getting it out of his glovebox and finding someplace to sit down with the syringe and poke himself. He wanted to go home. His real home. He was besieged by memories as he started the truck, snow rapidly plinking the windshield. There were still streets to plow, but Karl headed north out of town toward his cabin. He'd not been there since fall.

Karl knew Maureen would try and return to the cabin the instant he read about her being missing. The snow was so fierce that even in the pickup truck, with proper tires, Karl had to take it slow out of town. He headed up LaFleur Highway past all the old farms. The drifting, blowing snow was even worse in the open fields. There were no other vehicles. The cabin was set off two miles from the nearest road, and since he'd been living in town no one plowed the drive. The blade was on the truck, but it would take too long to plow. He knew where the turnoff was but didn't stop. Through the snow whipping in his headlights, he saw the rear end of a vehicle up ahead. The car's front end had rammed into a snowbank and was slanted in the road. The roof and hood of the car were covered with snow. At first, Karl couldn't determine the make, but when he did, he wasn't surprised it was a Cadillac.

Karl brought his pickup to a halt. The sky was brightening now, though the morning sun was hidden behind layers of snow and clouds. He still couldn't see if there was anyone in the car. Karl yanked on his gloves and slowly walked over to the car and noticed that the driver's side door was open just enough for a woman to escape. The Caddy was empty. The blowing snow had mostly covered any footprints, but Karl had always been a keen tracker. There had been five inches of snow on the ground even before the storm that day, which added four or five more inches. The footprints led across the field toward the cabin, messy impressions sunk deep in the fresh snow, but filling up fast as more snow fell. The trail was jagged like a person walking with great difficulty. In the summer, the field was tall grass and wildflowers. He pictured her sitting next to the fire in the rocking chair. In his imagination, she didn't appear how she looked in the newspaper picture, but as she did when he last saw her in the full bloom of womanhood.

He grabbed snowshoes and a flashlight from the bed of his pickup. The sky was lighter now, but it was still difficult to see. He went for his insulin packet, which was supposed to be in the glovebox, but wasn't. Karl cussed and banged the dashboard, but he was more afraid than angry. He was already feeling dizzy. His insulin was on the dresser in his little room at Lars's house, he realized. But he felt like he could make it even if he was due for his shot an hour ago. Karl strapped on the snowshoes and started following the tracks in the snow across the field. The cabin was about a mile away. It was slow going. Karl had to stop and catch his breath a few times. Then he saw something in the distance through the frenzy of falling snow that made his stomach drop—a dash of red in the whiteness. It took his breath away again. His heart was pounding as he plodded through the snow closer to the redness. It was her robe. She had fallen over on her side, her leg stuck in the snow. He could see her face, eyes still open but with no life. Her face was changed by age, smaller and filled with wrinkles, her hair short and a darker shade of white compared to the snow. Karl was afraid to touch her at first. He began to softly weep.

Maureen was frozen stiff in the fetal position. Even her red robe was solid. He finally picked her up but kept his eyes on the sky instead of looking at her. Karl felt dizzy but managed to carry her body toward the cabin one step at a time until he reached the woods and then the clearing. He was sweating and breathing hard, great billows of steam coming from his mouth. The sight of the cabin brought him comfort despite the circumstances.

He wasn't sure what to do with Maureen. If he brought her inside and started a fire, she would thaw. But if he stood outside holding her like this while thinking about it, he could faint and freeze to death. Maybe it would be for the best, though. He thought quickly of his life in town, living at his nephew's, plowing the streets, listening to the children talk and play Ping-Pong. He didn't have his beloved solitude anymore. He didn't have Maureen or love anymore. Maybe it made sense for them both to die out here together. And yet, standing there with her frozen body in his arms, there was still a desire to go on. And that was the greatest mystery of all, one Karl had never been able to reckon in the decades he spent alone thinking about such things. Why, despite everything, do we go on?

Karl went into the shed and found the sled he used for gathering wood out in the forest during the winters and tied Maureen's body to it. First, he needed to warm up and rest until the dizzy spell went away, then he'd pull Maureen back across the field to the truck.

He left Maureen on the sled outside and went into the cabin, where he started a fire and sat in the rocking chair. He rocked and rocked while he warmed up, but he was still feeling weak. There was a blackness that seemed to be beckoning him. It made sense to close his eyes for a few minutes. He wouldn't sleep; he just needed to rest.

When he came to, it was full daylight and he realized he'd been unconscious. He was starving and dizzy. The fire had burned to embers. He went out to check on Maureen, who was still strapped in the sled by his wood-chopping block, her body covered in an inch of fresh snow. It was still coming down as hard as ever. Karl stood on the porch not knowing what to do. He thought about going out to Maureen and dusting the snow off her but didn't feel like he had the energy to put his boots on. He went back inside and shut the door. There was no way he could cross the field again, not in his condition. Karl knew he needed food and insulin. He opened a can of chicken noodle soup from the pantry and slurped it down cold. It only nipped at his hunger, so he had another. The insulin problem wasn't solved so easily, though.

He went back to the rocking chair and sat down, still dizzy. An idea presented itself. There was only one thing he could do if he wanted to make it out of the storm alive and return Maureen's body to her family for a proper burial. He'd thought about it before, during his long hours, days, and years at the cabin, increasingly so when he got older and weaker. Even if it killed him to have every firefighter and cop in Bear County out on his place, he'd have to do it.

Karl put on all his outdoor gear, including the snowshoes. He pulled Maureen on the sled into the small shed with openings on both sides, a couple feet of hard brown earth. He searched the shelves of the shed and grabbed a red metal gasoline can and left Maureen for the cabin.

It was still warm inside. The cabin was the most familiar place to him. Every other place in the world felt foreign and unpleasant. But Karl couldn't think of any other way out. He tipped the gas can and started dousing the wood. The floorboards. His bed. His table. His entire world. Ned and Ethel Stonecipher, who lived in a farmhouse a few miles down the road, would be sure to see the flames, smell the smoke, and call the authorities. Karl was feeling weak and shaky by the time he pulled the matches from his coat pocket and lit a rolled-up newspaper. He started weeping again as he stood on the gas-drenched porch and dropped the flaming newspaper.

The cabin went up quickly. Sobbing, Karl sat down next to Maureen's body in the shed. He covered himself up with a thick blanket he'd taken from the cabin and watched it burn through the opening of the shed. He blacked out again, but when he woke he heard sirens and saw flashing lights. Across the big white field, he saw a uniformed man on a snowmobile moving toward the cabin, then everything went black again. Karl somehow slept with knowledge that he'd been saved.

The Standoff

Bear County Sheriff Duane Bobbins knew he was going to die. Not anytime soon, though at sixty he was a little farther along than others. His greatest fear was that he would die unhappy. Married for thirty-five years, he didn't think he'd die alone.

Bobbins never had these types of thoughts until Jill Bonecutter came along. She would save him. He was sure of it. One summer evening he surprised himself and his wife when he said, "I'm leaving you, Val. If I don't, I'll die."

"Go ahead," was Val's first reply.

Bobbins couldn't be sure if she meant to go ahead and leave or go ahead and die. She was hidden in her full-brimmed straw hat, stooped over in one of their property's many flowerbeds. She looked up for a moment, facing him with her broad nose and twinkling green eyes that remained sharp even as the rest of her had aged and taken on softer angles. The girl he'd fallen in love with was still in there, but Bobbins didn't know where. She went back to her roses. She had caressed them more than Bobbins for the past ten years, he thought, twice winning ribbons at the Bear County Fair.

"I'm serious," he said.

"If that's what you think is best, Duane," she said finally, rising and looking him in the eyes, the trowel held like a weapon at her side. "I know about you and the girl at Bucky's Laundromat. Everyone in town does. But you'll be back. She'll break your heart and you won't win reelection next year, either. You'll be back, but I might not be here."

Bobbins felt shame creep into every part of his body. Val returned to her flowers.

He spent a sleepless night on a cot in a sergeant's pole barn to avoid the scandal of renting a local motel room. The next morning at six the light was already on in Jill Bonecutter's apartment above the row of three storefronts just outside of town on US 31 as he approached in his black Crown Victoria, marked with the official gold Bear County Sheriff's Department seal on the side. Downstairs in the laundromat, the industrial-sized washing and drying machines were silent in the dark. There were rows of chairs and the occasional table with old, crumpled magazines on them. Bobbins parked his patrol car at the gas station across the highway and hustled across the street to Bucky's. There was a flimsy wood door behind the building that led to the apartments above. Sheriff Bobbins had a key. The closer he got to the door at the top of the staircase, the more it smelled like marijuana smoke. He could also hear a guitar softly being strummed. She was already awake.

Jill Bonecutter had been bringing him back to life for the last six months, ever since hoodlums broke into the laundromat and cracked open the change machines and made off with about a hundred bucks. Bobbins got involved with the investigation partly because he was short-staffed. When he found out where it was, he was more eager to help than usual. He'd seen the young, attractive girl at the laundromat and wanted to meet her. It was his first dance with adultery and it was exhilarating.

"Don't start getting all sappy on me," Jill had said to him. "This is just about sex and for any future speeding tickets I need to get out of."

No woman had ever spoken to him like this. It made him melt immediately. Now she was waiting for him in her messy bed, the room lit only with a flickering television, the electric guitar on her knee. There were music and fashion magazines strewn all over the bed and the floor. Jill would sometimes play while he was there, a jangled noise that didn't sound much like music to Bobbins.

Jill was thirty or so with a suspicious past she mostly refused to speak about. She was sullen, mean, nasty, and beautiful, standing nearly as tall as Bobbins, thin as a stem, the pronounced cheekbones of a magazine model. She had long, thin fingers she was always using to swipe her sandy blond hair out of her eyes. There was a silver stud in her nose and tattoos all over her body. There were other piercing holes on her face that had started to close. He knew she'd grown up in Bear River and disappeared for fourteen years, returning without any fanfare about eight months earlier and taking a job as manager of Bucky's Laundromat, owned by Buck Swineheart, a contemporary of Bobbins in town. Jill rented the upstairs apartment when she took the job and never seemed to leave. For the past year, Bobbins hadn't seen her anywhere else besides the apartment or behind the counter downstairs amid the furiously spinning washers and bounding dryers.

Bobbins found her how he did most mornings, sitting up in the bed, smoking marijuana in a small, glass-blown bowl and watching an old black-and-white movie on television while playing the guitar. She leaned the guitar against the wall when he walked in, then took a toke from the bowl and blew out a large cloud of smoke and said, "Morning, Chief."

Bobbins began undoing his pants.

"I'm the sheriff, not the chief."

"Whatever," she said.

Even when they were finished and naked in each other's arms, Bobbins didn't have the courage to tell Jill he'd left his wife. She frightened him more than the countless criminals he'd arrested in thirty-plus years of law enforcement.

Tyrell Winter Bear waited until the warm winds of summer blew in across Lake Michigan to annex Al Vollmer's beet field for the tribe. The land had been disputed in Bear County ever since 1847, when the first Vollmers came and squatted on the eighty acres that had been set aside as an Indian reservation. The Vollmers didn't have much love for the native inhabitants—or anyone else really—but they found allies in the United States government of the nineteenth century, which tended to side with despicable characters.

The Bear River Band of Ottawa Indians only managed to hang on to a hundred acres of the two thousand that were promised to them. There was an impoverished Indian village, where in the 1960s, in the middle of the rolling hills of northern Michigan along the great lake, they built the ghastly low-income projects where Winter Bear grew up, a sprawling collection of cheaply built townhouses visible from the back end of Vollmer's field. Officially called Bear River Tribal Housing, the buildings fell into disrepair so quickly everyone had called them "the Ruins" for years.

Even in the early 1990s, when the tribe was federally recognized and wealthy backers from Chicago and Detroit helped purchase more land around the original hundred acres to enable the construction of a luxury casino, stubborn Al Vollmer refused to sell despite the millions offered. Then in 1995, a team of anthropologists from the University of Michigan determined that his acreage wasn't just part of the land set aside for the Indians in the Treaty of 1855 but also the site of the longtime semipermanent village predating the arrival of Father Gabriel Pierre LaFleur and the white men. In other words, the beet field was the tribe's true home. Tribal leadership sent Vollmer a letter stating as much but received no response. The ogema didn't pursue it any further.

These last two events occurred when Winter Bear was growing up in the Ruins. Young Winter Bear and his friends—especially Derek Muskrat and Billy Waters—declared war on the Vollmers when they were fourteen years old. Back then, all they had were toilet paper, water balloons, and firecrackers. Vollmer had made it known he had a shotgun waiting by the sliding glass door near his patio for anyone—especially Indian kids—trying to come on his land. He wasn't kidding. Whenever Winter Bear and his buddies decided to play a prank on the old man, he'd totter out with his gun and shoot a couple shells off into the air. Police were frequent visitors.

It was all harmless until three years ago, when ten-year-old Little Sammy Barefeet was found dead on the side of Vollmer Road, his body crumpled up in a snowy winter ditch, his feet literally bare. The Nikes he'd been wearing as he walked back to the Ruins from basketball practice had been knocked off, as had his Detroit Pistons knit cap. Blood gelled from his brow into the snow. A group of partiers from the casino found the body late at night, about a hundred yards down the road from the Vollmer place, the only nontribal structure in a two-mile radius. It was commonly known that Little Sammy Barefeet was found on a stretch of the road carelessly traveled almost daily by Al Vollmer in his white Lincoln when he made trips into the town of Bear River to purchase his lottery tickets—he was a gambling man, but refused to go inside the casino.

Everybody at the Ruins blamed Vollmer, who adamantly denied it. While they couldn't prove it, local law enforcement agencies also suspected Alvin Vollmer. They'd pulled him over numerous times for drifting off the side of the road. And since this was a tribe kid, and everyone knew Vollmer had no love for them, it was conjectured it wasn't an accidental slide.

Everyone in Bear County suspected Vollmer. Anyone other than the spiteful beet farm owner would have felt remorse and stepped forward. Only Al Vollmer, it was decided, was cruel and bitter enough not to turn himself in.

Vollmer blamed the carload of casino partiers, two guys and two girls from the Detroit suburbs, even though an autopsy confirmed Little Sammy Barefeet had been dead five hours when the group found him.

Before moving on Vollmer's beet field, Winter Bear and his buddies acquired a half-dozen automatic firearms through a criminal connection of Muskrat's down in Muskegon. They recruited a dozen or so male members of the tribe. Some of them legitimately cared about forcefully reclaiming the site of their historical home and avenging Sammy Barefeet. Many of them had been members of the now-defunct tribal gang, the Kick-Ass Boyz, including Winter Bear. Others, like forty-eight-year-old Billy James, a drunk who was in and out of the Bear County jail, would participate in anything as long as they could stay drunk and out of county lockup. Others were just the kids who hung around the Ruins selling and buying drugs.

Winter Bear didn't bother going to tribal leadership. He thought many of the elders—especially quarter-breed Ogema Bob Kowalski—had been corrupted by casino money. Instead, the group struck without warning one night, sneaking barricade wire, lights, tents, weapons, and Winter Bear's pack of wolf dogs from the Ruins, about a half mile through the woods. They rolled out generators, televisions, video game consoles, coolers of food, barbecue grills, and numerous cases of beer. They set up the barricade so they could use the mile of woods between the beet field and the casino as shelter. The concertina wire was stretched out across the entirety of the field about two hundred yards from Lorraine Vollmer's tomato patch next to the patio. They even put the wire between them and the casino, creating about a square mile the splinter group of the tribe was claiming as their own. They intended to reclaim the entirety of the historical village, which included Vollmer's house and part of Vollmer Road. Winter Bear and his men stayed hidden, and once they had the barricade unrolled, sought shelter in the woods, where they popped tents and cracked beers and waited for morning. It seemed they would stay all summer.

Throughout the night, Al Vollmer watched from his back window clutching the old shotgun. He could occasionally make out the lean figure of Tyrell Winter Bear, his huge Afro swaying with the pines as a heavy wind blew in off the nearby lake. Winter Bear was half-Indian and half-Black. America hated him twice over, he liked to tell people.

The next morning, Al Vollmer and Sheriff Duane Bobbins could only see the concertina wire barricade, two posts topped with searchlights, and bonfire smoke rising from the patch of woods. Three large wolf dogs prowled the open beet field between the tree line and the fence. The men stood at the edge of Vollmer's patio. Through the open window Bobbins could smell the coffee Lorraine was brewing in the kitchen.

"These cocksuckers can't get away with this, Dew-ayne!" Al said.

Bobbins knew Winter Bear and his wolf dogs could be sons of bitches. But the sheriff didn't have much love for Vollmer, either. They graduated a grade apart from Bear County High School. The entire Vollmer family was known for their general lack of height (the men barely broke five feet) and nasty dispositions. Al, the oldest son, had inherited the original family farm. Other Vollmers were scattered throughout Bear County. About their only redeeming quality were their devilishly cute faces. In high school, Al Vollmer was known as a heartthrob. If you could make a Vollmer smile, it would melt your heart.

"What happened to hard work? When we was coming up, you worked hard and you were rewarded. You didn't just take what you wanted. You didn't wait for handouts."

Both men were neither fat nor skinny. The crinkles and creases of age were wiping away the personalities of the faces they once were, old men becoming indistinguishable like babies in the maternity ward. The only thing strikingly different about the two was the way they were dressed. Bobbins wore his brown sheriff's uniform. Vollmer was dressed in blue jeans and a flannel shirt despite the heat.

"Well, what are you gonna do, Duane? Aren't you gonna call in the goddamn SWAT team, or whatever it is you've got, and get these goddamn kids off my property! What's your plan?"

Bobbins stared thoughtfully at the barbed wire two hundred yards off.

"We don't do anything right now," he said.

"What!"

"I'll have a chat with Ogema Bob and some other tribal leaders. He'll talk some sense into Tyrell. We'll do this peacefully," Bobbins said.

"The time for talking is over! Don't you see what's right in front of you!"

Bobbins looked down at Al, who only came up to his shoulder. He tried to give him a reasoning glance.

"I can't just start shooting at kids, Al. You know that."

"Why not?" Al said nastily.

Just then, the wild crackle of tires tearing up the gravel drive at the side of the house interrupted them. It was a blue Michigan State Police patrol car that parked directly behind Bobbins's car. The sheriff sighed inwardly. The state police post had been tipped off about the situation, too, and sent out none other than trooper Artie Dunn.

Dunn struggled to get his six-foot-six frame out of the car, then popped up to his full stature and charged at the men. Dunn was known around town as a stickler for every minor rule and regulation in the book. He wouldn't have a speck of dirt or lint on his blue uniform while he wrote you the stiffest possible ticket for not wearing a seatbelt. Everyone in law enforcement circles knew he'd been reprimanded twice for using excessive force.

Bobbins was privy to such knowledge and wasn't too fond of the state police trooper. Still, they exchanged a fraternal police nod as Dunn joined the men.

"I'm going to call in SWAT from Lansing, Sheriff," was the first thing he said.

"Yes! Now we're talking," Al said.

"No," Bobbins said.

"Do we even know what they have back there? They could have semiautomatics!"

"They could also just have pellet guns," Bobbins said.

Bobbins was all for cool heads. Dunn had a big dumb one. Bobbins didn't know how Post Commander Lt. Walter "Lew" Lewandowski put up with him. Lew was a good enough guy. His only weakness was putting Dunn in charge when he was down in Lansing like he was now.

"So, what are we gonna do?" Dunn said. "Those kids aren't gonna do anything. I say we just walk across the field, guns drawn, and arrest them."

"Is that what Lew would want us to do?" Bobbins said.

Dunn looked at the sheriff with spite. He didn't enjoy anyone having authority over him and it showed, especially when Bobbins wasn't technically his boss.

"Well, it's your show," Dunn said. "For now."

He looked spitefully at the sheriff, then turned and stomped back to his patrol car without saying anything and aggressively peeled out of the driveway, spraying pieces of gravel into the summer grass.

"Well? What we gonna do here, Duane?"

The sheriff didn't know. It could be a quick prank and the tribe kids could disappear overnight. Or Dunn could be right. They could have semiautomatics and be ready for a shootout. He needed to get into contact with the tribe. He also knew Dunn had a point. This incident would draw attention first from Lansing and then from Washington. Bobbins wouldn't be the highest-ranking law enforcement officer in Bear County for long.

He comforted Vollmer for a few minutes before excusing himself to his patrol car, where he finally got Ogema Bob on the phone. The ogema was completely bald and had promptly gained a hundred pounds after being named head of the tribe because he ate at the casino buffet free of charge three times a day. He claimed a quarter Ottawa blood, the rest a mixture of Polish, German, and Scots-Irish. Bobbins knew him as a mostly reasonable man who, though head of the tribe, usually put casino interests first. With annual profits of $300 million, it was hard not to. Bob Kowalski had been named ogema in part because of his business acumen and prowess for increasing profits at the car dealership he used to manage.

Ogema Bob agreed with the sheriff. Wait it out. Let Winter Bear make his point. The boys will get tired and want to go back to their wives and girlfriends eventually. The only thing they could be charged with at this point was trespassing. In the meantime, the ogema said he'd try to get some other tribal leaders inside to talk some sense to the boys—and maybe see what all they had back there. He agreed: they could be armed only with slingshots and BB guns.

It upset Al Vollmer, but Bobbins decided to put only one man on it overnight, telling Deputy Raul Ramirez, who had the night-time shift, to stick around the house and answer any nearby calls. The sheriff had no reason to believe the situation would get violent or explode into the fiasco it did.

Bobbins had other things on his mind. He had to tell Jill. Over the years, he had told innumerable family members their loved ones had died in farm equipment accidents and drunken driving crashes. Now, he was more terrified to tell the young woman he had left his wife for her. He was honestly afraid she would laugh.

Before heading to Bucky's, Bobbins drove by his own place. He knew his marked vehicle was conspicuous but didn't care if Val knew he was checking up on her. He drove the car faster than planned, abruptly stopping when he saw a For Sale by Owner sign stuck in the front lawn. The garage door was closed; the house was still. She was either not home or inside washing her hair. Bobbins interpreted the real estate sign as a harmless threat and drove on.

Maybe if they had kids they wouldn't have drifted apart, he thought while driving to Bucky's. His wife had become harder, meaner with age. Maybe all women did. But that didn't make any sense because Jill was already like that. Maybe that's what he liked about her. Maybe it felt good for him to be able to let go and let someone else take charge and make the decisions. Maybe Jill was nothing but a younger version of his dear wife.

He pulled into Bucky's not knowing what to expect. He was hoping she would let him stay the night, at least. Sleeping in his sergeant's pole barn wasn't exactly comfortable. A motel sounded dismal and lonely and was bound to start rumors. "I heard the sheriff stayed at the Lakepoint Motel. What's that all about?" Bobbins was more worried about being lonely. While women got tougher with age, Bobbins was becoming weaker and needed more attention. Bobbins wanted to strip off his stiff uniform and be held naked like a baby.

From the parking lot, he watched Jill close the laundromat for the evening. She went about her work methodically and laboriously, counting out the register till like she was forcing herself to do it. Bobbins eventually got out of the car and went inside. The business was still open for another ten minutes, but it was empty. When Jill looked up and saw him, she didn't smile.

"We've got to talk," he said. "You almost finished?"

"Go upstairs and wait," she said. "And no snooping around. None of your cop detective bullshit."

Bobbins had never been alone in Jill's apartment. He'd also never been there in the full blaze of day. The summer sun was still high in the sky at six p.m., poking through the slated miniblinds of the room's windows. Bobbins did as he was told. He didn't snoop. He sat at the foot of the messy bed next to her guitar leaning against the wall and placed his hat in his lap like he was waiting to meet with the governor.

Jill finally came up, lighting a Newport as she walked into the room.

"You hungry?" she said. "I was going to make some noodles."

Bobbins was suspicious of any type of cooking that could be done by a person like Jill in a place like the grungy apartment with the tiny, stained stove. Valerie would be cooking a pot roast with fresh vegetables from the garden. Bobbins was hungry.

"How about we order a pizza?"

"You plan on staying that long?" she said, moving across the room and sitting down on the loveseat and flicking her ashes into an ashtray.

"Well that's what I wanted to talk about."

"Don't tell me you did something stupid like left your wife."

Bobbins clutched the hat in his lap with embarrassment. He nodded.

"I'm sorry to say, but that's exactly what I did."

Jill took a deep breath of smoke and blew it out all over the small room. Bobbins watched dust motes swirl within the gray and blue waves as the smoke drifted over to him.

"Well, that was pretty fucking stupid," she said. "You left your wife of how many years who probably had her shit together for me? Look at where I live, Chief. I'm a fucking mess."

"But I thought we felt something for one another," Bobbins said. "I certainly feel something for you. I feel alive."

"That's just the sex," Jill said. "Sex will make any person feel alive."

He looked down at the top of his hat, feeling ashamed and uncomfortable. It wasn't going as planned, but he wasn't surprised.

"So now you're going to swoop in and take me away from all of this?" she said. "Was that your plan? That this town would accept *me* and *you*? Like I could walk into the fucking policeman's ball on your arm and everyone would just think that was cool?"

"I don't know what I thought."

"Well I hope it's not too late for you to go back home."

"It might be," Bobbins said. "I'm not sure. I haven't spoken to Valerie since I left."

"Wait. You came here after you left her? And didn't tell me?"

"I did."

Jill stamped out her cigarette in the ashtray and reached for her marijuana bowl on the nightstand table between the loveseat and the bed. The table was littered with beer bottles, cigarette butts floating in an inch of swill.

"You're one dumb cop," she said lighting the bowl and inhaling the marijuana smoke. "You've never even asked me what I thought about this? Or what my plans are? I probably won't even stay in this shithole town. I hate this fucking place."

"Then why are you here?"

Jill set the bowl down and abruptly got up. She went over to the stove and started noisily clanking pans together, trying to pull them apart from one another. Bobbins could see she was rattled. He wondered why he never thought to ask her the question before.

"I don't want to talk about it," she said.

Bobbins stood at the threshold of the tiny kitchen and the bedroom, which comprised pretty much the whole place.

"I know it's not your fault I left my wife, but maybe if we had communicated before, none of this would have happened," he said. "Maybe if we are just straight with each other for once, no one will get hurt."

Her back was to him as she put water on to boil, but Bobbins knew she was starting to cry. Her show of emotion startled him. He took a step toward her but stopped.

"You're right," she said. "I should tell you about Caden."

Here it comes, Bobbins thought. She's got a husband or a boyfriend of a more suitable age.

"Who is Caden?" he asked.

"He's my son," she said. She kept talking, all in a rush. "He's fourteen. I've never met him. He was taken from me. I was young and stupid, so I ran. But now I've come back to town for him. And once I find him and convince these courts he's mine, we're leaving for good."

Bobbins went and sat on the loveseat, trying to ignore the smell of tobacco and marijuana lifting from the table. To his surprise, Jill came and sat next to him, allowing their thighs to touch.

"Well, maybe I can help," Bobbins said. "You said he grew up in Bear River. What's his last name? Maybe I know him."

"Caden Radke."

Bobbins shifted uncomfortably in the loveseat. Jill blinked a few times watching him, sensing his disappointment.

"What's wrong? Is he OK? Do you know him? I've still never even met him. The courts won't allow it."

"I know Caden Radke," Bobbins said.

"That doesn't sound good."

Bobbins knew him as one of the youngest drug dealers in Bear County, a rich kid who got caught up with the mixed blood dealers over at the Ruins, helping front large sums of money for drug exchanges. The dealers at the Ruins didn't have much respect for the boy, just liked him for his money. Late last year, Caden Radke had been arrested with a bag of molly and two thousand dollars while illegally driving a tricked-out Jeep Wrangler that belonged to his dad. Bobbins threw the book at the kid, but nothing stuck because he was a juvenile and his family retained the best local attorney money could buy. During a briefing about the standoff, his detectives went over every person believed to be with Winter Bear. Caden Radke, with his known association with Derek Muskrat—Winter Bear's best friend—was believed to have helped front some of the money for the supplies. Bobbins didn't know how much of that to explain to Jill, sitting there looking at him with squinted, searching eyes.

"He's been in plenty of trouble. Hangs out with all those druggy types over at the Ruins."

Bobbins also suspected the Radke kid was with Winter Bear's gang on Vollmer's property but didn't tell Jill because it might raise too many questions. Jill didn't react as emotionally as Bobbins anticipated. She lit another cigarette and blew out a noxious cloud, got up from the loveseat, and went over to the stove.

"Better than being an altar boy. I'm turning the noodles off," she said. "Let's order a pizza. You can stay tonight if you want."

Bobbins smiled at the thought of Jill telling him everything. They would talk more in depth about her problems. He would get her son back. He would promise. They would hold each other all night long.

On the front page of the *Bear River Dauntless* the next day was a picture of Tyrell Winter Bear standing behind the barricade wire with his fist in the air and a machine gun slung around his shoulder. Bobbins recognized such poses from the turbulent 1960s: the Black runners at the Olympics, Che Guevara, and Malcolm X. He'd been a boy then. Bobbins wasn't altogether sure it was such a bad thing. He didn't care for the flagrant abuses of sex and drugs that came out of the 1960s but had always fancied that it was his job to preserve a country where people could live free and happy, as long as it wasn't hurting anyone else.

He stood outside of Bucky's at five-thirty the morning after Jill told him everything and they made love three times. He felt warm and good inside, descending the staircase into the summer dawn. Jill had told him about the Radkes, a wealthy old Bear River family that seemed to have taken advantage of the young Bonecutter girl when their boy knocked her up. She told him about leaving town and touring the country in a punk rock band. She told him about the insufferable sadness of knowing that her child was out there the whole time and not being able to take care of him. Despite his feelings for Jill, he had heard a lot of stories during his time as a cop and he was always an instant skeptic. Her story didn't seem that outlandish, but he could check into it after all this trouble with Winter Bear was resolved.

Bobbins kissed the sleeping Jill goodbye and grabbed a fresh paper from the news box outside the laundromat. He wanted to be out before day broke and they opened for business. Now he stood in the parking lot's floodlights looking at the big picture of Winter Bear on the front page. The reporter over at the *Dauntless* had gotten an exclusive interview and the chance to photograph Winter Bear, which made sense because the whole thing seemed like more of a publicity stunt than anything else. Bobbins had given an interview with the reporter the day before too, but his professional quotes were impotent next to Winter Bear, who spoke in the seemingly forgotten rhetoric of the 1960s: "This is a revolution. We are taking back the land that was swiped and swindled from us hundreds of years ago. We are not the criminals. All of you on the other side of the fence are the criminals."

What most took the sheriff's attention were the semiautomatic rifles visible in the picture. So, they had more than slingshots. The state troopers would be all riled up. He guessed Dunn was already out there with a bazooka pointed at the barricade.

Bobbins felt a headache coming on.

The cell phone buzzed in his pocket. He knew it was an emergency. It never rang this early. The normally calm and stoic Deputy Ramirez was in a panic.

"What is it, Raul?" Bobbins asked, tucking the paper under his arm. He felt his chest tighten as Ramirez explained. That morning, Al Vollmer and his wife were found in bed with their necks slit and heads scalped. While scalping wasn't a historical accuracy for any Michigan tribe, the message was clear enough.

Lorraine Vollmer was a good seven inches taller than her husband and required a king-sized bed. There was a little step stool on Al's side of the bed because it seemed he couldn't get in without help at his age. Bobbins winced at a painful tingle in his own back, no doubt from sleeping in Jill's rickety sofa pullout.

Both Vollmers slept in nightgowns, Bobbins noted, standing over the two bodies in the bed as various forensics technicians went to work around him, transforming this once peaceful domicile into a crime scene, a place for work, not sleep.

Lorraine was on the right side of the bed, her body on its side with her back to Bobbins and her husband. Her arms were down, and her head cocked up like she was gasping for breath. A patch of her gray hair including a piece of scalp had been sliced away leaving behind a red raw wound. The way her body lay, Bobbins could tell she didn't put up a fight. She probably never even woke up.

Al Vollmer lay flat on his back, his chin doubled over on his chest hiding the gaping slice mark in his neck, hands resting on his stomach. The bed covers were completely pulled away and on the floor. Their heads both rested inside two big red circles of blood like halos. A piece of Al Vollmer's scalp had also been cut away. It didn't look like there had been a struggle. Bobbins couldn't find a point of forced entry. It was as if a spirit had slid in, cut their throats and left. They were the first murders in Bear County in two years.

There was a large knife pinning a bloody note to the sternum of Al Vollmer.

Bobbins had to wait for the state crime lab to process all the details before getting his hands, clad in latex gloves, on the note, written in pencil on white, blue-lined notebook paper. The handwriting was impossibly neat and meticulous:

Dear Imperialist Americans,

You will undeniably construe that what occurred to the Vollmers was murder. It was not. He was tried and found guilty of, among other charges, the murder of Sammy Barefeet and sentenced to death. His wife was found to be an accomplice. They were merely executed under our law, which predates yours on this soil, and is therefore found to be superior—the law of the land.

> *The Vollmers were also found guilty of theft. According to the Treaty of 1855, the land his family has resided on was set aside for the native inhabitants of the region, now recognized by your government as the Bear River Band of Ottawa Indians. This land was stolen by the Vollmers. The United States government was an accomplice in this. Despite the ominous presence of that government, this doesn't make that theft any more justified, even if a thousand years had passed.*
> *A crime is a crime forever, sirs and madams.*
> *You are the murderers and thieves. Not us.*
> *You tore us apart, now it's time for us to tear you apart.*
> *Just leave us be and go away and we will be in peace.*
> *Be on the side of justice for once.*

Tyrell Winter Bear

The kid made some solid points, Bobbins thought.

Ten years ago, the sheriff might have been annoyed to have federal agents come in and take control. Now Bobbins was relieved. More law enforcement kept showing up. Outside, Bobbins saw the towering state police trooper Artie Dunn approaching with a guy in a dark suit. A fed for sure, Bobbins thought.

Dunn was soon before Bobbins with the man in the suit. His dark hair was perfectly sculpted. Around forty, he had straight white teeth. An Ivy Leaguer who probably wanted to be a senator someday, Bobbins thought. Walk around Capitol Hill with a limp from when he was a marshal.

He vigorously shook Bobbins's hand.

"United States Marshal Roger Narsh," he said. "These fellows over here are violating a serious federal law, not to mention murder. They are in violation of the Bear River Treaty of 1855 that was made with the federal government. That makes them terrorists, Sheriff. And we don't negotiate with terrorists."

"No one has negotiated anything yet, Marshal," Bobbins said.

Narsh scanned the field, ignoring Bobbins.

"Obviously, I'm in charge now. We have more marshals on their way. The FBI too. But we'd appreciate it if you and your boys could stick around. We'll need the manpower. And we'll need you, the state post commander, and tribal police chief for intel. Dunn here has offered to assist me. He's filled me in on everything. He's a good cop," Narsh said.

Dunn beamed. Bobbins sighed.

"Come on, walk with me, Sheriff. You too, Dunn."

Dunn immediately followed the marshal, who started across the field toward the concertina wire. The sheriff reluctantly went along. He didn't know what Narsh was up to and didn't like how reckless he was.

"Standoffs aren't as common as they once were. Most recently, you have the Christian cults. Ruby Ridge. Waco. Usually one man has duped the people into following him and is doing it purely out of motives for power and sex. Take out the man, and the rest instantly fall. To find something close to our current situation, you'd have to look back to 1973 and the situation at Wounded Knee in South Dakota. The American Indian Movement took the town by siege for seventy-one days. They were shot and killed. US marshals were shot and killed. And what point was proved from their deaths? I'd argue they died in vain. Now, I don't plan on being here for seventy-one days, that's for sure. We need to settle this immediately."

"And how old were you in 1973, Marshal?" Bobbins asked.

"Does it really matter?"

They were getting closer to the barricade. It wasn't easy walking. The three men stumbled over uneven furrows and clumps in the field. Bobbins had bad knees and was suddenly trailing behind the two younger men, who went quickly past the obstacles.

"You can't treat this delicately. You go in there with as much force as possible and end it as quickly as possible."

"I agree completely," Dunn said.

The trooper had a crush on the marshal.

"Every standoff you mentioned ended disastrously for both sides," Bobbins said.

"I don't care about public relations. You go in with force and end it as quickly as you can. Besides, what's the alternative? Wait it out indefinitely? What would you suggest, Sheriff?"

Bobbins was at a loss for words. He wasn't exactly sure what should be done. The older he got the more indecisive he was becoming. Too many competing thoughts clouded his head. He didn't answer. Instead he said: "So, are the three of us going at them right now?"

There was movement in the woods, only about fifty feet off now. Two wolf dogs emerged, stopped, and stared at the approaching men from behind the fencing. The dogs sat politely, menacingly on their haunches. Bobbins had seen the creatures locked up in a giant pen Winter Bear had built at the Ruins. The animals looked like wolves but had somewhat tamer blood due to crossbreeding with domestic canine species such as German shepherds and huskies. But the domestic blood didn't exactly make them lapdogs. They still looked mostly wolf and had the same swagger. Winter Bear only ran into trouble with the law if he took them off tribal land, where they weren't listed as an illegal species like they were in the rest of Bear County.

The two dogs started barking ferociously at Bobbins, Dunn, and Narsh. Winter Bear and his men were standing at the tree line with their weapons when machine gun fire suddenly cut through the sky. They were shooting upward as a warning.

Bobbins and Dunn both ducked. Narsh didn't, though he did stop walking.

"We're testing them," he said.

Narsh cupped his mouth to yell. "My name is US Marshal Roger Narsh and I represent the United States government!" he shouted at the woods. "You are in violation of a treaty your tribe made with the federal government in 1855 and are suspects in a double murder. I will give you three hours to surrender, or else we will come in with all we've got. Understand?"

Bobbins was embarrassed. He turned around and looked at the officers in the Vollmers' backyard. There was a group of US marshals in navy windbreakers amid his guys and a few state troopers now. No one was moving. All two dozen officers were on guard, with guns drawn or hands on hips.

Winter Bear's response was plain to interpret: the single report of a rifle, the bullet of which landed in an uprising of dirt a few feet from Narsh's dress shoes. The marshal didn't react, just turned and started walking back to the house.

"They'll come around if they know what's good for them," he said.

Dunn scurried after him like a puppy.

Bobbins was stuck in the middle of one incomprehensible mess indeed.

The high drama of morning settled into a simmering détente on either side of the standoff as the afternoon wore on. It was 90 degrees now and both sides seemed like they needed a cooldown. Narsh went about organizing all the officers and holding meetings in tents and mobile command units. National media vans showed up and lined Vollmer Road, their chiseled and attractive correspondents running around confusedly, trying to figure out where to set up their shots. Bobbins stole some evidence from the Vollmers' house and went back to the air-conditioned department to look at it while eating a roast beef sandwich.

He locked himself in his office with a box of papers he took from a fireproof box in the bottom of the Vollmers' closet. The stack rested on his desk next to his sandwich. On top were Al and Lorraine's birth certificates and marriage license. Bobbins would try and do some work that could maybe prevent more deaths. If he could be first to find Al Vollmer's last will and testament to see who inherited the land, further bloodshed could possibly be avoided. Winter Bear was bound to go after any other Vollmer who laid claim to the disputed land.

Bobbins missed his wife as he went through the papers. He and Val had a similar cache of documents that chronicled their lives together: certificates, deeds, and proofs of insurance. The phone was right next to him. All he had to do was call her and they could talk it out. But he didn't. Instead, his attention was taken by the fat, sealed envelope at the bottom of the pile: "My Last Will and Testament, Alvin Vollmer."

Jackpot.

Bobbins tore open the envelope, the legality of the action be damned. He wanted to see what he was dealing with. The will was handwritten on one side of two pieces of yellow legal pad paper but dated and signed by a notary public only six months before. Did Al know he was going to die?

After skimming the two pages, Bobbins noticed with a shock what may have happened in the last year to make Alvin Vollmer change his will. After bequeathing his worldly possessions— money, shotguns, his Lincoln—to various relations, Al stated who stood to inherit the house and all surrounding properties if both he and his wife died. Bobbins didn't finish his sandwich. Instead, he fled through the back door of the department without telling anyone, hopped in his car, and drove straight to the laundromat, where Jill Bonecutter was cleaning out lint traps.

Jill Bonecutter was an expert on sorrow. She had accumulated plenty herself and quickly identified it in others. No category of people was more sorrowful than old men, she'd decided. While most women were attracted by money, good looks, and athletic bodies, what turned Jill Bonecutter on was sadness, especially the lazy malaise of men over sixty. Their weariness was her weariness. Their fatigue her fatigue.

The strange fetish hadn't manifested until she moved back to Bear River after fourteen years. She suddenly found herself attracted to their sagging bodies, hair turned gray in their noses, their frequently impotent dicks only her youth could coax into action. They were so much more settled into themselves than the younger guys who tried picking her up. Jill knew she was a dream for these oldsters. She wasn't just a toy for them. She was affecting their lives in monumental ways.

It had started when she was looking for a job. The economically beleaguered town seemed shut of any employment. She was sipping a drink at Lester's Bait and Beer after a failed attempt to get a job bartending when she ran into Bucky Swineheart, who owned the laundromat. She remembered carrying baskets of laundry there as a kid with her grandma and seeing Bucky and his wife, who was now dead, behind the counter. Bucky always gave her a Dum-Dum.

She brought this up at the bar. They got to talking. They ended up grabbing a six-pack at the gas station and going up into the unrented, furnished apartment over the laundromat and having sex and talking until the sun came up. Bucky, who was sixty-seven, said it had been ten years since he last had sex. His wife died of breast cancer eight years earlier.

The glow that enshrouded the man was the first thing that made Jill Bonecutter smile in a very long time. Bucky offered her a job and use of the apartment.

"No strings attached," he said.

Jill was wary, but it had turned out Bucky needed just this one screw to revive him. He was so appreciative that he hadn't been back for more in the past year, even though Jill would probably have been up for it.

Instead, she took in other elderly suitors. As far as she knew, even though a few of them swilled beers with each other at the vets' hall and played cards together in a pinochle club, none of them knew what the other was up to.

She never intended on getting anything in return, but her chosen fetish had an unintended consequence: old men gave her things. They helped her out. She needed the help, sure, but she didn't want to screw her way there. The idea made her sick. Was it just Craig Radke all over again? Was she screwing an older boy to elevate herself in some way?

Jill saw the sex—not to mention the copious amounts of marijuana she smoked—as ways of alleviating her psychic pain, much of it brought on by a folded letter in the top dresser drawer of her apartment. It was what had brought her back to Bear River, crumpled from hand grease after having been read and reread hundreds of times since she received it a year ago. It was from her son, the child she thought had been taken out of her breathless and lifeless. That's what she had been told by the family of Craig Radke when she was a poor, friendless fifteen-year-old girl.

That's how Jill Bonecutter went from jilted jailbait to front lady of the punk band Monthly Blood Bath, and then made her return to Bear River.

The first epic experience in the annals of Jill's life was when her parents drowned in an ice fishing accident when she was twelve. They were both drunk off bucket-loads of beer and Hot Damn when her dad decided to push their shanty onto some unsafe ice. They sank and died. The bodies were bloated and unrecognizable when the state police finally recovered them.

Her second life-altering experience was when town golden child Craig Radke, of *that* Radke family that hailed from the Hill, took a shine to her. He was twenty and horny. She was fifteen and needed some of that shine in her life. The Radkes had employed several Bonecutters throughout the years. It was unavoidable: historically the Radkes owned one of the lumberyards that thrived along the banks of the river. They were among the most successful families in town, those who built mansions on the Hill, one of the only places with a view of the big lake.

They'd met, fittingly enough, at the now-demolished Radke Roller-rama that had been next to Sorenson Groceries. It was a brief but intense affair executed while Craig was home from the

University of Michigan one summer. No one could understand why he was messing around with a skuzzy Bonecutter girl. She was young. She came from a bad family. Everyone may have questioned it, but it was understood among boys on the Hill that poor girls put out.

Jill could never say for sure, but she always thought that the impregnation occurred the night they whipped through the backwoods in Craig's dad's Land Rover with a case of beer between them. They parked alongside some fishermen's trucks down at Powers Bend on the river and had sex standing up while Jill held on to a tree. At the time, she counted it as a fun, wild night. A few weeks later, she peed on a stick and discovered she was pregnant.

No one in her family cared. Craig's parents up on the Hill, though, were horrified.

Craig's mother, who was known for her religious zealotry, treated Jill in a way no fifteen-year-old girl should be treated. She had no one to fight for her, especially vile Craig who never crossed his mother. While Jill would have preferred an abortion, it was something she could not afford or figure out how to do on her own at that point. Her own family—two brothers and a grandma—were no help. Besides, the Radkes seemed to be acting very kind to her. They let her move into their giant mansion on the Hill. Betty, a servant, would bring Jill whatever she wanted to eat, even ice cream, whenever she wanted it. Abortion, Jill learned, was not an option for Craig's grandmother, Marion Radke. Jill would have the baby and it would be absorbed into the Radke family's largesse.

Jill was scared, though contented with ice cream. She began to trust the Radkes and ignorantly signed any paper Marion placed before her. The day of delivery was chaotic. She was drugged, whisked to the hospital, and drugged again. When she woke up, she was told the baby had died. After she was released from the hospital, she was turned away at the Radke door. Marion said now that there wasn't a baby, there was no issue. God had taken care of it. In short, have a nice life.

After she was scorned by the Radkes, Jill hitched down to Chicago to live with her punk rock cousin, Gina. Jill soon got caught up in the scene. She learned she had a knack for singing, playing the guitar, and writing songs. She started a band with some other girls, all of whom had similar pasts of broken homes and traumas. They called themselves Monthly Blood Bath. Since she put on such an energetic stage show, the once meek Bonecutter girl was now called Jill the Thrill. With nothing to lose, they hit the road in an old van and cultivated a medium-sized cult following across the country. They sold plenty of merchandise. It was nothing to retire on, but it kept them in the bare necessities. There were a lot of barrooms, drugs, and men. She'd had a few long-term boyfriends, none worth mentioning.

But there was also a baby. Fourteen years after she left, she called one of her brothers to check in and they said something had come for her in the mail. They had opened it (Jill loathed her brothers) and shared the news with her. She was in Cleveland at the time, still on tour. Always on tour. Running.

Jill the Thrill was already worn out from life on the road. Too many drinks and nights in sleazy motel rooms with questionable dudes. Too many tampon-littered stages. She wanted to come home. She wanted to meet her son.

So, much to the consternation of Monthly Blood Bath, she quit right then and there and came immediately to Bear River. Jill retrieved the letter from her old house on Ninth and Elm and promised herself to stay away from there while she was back in town: her grandma was stoned off her ass on Oxycontins. It was obvious one of her brothers was taking advantage of her clouded state and stealing from her. Her other brother was perpetually sleepy looking. More drugs, she figured. She got the letter and left.

It was written in a style befitting a fourteen-year-old, which was to say it was short on details. The boy said he recently learned the woman he thought was his mother was not his mother. "After a little digging, I think you are my real mother. I'd like to meet you." It gave absolutely no hint of where Jill should seek him out. No address. No meet-me-at-the-McDonald's-at-this-time type of information.

Jill found herself once again pounding on the door of the Radke mansion. Marion Radke didn't recognize Jill when she answered the door. Why would she? When she had left town, she had long, brown hair and wore jeans and T-shirts from the Goodwill. Now, her hair was blue, cut in bangs, tattoos up and down her arms, an arsenal of metal all over her face.

Marion, now old, reeled from the woman's appearance. "Can I help you?" she said, trying to be as pleasant as possible.

"Where's my son?" Jill said. "I know what you did."

Marion looked deeper into the face.

"Jill *Bonecutter*?" she said, disbelievingly.

It was the way she said the last name that made Jill tremble with anger. That tone of superiority. The amazement that a stupid, smelly, no-good *Bonecutter* should step up onto the porch of a well-bred Radke. That's what made Jill hawk a loogie in the old bitch's face.

"Oh, my," Marion said, backing up and slamming the door.

"Where is my son?" Jill yelled.

"You'll never see him," Marion yelled back from behind the closed door. "You signed all the papers giving him to us! Now, get out of here! I'm calling the police. You assaulted me."

"I just spit on you, that's not assault."

"We'll see about that!"

Jill banged on the door before leaving just to strike some fear into the hag's heart. She decided to walk around a little and was soon picked up by Bear River's finest and charged with assault. It was a bullshit charge, soon dropped, but it did put Jill in touch with the prosecutor's office, where she told them the entire story. They gave her some advice, and she eventually wrangled a hearing in the probate court, though in hindsight she should have waited. Craig and the boy weren't even there, just Marion and their loud-mouth attorney. Jill couldn't afford an attorney. She'd rolled into town from Cleveland on a bus with $128 and a box of Blood Bath T-shirts no one wanted in country music–heavy Bear County.

And this was why, for a year, she still hadn't even seen her boy. The Radke's loudmouth lawyer argued Jill was an unfit mother. Jill hadn't thought about it from that angle yet.

"She's got no job, no car, no home. And she was arrested on an assault charge for spitting on my client. The child's lived in the same comfortable circumstances for fourteen years. Why would we release him to this *woman*?"

Jill—who had cleaned up for court, hair dyed brown, piercings removed—wished she could hawk a loogie in his face too. She presented her case: the ice cream, the papers she unwittingly signed, the drugs on delivery day, and how she was told the baby hadn't made it. Near the end of the spiel, she realized the story sounded hysterical, conspiratorial.

"Unsubstantiated claims, Your Honor!"

"Ask the doctor, then," Jill said.

"Let's do just that," the attorney said, waving to someone in the back of the courtroom.

Jill turned. The large Turkish man in the back was none other than Dr. Demir, who went before the judge and lied. In his thick accent, he said he never told Jill the baby had perished and questioned her mental stability—then and now.

This shit just isn't fair, Jill thought.

The judge not only decided that the boy shouldn't be given to Jill, but that she was dangerous and should be given no visitation rights. Even after she got the gig at Bucky's and started living in the apartment upstairs, the judge continued to side with the Radkes every time she appealed. She'd been in Bear River nearly a year and still hadn't been united with her boy.

But another hearing was planned, and this time Jill was coming with heavy ammo.

A few months earlier, as Bear River thawed from a fierce winter, she finally caught a break. As Jill was tending the laundromat counter one day, a hunched, elderly woman came up to request the bathroom key. Jill recognized her immediately.

"Is your name Betty?"

"Yes," the old woman said, smiling.

"You worked for the Radkes?"

"Oh, I did a long time ago. They fired me. Accused me of stealing."

Jill explained who she was and what was happening with the child. She asked Betty if she remembered the events fourteen years ago. Betty became very solemn.

"Yes, I do," she said. "It wasn't right. I bit my tongue because I needed the money. Didn't last there much longer anyway. I never knew what became of you."

Betty agreed to join Jill in probate court and tell the judge what she remembered. Jill planned on keeping her a secret until the day in court—about a month away—just like the loudmouth lawyer and Marion Radke had kept Dr. Demir and his lies in their back pocket. And if that didn't work, she'd try something else. She'd keep fighting.

In the meantime, Jill began taking old men on as lovers to ease the boredom and sadness. The sex, the weed, and the hum of the washers and dryers all day long made her sufficiently somnambulistic. She dozed through her days, biding time until she could get back what was taken away from her so many years before.

And if she was subconsciously using these old men for favors, it was fine by her. So much had been taken from her in life that it was time she became the taker.

Jill sat on a stool behind the laundromat counter with a closed, half-read Kurt Vonnegut novel—*Cat's Cradle*—in her long fingers. Instead she watched the television mounted high on the wall on the other side of the room. It was one of the daytime court shows. Ever since her own legal struggles began, Jill tried to watch court shows. But the problems on court shows were always petty and often ridiculous. She could only take fifteen or twenty minutes of them. In her mind, she was always rereading the letter in the dresser upstairs.

By noon, she only had four customers, all of whom were well known to her. One was a semi-itinerant woman around sixty who lived out of a Buick station wagon filled to the brim with newspapers, food wrappers, and garbage bags full of bottles and cans she collected to return to the grocery store for the ten-cent deposit. Jill could usually smell her coming.

Down the row of dryers from her sat an obese woman in a motorized scooter whose two snotty kids banged on the candy machine, hoping to dislodge a Snickers bar they hadn't paid for. The woman would smoke cigarettes outside the laundromat, sitting in the Rascal, the oxygen tank she needed for her emphysema left inside so she wouldn't blow herself up. There were always bits of food and tobacco in the washing machines when she finished with them.

Then there was the quiet young kid who worked as a busboy at the Chinese restaurant. He and his girlfriend, who stocked shelves at the Dollar General, lived in an apartment with no washer or dryer units and came in once a week. They looked at magazines and barely spoke to each other, let alone to Jill or the other customers.

These were her people now. She had no other social contact, besides her old men. And here came one of them now.

Out the window, Jill saw the sheriff pull up and park his cruiser in the small, six-car lot. Something was up. He usually parked across the street at the gas station. His face wasn't right as he pushed through the door. It was furrowed with worry. Whatever was bringing him back after last night wasn't good. He came up to the counter, looked around at the clientele for a moment, and spoke in a serious whisper.

"You realize Al Vollmer and his wife were killed this morning?" he said.

She set the book down on the counter and forgot how to move for a moment.

"No," she said.

Tears formed in her eyes as she thought about handsome little Al Vollmer, who would caress her body in a rented room at the Lakepoint Motel and say he loved her more than anything, that she was the best thing to ever happen to him. She knew he was a jerk to everyone but her, but she was captivated by his mischievous smile that turned modest when she undressed.

"Well, that's not as strange as who he left his house and property to in his will."

"Who?"

"You."

"Me?"

"We've got to get you out of here, get you someplace safe. If Winter Bear and his friends find out, they might come after you."

She stared at him but didn't move.

"So, let's go," he said.

"I have customers. Bucky will be pissed. I'll lose my job."

She looked at him deeply.

"We'll work that out. I'll talk to Bucky," he said, then turned around to face the noontime laundromat clients. The obese woman was alternately coughing and screaming at the boy and girl. The rest in the laundromat just sat looking drowsily at magazines.

"All right everyone, place is closed," Bobbins said. "Get moving. Out. Everyone out."

Bobbins didn't know where he was going to take her but knew they couldn't stay at the laundromat. Before he even had time to think, his cell phone rang. It was one of his sergeants back at the standoff.

"Better get over here, Sheriff," he said. "I think they're going in."

"Shit," Bobbins said.

Bobbins explained as much as he could to Jill, including that they believed her son was with Winter Bear and his crew behind the barbed wire, shouting to be heard above the sirens, as they raced to the farm where any sense of logic had unraveled. He told Jill to stay in the car no matter what.

"No, I'm coming with you. My son's over there," she said desperately.

They parked behind dozens of other emergency vehicles and raced toward the backyard, where Narsh was addressing a team standing in a semicircle, buttoning up their Kevlar vests and putting on helmets. Narsh was already geared up, though still in a dress shirt and suit pants. He probably sat in an office down in Grand Rapids his whole career waiting for this, Bobbins thought.

The sheriff went and stood next to Lewandowski, the well-postured state police post commander, who looked just as frustrated as the sheriff. Jill blended in with the crowd on the patio and peered across the field.

"We're going in, Sheriff," Narsh said. "Care to join us?"

"I'm not shooting at those Indian boys," Bobbins said. "Even if they did kill Al Vollmer. There's got to be a better way to solve this."

"I agree," Lew said.

"Why can't you fellas be more like your trooper Dunn here?" Narsh said.

Artie Dunn was one of the eager, intent faces in the semicircle suiting up.

"No thanks. Good luck," Bobbins said.

Narsh shrugged and went back to addressing his men.

"No one else from here going in there, right, Lew?" Bobbins asked him aside.

"No one wants to except Dunn," Lewandowski said. "He's been applying to the FBI and US Marshals for years. This is his opportunity. Who am I to take that away from him?"

The tactical assault began a half an hour later. Bobbins stood watching with Lewandowski from the Vollmers' patio as Narsh sent two squads around either flank. They moved in teams of three stealthily through the sparse groupings of trees. Media helicopters clacked overhead. The cameras trained on the operation were permitted and encouraged by Narsh, not realizing the Indian kids had TVs running on generators carrying the local news stations. In this way, they knew the feds were coming and watched their advance.

Narsh knew about Winter Bear's pack of wolf dogs but underestimated them. Bobbins, watching with binoculars, caught sight of the mangy pack rounding the woods next to the barbed wire and blazing a path like hellfire toward the open field. As if they were operating by divine command, the pack split in the middle. A half-dozen dogs headed straight to where one squad was trotting through mud alongside a fence. The other half of the pack went straight to the unit flanking around the opposite side of the field.

The feds didn't even notice the animals, didn't hear their stampeding paws thumping the ground. Bobbins marched around Vollmer's property, looking for Narsh. Despite his gear, Narsh stayed behind to direct the operation and was on the other side of the house, commanding his ill-fated invasion through a radio.

"There's wolves," Bobbins said.

Narsh was distracted and barely looked at him. He kept the radio close to his mouth.

"What?"

"Those tribe kids got a pack of wolf dogs, about a dozen of them. Just unleashed them on your guys."

"So what? What's a couple dogs going to do?"

"For one, it's not just a dog. It's a dog bred with a wolf. They'll tear a man up even when they're shot. Especially when they're shot."

Just as Bobbins finished his sentence, a crackling man's cry and a wolf howl came in over the radio. Beyond the barricade, the tribal kids starting cheering. They sprayed the sky with machine gun fire, narrowly missing a news chopper.

Bobbins brought his binoculars to his eyes and saw two wolf dogs pounce on an unsuspecting deputy marshal and drag him to the ground. Bobbins and Narsh heard the deputy's cries of pain over the radio as the creatures ravaged him. Many of the officers were now busy with the wolf dogs. One deputy finally got away and ran back to the house minus his gun and cursed while catching his breath. Other agents who had remained behind took aim on the wolf dogs but couldn't hit the moving targets.

Finally, Narsh screamed into his radio, "We've got wolves, boys! Real wolves. Be careful out there."

One by one, the deputies returned—limping, bitten, and bloody. There were no casualties, but numerous injuries. After a sharp whistle, the wolf dogs quickly disappeared back into the safety of the woods. Victorious howls were heard for an hour after the battle. Winter Bear and his crew shot off their guns in celebration.

They all returned except Artie Dunn.

Bobbins saw a tall figure on the field of battle, taller than all the rest. The figure jerked and bounced and, as a wolf dog attacked him, struck it down with the butt of his weapon, and kept running without missing a beat. He'd dealt with wolf dogs before.

Dunn ran at the barbed wire, trained his weapon on the woods where the yipping came from and started firing like mad. The cameras above caught it all. It was only after the news media had time to edit the footage that they could analyze what happened. It was endlessly replayed throughout dinner and primetime viewing hours: Dunn running, aiming his semiautomatic rifle somewhere in the woods and firing. Eventually, he tripped and fell. Two boys slipped through an opening in the barricade, pounded him on the head with the butts of their guns and dragged the long, lean state trooper by his boots onto their annexed land.

Dunn was now a captive.

Bobbins drove Jill to the nearby casino where he would put her up in a room. It would be the last place Winter Bear and his crew would think to find her if she was identified as the inheritor of the land. Besides, by the time he left the casino, Bobbins hoped to have struck a deal with the official tribe that could possibly put an end to all this nonsense. He'd already called ahead. Ogema Bob was waiting in his office.

First he had to deal with Jill, who was becoming more a part of his workday than he would have liked. She looked different sitting in his passenger seat, a maternal being despite smoking in the patrol car without asking, flicking ashes out of the open window. There was still one thing he had not asked because he was afraid of what the answer would be.

"Why are you in Al Vollmer's will? I don't understand."

"Because I was fucking him," Jill said flatly. "I hope you didn't think I was just screwing you. I told you not to leave your wife."

Bobbins gripped the steering wheel with moistening palms.

"Who else?"

"Who else what?"

"Who else were you sleeping with?"

Jill looked out the window with a bored look.

"More than you'd care to know. It's my body. I can do what I want with it."

Bobbins gripped the wheel tighter. He had dumbly thought he was the only one. He couldn't look her in the face, so kept his eyes straight on the road, which lessened the humiliation by a slight degree. He needed to change the subject, get the topic off his burgeoning heartbreak and back on the mission.

"So, there are some options."

"I don't care how you do it, but you have to get my son. Those agents are pissed. They're going to go in there and kill all of them. My son will be dead and I'll never get to meet him."

"I think I have a way to end this peacefully, but it involves a decision you will have to make," Bobbins said. "It's a very simple solution. Winter Bear wants that land. The only thing that was standing in his way was Al Vollmer, who refused to sell. We all know that obstacle has been removed. But if you were willing to sell the land and agreed to it today, this could all go away. You'd get a nice chunk of money from the tribe. Then they can deal with Winter Bear."

Jill flicked the cigarette out of the window.

"How much you think I could get?"

"Enough to convince a judge you can take care of your son," he said.

Jill kicked her feet up on the dashboard and thought about it.

"And how would it work?"

"I'm going to meet with the ogema after we get you in a room at the casino," he said.

"Tell him I'll take a million dollars. They make enough here. A million dollars and it all goes away," she said.

Bobbins nodded and said nothing as he pulled his car into the vast series of casino parking lots. The Bear River Casino was five stories tall with a rushing waterfall in the center of it, the most luxurious building in a hundred square miles. It boasted four bars, a theater, an auditorium, three restaurants, and two hundred hotel rooms. Bobbins generally avoided the place. It was usually filled with retirees smoking cigarettes and plunking their pensions into the slot machines. It did huge business and contributed handsomely to the Bear County tax base. One of the restaurants made a good chicken parmesan too, Bobbins admitted.

He made sure not to touch Jill, even on the arm, as they walked in. It was awkward. He knew they both felt it. It was becoming clear to the sheriff that the situation between them was changing. She would never hold him again.

The lobby was bustling. As they stood checking in at the reception desk, Valerie and a group of her old cronies rounded the corner. Bobbins forgot her cribbage club rented out a small conference room at the casino each week. He knew what it looked like—standing there with his arms up on the counter, credit card in hand, talking with the hotel clerk about the room while Jill stood by his side, her tattooed arms bare in a tank top. Valerie and her pack of five friends stopped at the sight. They were all ladies in their sixties dressed in colorful summer clothes and sandals. They looked like they all went to the same beauty salon to carefully mold their short hair. The group emitted a collective gust of heavy perfume while clutching their large purses. The sound of jingling jewelry could be heard even when they weren't moving.

Bobbins locked eyes with his wife.

"Val?" he said.

She gave him a hurt look, but then smiled.

"Out winning votes for the next election, Sheriff?" she asked.

Her friends snickered. Even Jill was smirking, looking between Bobbins and Val.

"Wait, Val," he said turning to her and putting his back to Jill. "This is for work."

"Are you arresting this young lady?" asked Val's friend.

The pack of ladies again giggled.

"You're such a cliché, Duane Bobbins," one of the women said.

They again erupted in a group laugh.

"See you around, Sheriff," Val said, before leading her friends out the front doors into the sunshine. "Good luck in the next election."

Ogema Bob was in his office working on a plate of mostaccioli and tacos when Bobbins knocked on the door. Bobbins explained the situation to the tribal leader, who pushed aside his food. Bobbins got down to business.

"A million bucks is a lot of money." Ogema Bob looked large even behind his huge oak desk in the capacious office. It was decorated in a native theme with blankets and eagle feathers on the walls amid framed pictures of Bob Kowalski shaking hands with various members of the nontribal Bear River business community. In the corner was a giant life-size carving of the sacred bear on all fours in a relaxed, meandering pose. It was big enough to startle Bobbins.

"A million bucks and it all goes away," Bobbins said. "Winter Bear and his buddies can't be good for business here. You buy up the land, build a memorial—or whatever Winter Bear wants—and you're back in business."

Ogema Bob lit a cigarillo. He offered one to the sheriff, who declined.

"You know we've had a standing offer on Vollmer's property for about twenty years now, but it's nowhere near as much as that," he said. "How about $800,000?"

"This isn't a negotiation," the sheriff said.

"Everything in life is a negotiation. $500,000?"

"Let's go back up to $800,000 and shake on it," Bobbins said.

Ogema Bob shot his arm out and they shook hands.

"So how do we get word to Winter Bear?" the ogema said.

"I don't know. I figured you were in contact with him."

"We haven't been. I think he hates us more than you. But if we get the land, I'm sure I can get him to come around," he said. "He won't let any of my guys in there, though. I thought the feds had been talking to him."

Bobbins remembered Narsh screaming about how they didn't negotiate with terrorists.

"No, we haven't either," he said. "And I don't think the feds need to know about this yet. We're not even sure Winter Bear will go for it. I assumed the tribe was on speaking terms with him."

They thought for a moment.

"How about you, Sheriff?" Ogema Bob said.

"You want me to get in their camp and talk to him?"

"You've known Winter Bear since he was a kid. He'll listen to you."

He might, Bobbins thought. It was worth a try.

Jill had rolled up a wet towel and placed it where the door in the nonsmoking hotel met the floor to soak up the marijuana smoke she was constantly puffing from her bowl. Bobbins nearly tripped on it when he she let him in. He explained the mission to her.

"What about my son? Will you bring him back with you?" she said, enthusiasm breaking through her placid stoned demeanor.

"I can try. I don't know if I'll get to talk to Winter Bear. If I come from the direction of Vollmer's house, the feds would see me. I'm going to have to come around from this side of it. There's no telling those kids won't shoot at me, though."

Bobbins stood by the closed door with his arms crossed. The white towel was twisted like a rope at the bottom. It gave Bobbins an idea.

"Hey, you got clean towels in there?"

Jill, who had been sitting cross-legged on the bed, slowly rose and stepped into the bathroom, grabbed a towel. She moved to Bobbins and flung the towel around his neck and pulled his face close to hers, a smile on her face. Bobbins had the strength to resist, but not the heart. Her mouth opened and her eyes closed. They kissed while Jill pulled him in tighter with the towel.

"I'm really sorry how this all turned out between us," she said. "You old guys fall in love too easy. But it was just sex. And now it has to be over."

"But why?"

"You shouldn't have left your wife. It's weird now. We connected for a short time on some forbidden level and now it's over. There is no real future here and you know it."

"I think there could be. I have real feelings for you."

"That's normal. You're a decent man, Duane, which is why you're going to bring me my son. But I'm not decent. I never have been. I'm a different creature. Not better or worse, just different. And you can't save me by making me more like you."

"But I can save your son, right? Is that why you were with me?"

Jill didn't answer right away, just sneered at him with her eyes. She still had the towel around his neck in a forceful embrace.

"That's not why I was with you."

"You're saying it never crossed your mind that there might be advantages to sleeping with a cop while you were trying to get your son back?"

"It was just a coincidence."

"Then why were you with me?" Bobbins said, feeling burned and betrayed. She leaned up and kissed him again, then pulled back, her hot breath on his lips.

"I liked how you looked in your uniform. And I liked your eyes. I could tell that under that big tough uniform you're nothing but mush. I wanted to see what was behind all those doors. Haven't you ever slept around just for fun? Just to explore a person for a short time, then move on?"

Bobbins shook his head.

"Well now you have."

She leaned up and kissed him again.

"Go get your wife back. She looks nice. Because this is the last kiss."

Bobbins kissed her, bowed down into her face feeling like he might cry.

"I've been a fool."

"Was it worth it?" Jill let the towel go lax and took a step back from him, then put the towel in his hand.

"Yeah. I guess it was."

She was right. He would rescue her delinquent son out of a sense of duty and obligation. Jill would move on. He would put his life back together somehow, with or without his wife. Bobbins folded up the towel into a tight square, tucked it under his arm. Jill went back to the bed, flicked on the television, and relit her bowl.

The sheriff needed to restore his powers. He also wanted to wait until nightfall to crawl around the retention basin between the casino and the back end of the land annexed by Winter Bear. The media cameras couldn't see in the dark. It would be tricky navigating the swampy land, but that way Narsh and the feds wouldn't see him on his envoy mission either. They did not need to be involved.

Bobbins went back to the department and took a long hot shower in the locker room. He dressed in a pair of cargo pants, a polo shirt, and a sturdy pair of boots from the closet in his office, where he had essentially been living since walking out on Val a few days earlier.

Was she really trying to sell their house? It had only been a few days. It had to be a bluff. She was right in one regard—he probably wouldn't win reelection next year. He didn't even know if he would bother to run. Maybe after thirty-five years with the sheriff's office, it was time for him to retire.

Bobbins decided to disarm before crossing the swamp. He left his gun behind. Instead, he dug out a knife holster in the equipment room, took off his pants, and strapped it around his calf. When he put the pants back on, he was satisfied to see the six-inch knife didn't create a bulge. The cuffs were loose enough to lift and quickly grab the blade if need be. He practiced it several times in front of the full-length mirror in his office.

The sun began to go down. Bobbins watched television and waited until dusk. Coverage of the standoff had grown more intense. There were more news vans, more reporters, dozens of cameras trained on the exact same image of the field with the tribe kids on one side and the feds at Vollmer's house. It seemed redundant to Bobbins since the cameras were recording the exact same thing. Bobbins was glad to have handed off all media communications to the feds. He wanted nothing to do with it. It was spectacle for the sake of spectacle. They were putting on a show. Both sides.

At dusk, Bobbins drove back to the casino and parked near the entrance closest to Jill's room. But he did not go inside. Clutching the white towel, he walked across two parking lots and into the swampy area around a large retention pond he would have to circumnavigate to get to Winter Bear. It was the only area surrounding the woods occupied by Winter Bear that law enforcement didn't have men stationed at, partly because it was such difficult terrain. It was also tribal land, but Bobbins had asked Ogema Bob to have tribal police look the other way for the night.

Bobbins got on firmer ground and walked slowly toward the woods, where smoke from grills and bonfires lifted above the tree line. He could hear heavy metal music and a few voices shouting and laughing. As he got closer, he saw a concertina wire fence, the same as in the Vollmers' yard, and two wolf dogs on patrol. They sensed his approach and started howling. The heavy metal music stopped. Two human figures jogged out to where the beasts were barking.

Bobbins put his arms in the air and waved the white towel and continued walking toward the boys, one of whom he soon recognized as Derek Muskrat, a tall handsome young man with buzzed black hair.

"Sheriff Bobbins?" Derek said with confusion.

The boy had a semiautomatic at the ready but not aimed. Bobbins did not know the other guy, a skinny biker with long hair, a jean jacket, and a five o'clock shadow. He was closer to Bobbins's age.

"Hello, Derek." Bobbins didn't stop until he was a few feet away from the fence. He kept his arms up. "I'd like to speak with Winter Bear. I have an offer for him."

Derek thought about it for a moment.

"How do I know this isn't some trick and you got all those marshals right behind you?"

"This isn't an official offer. The feds don't know anything about it. This is between Ogema Bob, me, and Winter Bear. We're going to get you what you want, this land, and we'll get what we want—peace."

"It's a trap," the biker said. "Don't listen to this pig."

Despite their age difference, Derek was in charge. Before getting mixed up with drugs and crime out at the Ruins, Derek ran track for Bear County High and was still fit and muscular. Like his buddy Winter Bear, Derek was mixed blood. Bobbins had sat in the interview room hammering Derek about various narcotic cases over the years and considered him one of the brighter young criminals in Bear County.

"This needs to end somehow, Derek. Don't you want to see your mom?"

Bobbins knew Derek's mother was a sickly woman in a wheelchair. After taking another moment, Derek turned to the older man and said, "Go get him."

The man didn't move. "You sure?" he said.

"I said go!" Derek yelled.

The man hustled off into the woods.

"So tell me about this deal. And you're gonna have to keep your hands up until we can pat you down. You know how it goes. You've seen the movies."

Bobbins explained the offer: the tribe would buy the land from the current owner and do with it whatever the group saw fit. The only charges filed would be for the double murder. The group would have to confess who did it, though.

"We'll make sure the rest of you guys walk," he said.

Winter Bear, flanked by two of his wolf dogs, came walking out of the woods. As he walked, he stroked the head and ears of one of the wolf dogs, who looked up longingly at its master.

"Welcome, Sheriff Bobbins," he said. "You can put your arms down. I hear you come to make peace?"

Bobbins nodded.

"It sounds pretty good," Derek said. "Kinda like what we were talking about."

"We'll see about that. Get him in and check him for weapons."

Inside the fence, it was much how Bobbins had imagined. There were about fifty guys essentially having a campground party. They blasted music, grilled burgers, and drank beer from coolers.

The only sinister difference were the guns leaning against every other tree. Politics seemed to be far from anyone's mind—except, of course, Winter Bear's.

Not being trained in security, Derek didn't do a thorough job of checking the sheriff for weapons, which was what Bobbins expected. He could tell the boy didn't feel comfortable putting his hands on him, that he was nervous to be touching the same person who generally held high authority over him and would probably continue to do so after this was over. Derek quickly patted his waist and ribs and said, "He's OK."

The knife was safe.

Bobbins was led to a bonfire in front of Winter Bear's tent at the center of the camp. They were left alone and sat down in two canvas camp chairs. Winter Bear laid the gun across his lap. A wolf dog came up and sat obligingly on its haunches beside his chair, staring at Bobbins.

"Cute dog," Bobbins said.

"He's a sweetheart," said Winter Bear, giving the dog a kiss on the head. The dog panted at the attention. "But with the right command, he'd rip you apart. He'd even rip me apart. We're just animals, Sheriff, some more well trained than others."

Winter Bear pulled a joint out of his pocket.

"Before we get to this offer, we smoke. My rules, Sheriff."

Winter Bear stuck the large joint between his lips and brought out a Bic lighter.

"You go ahead," Bobbins said. "I'm fine."

"No," Winter Bear said. "I'm not asking. You are on my land, in my camp. You want me to listen to your peace offer, you smoke with me."

Both Winter Bear and the wolf dog glared at him. Bobbins had only smoked pot once, at deer camp with Ronnie Blizzard just before becoming a deputy. It made him feel dizzy and out of control and he hadn't understood why everyone was crazy about the stuff, but now he had no choice but to accept the joint and take the pungent smoke in his lungs and exhale. He immediately felt woozy and struggled to keep his composure.

"Good stuff, huh Sheriff?"

Winter Bear took the joint back and toked. Firelight danced on his serene face. He stared in the distance and then abruptly said, "Are you ready to die for what you believe in, Sheriff?"

Bobbins tried to read the situation through the marijuana haze.

"I think there are less severe and dramatic ways to make a point," he said.

"Well, you're addressing the death part of it. I'm more interested in beliefs. I want to know what you passionately believe in."

Winter Bear handed him the joint. Bobbins licked his lips, didn't know what to say.

"You're at a loss for words because you don't truly believe in anything. You're a cop. Your knee-jerk response is something like 'maintaining order' or 'protecting and serving,' or some other silly platitude. But don't you ever wonder about what you're maintaining order for? Who you're protecting? You only maintain order for the rich. You protect their material wealth and their interests. Police forces were started to serve the interests of slave owners and protect their property—the slaves. These are the same white people who snatched this land from us. And look what you've created with this wealth? Look at this world. Your people sold their souls for what? Air-conditioning, internet pornography, and fake crab meat? My people were peacefully living here in harmony with the earth, not killing it with exhaust fumes and plastics. You decimated the beaver for fashionable hats in Paris. You clear-cut the forest to fuel more westward expansion. You stole all our land, usually for nothing more than a jug of whiskey. All you protect is money, sex, and power, Sheriff. You maintain an order of greed."

Winter Bear took the joint, flicked the red tip into the fire and set the roach on the arm of the chair. Bobbins took a deep breath and felt himself rolling on invisible waves as the marijuana started to take effect. He tried to change course.

"I understand you are angry, and maybe rightly so, but this isn't the way," he said.

"This is a struggle for the soul of this land, Sheriff. White people move boldly. We have to be bolder."

"You're making a martyr of yourself."

"And martyrs don't make a difference?" he asked rhetorically and leaned back in his chair. He stroked the wolf dog's head again, enough to make the animal coo and show its tongue. "So, tell me about this offer."

Bobbins watched the boy's lively eyes as he explained it.

"So if I turn myself in for murder, the rest of these guys will walk and the tribe buys the land?"

"Did you kill the Vollmers?"

Winter Bear looked off into the dark woods.

"I didn't want to get anyone else here in trouble," he said. "I hated that motherfucker."

"So you confess you did it?"

Winter Bear looked Bobbins in the eye and gave one quick nod. Somewhere in the distance came a gunshot. Winter Bear jerked around. The music cut off. The men scurried to see what was happening. The sheriff sensed the whole camp was terrified of another Narsh attack. Derek came running up.

"What's going on?" Winter Bear asked, jumping up from his chair and grabbing his gun.

"Don't know."

"I'm going to get a few more dogs and find out. Take the sheriff here to the pen for now. Sorry, Sheriff. We're going to have to lock you up until we figure this out."

Winter Bear disappeared. Bobbins woozily stood with the help of Derek, who led him past tents and fires through the patch of woods to an old deer blind that was locked from the outside. Bobbins couldn't make out the details of the structure in the dark. Derek used a tiny key to undo the lock and held open the door for Bobbins, who had no choice but to step inside the dank ten-by-ten-foot cage. The door was closed behind him and relocked. Derek ran off toward the brewing commotion.

It was black inside and smelled like mold. Bobbins immediately sensed he was not alone. There was movement. A figure rose but was too tall to fully stand in the small enclosure.

"Dunn? Is that you?"

In seconds, the trooper wrapped a ratty old army blanket around Bobbins's head. Bobbins could do nothing. His muscles and brain were jelly because of the weed. Dunn drew him to the ground in a submissive position. The blanket smelled like mold.

"Goddamn, Dunn," he said. "It's Sheriff Bobbins."

"I know who it is, traitor," Dunn hissed.

"I can't breathe, Dunn!" Bobbins said. "Get this goddamn blanket off my face."

Bobbins felt the trooper's hands all over his body, deftly searching for any weapons. Dunn came up with the six-inch blade from his calf holster. Once Dunn had the weapon he withdrew into the corner.

"Give me the knife back, Dunn!" Bobbins whispered.

"Come and get it, motherfucker."

They breathed in silence for a moment.

"Are they treating you OK?" Bobbins asked.

Dunn now had the army blanket on his own head and wasn't answering. The knife was hidden.

"Dunn? I asked if you are OK? We'll get you out of here soon enough."

Again, the trooper did not respond. Bobbins didn't know what to do. He could hear the commotion dying down. People with flashlights were visible through the windows. Someone was approaching.

"You hang in there, Dunn," Bobbins whispered. "Don't do anything stupid."

Again, there was no reply.

The door opened and light poured in. Derek waved out the sheriff. He threw the flashlight on Dunn in the corner, who was sitting cross-legged in his dirty blue uniform, hands resting gently on his knees like he was meditating. The green blanket was draped on his head. The knife was nowhere to be seen.

"He's been sitting like this since we brought him here," Derek said. "We've tried to feed him, give him hot dogs and hamburgers, whatever else we've got, but he refuses. Just sits like that with the blanket on his head not talking. He's a weird dude."

Derek shut and locked the door.

"Everything all right?" Bobbins asked Derek as they began walking back to the main camp.

"Yeah. Just some kid didn't know he had his safety off. Fired a round into the ground. Your buddies across the field didn't seem to mind."

The music was cranked back up. More cans of beer were pulled from coolers. Marijuana smoke drifted through the night air. Winter Bear, flanked by three of his wolf dogs, emerged from the darkness.

"I'll need time to think about your offer," he told Bobbins. "Come back at the same time tomorrow evening and I will have an answer. But just you, Sheriff. Don't bring anyone else."

Bobbins hoped for a more immediate resolution, but it would have to do. He didn't feel up to negotiating with the youth.

"Just don't do anything you're going to regret in the meantime," Bobbins said.

"Same goes for you guys," Winter Bear said. "Derek will escort you back to where you came in."

"One more thing," Bobbins said. "It's unrelated. You got a kid here by the name of Caden Radke? Young. About fourteen."

"I don't think so," Winter Bear said. "The name doesn't sound familiar."

"He's talking about Shit Head," Derek said. "That's Shit Head's real name."

Winter Bear rolled his eyes.

"Yeah. What do you want with Shit Head?" he said.

"I was hoping he could come with me. His parents are worried. I said I'd try to get him home tonight."

"Be my guest," Winter Bear said. "Kid's been nothing but trouble since this started. Smoking up everyone's weed and stealing their liquor. I don't know how he even snuck in with us."

"I think he's passed out somewhere," Derek said. "C'mon, let's go find him."

The boy was crumpled under a tree near a pile of trash buzzing with flies. He had shaggy hair and was wearing a T-shirt with a complicated glittery logo, blue jeans, and sandals. He didn't look much like a revolutionary. Someone had taken a Sharpie and written SHIT on the boy's forehead and HEAD on his chin.

It was all very puzzling to Bobbins.

"You think you can carry him?" Winter Bear asked.

"I'll manage."

Bobbins stooped over and gathered the boy up in his arms. He couldn't have been 125 pounds.

"I'll see you tomorrow," Winter Bear said.

Winter Bear and his wolf dogs walked back toward the center of camp. Derek led Bobbins back to the swamp near the casino. The boy started getting heavier in his arms. Shit Head stirred slightly, but still showed limited signs of life. The smell of alcohol and marijuana lifted from his young face. At that age, Bobbins would have still been spending the summer catching turtles along the river. He was always amazed at how young some kids got started on the substances. Rich kids like Caden Radke always started younger, it seemed.

Derek bid them a cordial goodbye after letting them out of the barricade and Bobbins began the difficult trek across the swamp. It seemed things were coming back into the purview of sanity. It would all end soon, he hoped. The only nagging thought was Dunn with the army blanket on his head and the knife.

Bobbins had hoped for a more joyous reunion between Jill and her long-lost son. Instead, he came through the hotel room door with the boy in his arms and laid him on the bed. Jill rushed over from the sofa.

"He's fine. Just passed out."

"Why is 'Shit Head' written on his face?" she asked.

"I don't know. A nickname, I guess. I don't think he was very popular at the camp."

For the first time since he'd been with her, Bobbins thought Jill looked vulnerable, with disappointed, sad eyes and a closed, worried mouth.

"What are we going to do with him?"

"I'll call a deputy to take him in to jail," Bobbins said. "You'll only have a short time with him. I'm sorry, but I didn't know he'd be passed out."

"Then what will happen to him?"

"He'll spend the rest of the night in the youth detention center," Bobbins said. "His guardians will be contacted and he'll be released into their custody. But with this kind of behavior, it won't be hard disputing the current guardianship. This kid is obviously running wild. I can testify to that."

Jill nodded, but was focused intently on the unconscious boy.

"I'll leave you for a few minutes," he said.

Bobbins stepped out into the hallway and called Deputy Ramirez, informing him a youth needed transport from the casino to the detention center, but that it wasn't terribly urgent and to get to it when he could. The sheriff then went to the check-in desk and got himself a separate room, which wasn't cheap. Bobbins could afford a room for himself and Jill for a night, but nothing long term.

Bobbins went back to Jill's room, where the boy was starting to wake up. He sent Jill into the bathroom. Legally, it would be messy if she was around.

"You'll have a better chance in court if he doesn't know anything," Bobbins told her. "It was probably for the best he was passed out."

She gave him a stony look but complied.

Now Caden was rustling, then rising and rubbing his face and looking around, thoroughly confused.

"What the fuck, man. Where am I?"

"You've been placed under arrest," Bobbins said from next to the bed.

The weary boy looked at him. His eyes widened with shock.

"Sheriff Bobbins? How the fuck did I end up here? Where am I?"

"You're at the casino," Bobbins said. "You're in the nerve center of a special police operation. This is where we have our undercover mission set up. An officer will be along shortly to take you to the detention center."

The boy sat up in the bed.

"You guys smoke weed in your undercover whatever-this-is?" he asked, pointing to Jill's glass bowl on the table next to the loveseat.

Bobbins walked over and picked it up.

"Evidence I confiscated from Winter Bear's camp," he said. "Everyone there will be taken into custody soon enough. You were easy to find, passed out under a tree."

"This is fucked up, man," the kid said.

Bobbins got him a glass of water.

"Watch TV until the officer arrives," he said, flicking on the set.

Caden settled into the bed in the narcotic glow of the TV and nearly fell back asleep. After Ramirez escorted the boy out of the room, Jill wanted no part of Bobbins. She came out of the bathroom with a worried look on her face. The sheriff could feel her bristling thoughts. All she wanted to do was sit down in front of the television with the marijuana to tamp her worries. Bobbins wasn't surprised. Maybe it was humankind's natural way to use things up to the extent of their value and then discard them, including people. Maybe it was always that way.

As he left, Bobbins thought about Val. Is that what they had done, used up every piece of goodness in each other? Once the energy of youth had faded, they had enjoyed the comfort of one another, but then that too had passed? Or had it? Bobbins didn't go to his room. He went out to the parking lot and climbed into his patrol car and drove home.

The house was dark. The For Sale sign was still stuck in the long, rolling yard. Bobbins had taken pleasure in mowing the lawn once a week in the summer for the past twenty years. Now, however, the sign had a Sold sticker on it.

Bobbins was baffled. She couldn't sell their house without him in just a few days, could she? The house was in both of their names. Had he accepted this fate every time he lowered his body onto Jill's? It surely wasn't legal.

The kitchen light suddenly came on. She was home. Bobbins threw the car into park and went to the house. It felt strange, but he knocked.

"Well, if it isn't the mighty sheriff of Bear County," she said, standing in the doorway, not letting him in. "Going door to door trying to win votes at such a late hour?"

"Can we cut the sarcastic bullshit for five minutes, Val?" he said. "Something important is going on between us. We need to talk. You owe me that, no matter what I've done."

The sincere desperation knocked her back on her heels. Her face went slack.

"Well, all right," she said, opening the door wider.

Bobbins stepped into his house. The familiarity of the blankets draped on the sofas in the living room and the baked-in smell of thousands of home-cooked meals made the sheriff sigh with comfort. This is what he had given up. It was too bad a man couldn't have it both ways—a wife and a lover, a home and the road. His father had tried back in the days when it was accepted that the man of the house could act in abominable ways. His dad would raise hell after his shift at the fruit packing plant ended for the weekend and wouldn't be seen until Sunday night, bleary and beaten with a hangover, smelling like the thick perfume of the whorehouse at the bottom of the Fifth Avenue hill. It caused considerable strife at home, and his dad would wail on the kids and Bobbins's mother if they crossed his path. Little Duane simmered with injustice. It's partly what made him want to be a cop, so he could help put an end to such domestic tyranny.

He had vowed to be a better man. Now here he was sitting down at the kitchen table with his wife after climbing into Jill Bonecutter's bed for months.

"I figured that For Sale sign would get your attention," Val said.

"We can talk about that later," he said. "I think I'd like to start by offering my deepest apologies, Val. I'm sorry."

"My great aunt didn't die, Duane. I don't need a sympathy card. You left me."

"Maybe I'm laying it on a little thick. But I am sorry. I don't want to hurt you. I just want to be happy. I really want you to be happy too."

Val folded her hands together. Bobbins nervously rustled that morning's *Dauntless*, which was on the table next to the mail. The paper had the headline "Police: 'No End in Sight' at Standoff."

"I heard that Bonecutter girl slept with a whole bunch of you old fellows, including Vollmer, who left her his house?"

Bobbins nodded. He figured word would get around.

"Seems like she played you all for fools," she said. "I'm sorry you got wrapped up in it."

"Me too, Val," he said. "I'm sorry. We can survive this."

Bobbins reached across the table and attempted to put his palm on Val's clasped hands. He felt reconciliation was imminent. But Val pulled her hands away and put them in her lap. She looked downward.

"I have a confession to make, Duane."

She wouldn't look at him. It seemed like her eyes were getting misty.

"I've been having an affair too," she said.

Val burst into tears and brought her hands to her face.

"With who? For how long?"

"Ted Bolger," she said. "For a long time."

Val had been friends with Ted's wife, Betsy, who passed away from breast cancer three years earlier. Ted, a retired teacher, was also a gardener. He frequently accompanied Val to the landscaping sections and the flower fairs in the summer while Bobbins drank beer and watched the Tigers. Bobbins had always assumed—and Val had always told him—she was spending time with him because Betsy was gone. Bobbins said that to Val.

"Well, it started off like that," she said. "But then it turned intimate. You were never around. And when you were, you didn't care, just wanted to flop in your chair and watch sports."

It was true. After a day of police work, Bobbins sat in the chair and distractedly watched football or baseball, attempting to shake off whatever terrible events of the day besieged his mind, the bruised and bloody faces of wives beaten by their husbands, emaciated animals neglected by their owners, children sexually abused by family members. A few beers and the monotony of a sporting event took away the sting.

"I've found a buyer for the house," Val said. "Of course, I can't proceed without you. But I propose we get a divorce, split the house fifty-fifty, and go our separate ways. You could do whatever you want, Duane. Go be with the Bonecutter girl."

Bobbins leaned back in his chair and realized he had never known what he wanted.

"That sounds a bit drastic. Why can't we try and work this out? We're not getting any younger."

"Ted and I are planning on taking a trip," she said. "We're going to Holland."

"Holland?"

"To see the tulips."

"Give me a fucking break," Bobbins said, using a rare curse word in front of his wife.

Val wasn't crying anymore. She glared at him defiantly.

"I'm happy with him, Duane," she said. "I'm not happy with you and you're not happy with me. I can live with the sinfulness of it all, as long as we're happy."

Bobbins didn't know what to do. He suddenly realized he had no wild hopes and dreams anymore and was just trying to get through one problem after another. He had no Ted or tulips at the end of his tunnel. That's what scared him the most.

"OK, Val," he said, rising from the table. "We'll figure this out. As soon as I get this standoff fixed up, we can talk about the house and divorce stuff."

"When's that gonna be?" she asked, picking up the newspaper and showing him the headline he'd already read.

Bobbins moved out of the room toward the front door.

"Soon," he said, before hustling out of the house. He didn't want to be tempted by its alluring comforts anymore. Bobbins went back to the casino, ate a chicken parmesan, and drank whiskey while playing slots until he couldn't see straight anymore. He went up to his hotel bed and passed out.

His head throbbed with a pounding hangover the next morning, the first in many years. He dragged his woozy body into the shower and felt very much like a man of inaction. As he was getting dressed, he got a call from Ramirez. Narsh was going back in, this time with more force.

"Goddamnit," Bobbins muttered, after finishing the call.

Now the sheriff had to move with urgency, skipping breakfast. He had to get out to the Vollmers' and let Narsh know a peaceful resolution was imminent. Otherwise bad things would happen for no reason. Stopping in to talk to Jill barely occurred to him.

Despite it being a beautiful summer morning, the dark, smoky casino floor was packed with senior citizens eating free popcorn and playing slots. Bobbins shuddered at the thought of a similar existence after a divorce. It was the first time he truly thought the word "divorce" in relation to Val. The two concepts didn't seem to match. He felt better to be out of the casino and in his car driving toward the Vollmer place in the bright sunshine, the crackle of the dispatch radio breaking in every so often.

The media vans were still parked along the road leading to the Vollmers', mixed in with marked and unmarked police cars. As Bobbins walked up the driveway, he saw that the marshals had gotten themselves an armored tank. Narsh was briefing a dozen of his men in front of the vehicle when Bobbins arrived. Besides a few state troopers who were there to show support for their captured comrade, Dunn, it was now just the feds.

The group broke up and the agents scurried off to their duties before Bobbins got within earshot of what Narsh was saying. Narsh was in close conversation with one remaining agent when Bobbins approached.

"Can we talk?"

"I'm kind of in the middle of something, Sheriff. But we won't need any of your men. We've got a tank," he said, slapping the side of the machine.

"I see that," Bobbins said. "Can we chat for a minute first?"

Narsh excused the agent and pulled out a pack of chewing gum. Bobbins declined a piece. Seeing the tank made him not want to tell Narsh about the deal he'd struck with Winter Bear. Watching Narsh bungle another attack might be worth it.

"You don't think it would be bad for the government's image if you go storming in there with a tank?" Bobbins asked when they were alone.

"That's the thing," Narsh said. "Some of the higher ups back in Washington did a quick poll with average Americans about this little situation. It turns out *no one cares*. They will all watch it play out on the news, but they don't care how it ends, just that it ends."

Bobbins was startled at first, then as the notion eased into him, he ceased to be surprised. Why would an "average American" sitting around watching golf in the suburbs care about a few derelict Indian kids in the backwaters of a hinterland state like Michigan?

"Well, the parents of those kids in that camp care. So does this town," Bobbins said.

"We understand that," Narsh said. "That's why we're sending in the tank. The agents inside will have nonlethal weapons. We'll scare them into surrendering. Then we can all go home."

Just as Bobbins thought about how he didn't have a home, a wolf dog howled ominously in the distance. And before he could launch into the negotiations he'd had with Winter Bear, someone on the tribe's side of the barricade shot off two rounds.

Bobbins and Narsh hustled closer to where agents were drawing their weapons.

"Everyone stand down," Narsh said. "Let's see what this is about."

With his hands on his hips, he stood where the concrete patio ended and the wide field began, regarding the line of trees where the shots came from. The marshals looked at him with frustrated desire. They hated any cautious inaction. They were ready to go in full force and put an end to the situation as quickly as snapping a dry twig. Bobbins stood to the side of Narsh, also scanning the field. Another shot sounded from the woods. Then there was motion from the tree line, the first there had been for days. Two figures were on the move, coming toward the house. They were indistinguishable at first, but then slowly revealed themselves the closer they got. State trooper Artie Dunn had Bobbins's knife to the neck of none other than Tyrell Winter Bear, dragging the younger man toward the farmhouse, shouting something inaudible. It seemed the state trooper had somehow escaped and taken Winter Bear hostage with the sheriff's knife.

There were three more cracks of gunfire in the distance. Officers began taking cover, ducking behind trucks and cars. They had firearms pulled, preparing for a wild ambush. More shots erupted from the tribe side. Dunn was not fazed. He was close enough Bobbins could hear his voice.

"You don't lock me up in my own motherfucking country!"

He sounded possessed. The two slowly continued their way across the field. Winter Bear's hands were held straight up. Dunn had a hold around his neck with one arm and the knife against the boy's jugular with the other.

"What do you suggest, Sheriff?" Narsh said.

"Let me talk to Dunn," he said.

"Think you can do that?"

"I can try," Bobbins said.

Bobbins was now in shouting distance of Dunn and Winter Bear.

"Artie Dunn!" he shouted.

Dunn did not answer. He couldn't be mentally reached at this point. He moved slowly across the field with Winter Bear, the knife against his neck. The two stopped in the middle of the field and Dunn spun them in a circle. "This is my country!"

Bobbins was a few hundred feet from them now.

"Dunn!"

"My country, goddamnit!"

It didn't matter. Winter Bear cocked his head and started whistling. There was a rhythmical pattern to the whistle, a sweet little melody. Dunn didn't seem to notice or care. Bobbins couldn't be sure, but he suspected Dunn had started crying.

"You can't disrespect me like this in *my country!*"

The wolf dogs' paws thumped the earth. They emerged from the woods in seemingly all directions. At first there were six, then eight, then a dozen charging the two men. Winter Bear whistled the same melody. The wolf dogs made a circle around Dunn and Winter Bear, who kept whistling the melody. The ears of his wolf dogs were cocked at him. Dunn was crying now, clutching the much smaller Winter Bear closer to him. It almost seemed like he was seeking comfort from the young man. The wolf dogs started to circle Dunn and their master, snarling and growling. Winter Bear smiled and closed his eyes and issued one last command. The animals immediately came at both him and Dunn, attacking from all sides, tearing away their flesh in a carnal and gruesome way. The animals continued to swarm in a flurry of gnashing white teeth and claws, ripping apart the clothes, the skin, the sinew, and the bones of the two men.

Marshals fired shots, felling several large wolf dogs who soon lay dying on their sides, panting in the dust. The humans were no longer visible. No matter how many rounds were fired at the dogs, it still seemed like they were bounding and leaping in every direction. By the time they were finished, a half-dozen wolf dogs trotted confidently back toward the tribe barricade. No more shots were fired. The air was silent. Officers were too stunned for words. More of the wolf dogs, some dead and others half alive, were scattered on the field. The two torn and tattered human corpses were crumpled on top of one another.

After covering up the bodies, after the ambulances, after calling in more officers to help make arrests, after taping off the scene and marking where all the rounds fell with plastic yellow cards—after all of it—Bobbins drove into the woods alone. It was past midnight. He flipped off the car lights in the pitch-black, no-moon night, letting the car rumble along the washboard road invisible. A smoky, haunted air blew in through the cracked window from the woods. Bobbins drove with no direction. He had no place to go. He couldn't go home and face Val. He knew Jill didn't want him. The impersonality of a motel made him shudder. He just wanted to drive in the dark woods and disappear.

But then he was compelled to pull the car over on the side of the road. There was nothing but the gray road in both directions for miles and woods on either side of him. He got out of the car and stood near the front bumper feeling very alone. Then he started to sob, slowly at first, then uncontrollably, doubling over on the hood of his patrol car. There was nothing left to do. All the fear and hurt poured out of him on the hood of the car. Poured and poured.

Afterward, it was like a storm had passed through his body. There was a certain peace, but with the knowledge that the storm had changed everything. His thoughts slowly returned. He couldn't cry in a dark road forever. He opened the car door, flipped on the lights, and headed back to town. He had to keep moving.

A year later, Bobbins sat on a dock watching the rusty water of the Bear River sluice past his feet. In retirement, he thought of his life as water. Life came at you like rushing water and slipped away like rushing water. He felt free for the first time in years. He hadn't bothered running for reelection. Despite the whisperings around town about his affair with the younger woman that drove his wife into the arms of Ted Bolger, he probably would have won. He had successfully helped end the standoff, albeit with two casualties. The tribe honored his deal. Winter Bear's suicidal demise made it an even neater package. The Vollmer house had been demolished over the winter, and construction was under way for a historical interpretive center where tourists could stop to learn about the native village that was once there.

Suddenly he had no clear goals for the future. Instead, he took his part of the money from the sale of his own house and bought a secluded cabin on the banks of Bear River. The future would present itself somehow in the currents of the water swirling past his dock. Retirement was lonely but peaceful. A couple times a week, he'd head down to the Chit Chat Grille for breakfast along with a dozen other guys his age. They'd eat runny eggs, drink buckets of coffee, and talk politics. Bobbins surprised himself by considering another run at elected office. He could see himself as a state representative, heading down to Lansing and bulldogging through the bullshit. He had the support of the fellows down at the Chit Chat, who urged him on.

"They need a man of your integrity down there, Duane!" they cried.

When they said words like "integrity," Bobbins instantly thought of himself undoing his trousers before Jill Bonecutter's parted legs. All the guys knew about the situation, but only mentioned it as "the trouble" that would soon blow over.

And it did. He only saw Jill around town a few times, driving or walking with the boy he'd rescued from the standoff. She'd stayed in town for the kid's sake. Bobbins knew through his friends at the courthouse that Jill had gotten weekend visitation rights and could eventually obtain partial or full custody of Caden. Bobbins was happy for her. The boy had problems and she had problems, but maybe they could help straighten each other out.

Part of the reason the probate judge couldn't ignore Jill's maternal claims was that the Radkes had been doing such a poor job with Caden, letting him run wild with the dealers at the Ruins. The judge also couldn't ignore Jill's sudden influx of relative wealth. While the Radkes' largesse was well known throughout Bear County for decades, the family could not characterize Jill as too poor to properly care for her son any longer. Jill took the $800,000 and bought a modest house on the north side of Bear River and started giving guitar lessons to children during the week and caring for her son on the weekends.

Bobbins was happy for Jill, though whenever he thought of her while sitting in his lawn chair on the tiny dock watching the moving water, he had those old urges again and forced himself to think about something else. Sometimes his thoughts turned to Val, who had hopped on a plane with Ted Bolger and flew to Europe to look at flowers. By the time they returned, the divorce was finalized and Ted and Val went to live in suburban Detroit to be near Ted's children and grandchildren. Just thinking about them made Bobbins lonely.

As Bobbins sat on his dock looking at his piece of the river, he tried to make himself not think. He tried to imagine all that water gushing through his head and washing away his thoughts, leaving his brain quiet and peaceful. He imagined that's what it would be like when he died. He wasn't sure he'd be happy or fulfilled, but maybe no one ever was.

ACKNOWLEDGMENTS

Most of all thanks to my family: mom, Catherine Counts; brother, Chris Counts; wife, Meredith Counts; daughters, June and Anna; and Kathy and Larry Codere. Thanks to Megan Stielstra and all the kind folks at Northwestern University Press for helping bring these tales to readers. Thanks to the places that published early versions of them either in print or digitally: "The Bonecutters" first appeared in *Kneejerk* (as "The Bonecutters of Bear County"), "The Final Voyage" in *Great Lakes Review*, "Lucy and the Bear" in *Hypertext*, "The Nudists" in *Joyland*, "The Skull House" in *Midwestern Gothic*, "Big Frank" in *Current*, and "The Women of Brotherhood" in *Printers Row Journal*. Special thanks to a few of the hardworking folks at those places, all of them fine writers too: Chris Maul Rice, Emily Schultz, Rob Jackson, and Robert James Russell. Thanks to Dylan Savela, Jodie Fletcher, and Matt Wenzel from the *Manistee News Advocate* days when many of these stories were hatched. Thanks to my longtime work family at *The Ann Arbor News* and MLive, especially John Hiner and Kelly Frick, who have always given me the opportunity to chase big news stories. Thanks to the writing professors who inspired me, encouraged me, and lent me money when I needed it the most: my mentors during my undergraduate days at Wayne State University, Osvaldo Sabino and Christopher T. Leland; and a few of the great professors I had at Columbia College Chicago during my MFA days, Randy Albers, Betty Shiflett, and Don De Grazia. Thanks to all my friends in the Detroit punk scene; my fellow Suburban Delinquents—Steve Toth, Howie Campbell, and Brian Galindo—who've been making music with me for thirty years. Thanks to my hunting and fishing

ACKNOWLEDGMENTS

friends Kurt Kuban and Perry Rech. And finally, this book owes a lot to my departed dad, Jeff Counts, who taught me to appreciate the backwoods, good stories, and interesting characters.